# AVENGEMENT

SAM BLACK

Library of Congress Cataloging-in-Publication Data


Black, Sam

Avengement/ Sam Black

TXu-1-789-225     2011

IN MEMORY OF MY DOG,
BROWNIE, MY LONG-TIME FRIEND

She died two weeks ago. The town can still hear the shock of the two cars—can still see a man running in the headlights, blood, and broken glass. The town awakens with her name on their lips. They had adopted her as one of their own and, now, the townspeople reach out as they mourn the injustice of her death.

# THE LAST DAY

# Chapter 1

## APRIL 1960

On the morning of the last Saturday in April, 1960, Joe Clark and his best friend, Brownie, a hundred-pound mixed-breed dog, had just returned home from Harry's Standard Oil Station, where he'd gassed up his pearl white 1959 Ford Thunderbird. Tonight would be Joe's first and only high school prom. He hadn't been able to attend the previous year because of obligations beyond his control. Sue Andretti, Joe's girlfriend for the past five years, wanted to make this a special night.

The radio in the garage blared out the lyrics of "Jailhouse Rock," by Elvis Presley, echoing throughout the neighborhood. The temperature had already reached 68 degrees and Joe had shed his extra large shirt. The hairs on his chest were the same as on his head—sandy red, which radiated when the sun touched his muscular body.

Brownie lay stretched out on the lawn under a large oak tree that shaded most of the front yard. Joe applied the soapy water to his pride and joy as he listened and sang along with Frankie Lane's, "The Wayward Wind." A smile formed on Joe's face as thoughts of Sue ran through his head.

Joe's T-Bird was extremely rare in these parts. T-Birds weren't exactly part of this conservative farm community's transportation needs.

Joe said goodbye to Brownie, making sure not to get dog hair on his clothes. He climbed into his gleaming car and drove to Sue Andretti's house, arriving with two minutes to spare. He wore a navy suit, black shoes, white shirt, and crimson tie, none of which had ever been worn before.

Sue's mother, Rene, came to the door seconds after Joe had made his presence known with a loud knock. "Hi, Joe, you look great." She smiled.

"Hello, Mrs. Andretti." Joe gleamed from head to toe. His face heated up and perspiration formed on his back. He wanted everything to be just right. Joe fumbled with his carnation, trying to pin it on his coat.

Panic crept into his body. Still, he fiddled with the flower, knowing he was too nervous to do it.

"Please, sit down. Sue will be down in a minute or two." Rene took Joe's large hand and led him to the staircase-facing sofa. Rene realized Joe's nervousness and quickly took the white carnation and pinned it on his suit coat.

"Thanks!" He winked and smiled at her—a bold attempt to hide his anxiety. Joe sat down; his heart pounding harder now as he watched the staircase.

"You're welcome, Joe. You sure have a nice corsage for Sue. Joe's smile stayed frozen.

Sue made her way down the staircase. She wore a sleeveless, yellow formal, with white shoes, and the necklace her father had given her. The sight of her made Joe's head go straight to stammer-ville. With every step she made, her silky black hair bounced off her shoulders. Her smile made Joe's head spin, or could it be the thought of her soft skin nestled against him? Joe took a deep breath.

"Wow! I'm the luckiest guy in the whole world." Joe forced his wobbly legs to hold his weight as Sue drew closer. Her beauty and grace gave her the look of a young movie star.

"Joe, you make me so proud to be with you tonight." She hugged him and kissed him on the mouth. She whispered in his ear, "I love you." Rene took the corsage from Joe, knowing he wouldn't be able to pin it on her. Joe beamed as Rene pinned the flowers on her daughter's formal.

"I love the corsage, Joe," Sue said, her white teeth gleaming through her red lips.

Rene reached for her Kodak camera from the end table and took several pictures of the young couple. Joe tried to regain his composure. His face felt beyond warm. Moisture ran down between his shoulder blades like melted butter. Their smiles showed a picture of long-lasting love. Joe managed to tell Sue, without stuttering, "You look fantastic." He whispered in her ear, "I love you very much, Sue."

Rene kissed her daughter on her left cheek. "I love you, baby." She kissed Joe on his right cheek. "Take care of my baby." Sue was all she had.

"I will," Joe replied, sparing a glance for Rene before returning his gaze to Sue.

Rene smiled. Joe, holding Sue's hand tightly, led her toward the door.

"Bye, Mother. I love you. I'll see you tomorrow," Sue said, smiling, as she stepped over the threshold.

# Chapter 2

# THE CRASH

Joe and Sue spent most of the evening dancing. When they weren't, they sat together holding hands and socializing with friends. Joe and Sue were very popular in school, even though Joe wasn't a jock and Sue wasn't a cheerleader.

The time was eleven thirty; the Prom would be over by midnight. Some of the students had already left. Joe and Sue danced to a Glenn Miller tune, "Moonlight Serenade."

"Sue, we don't need to stay to the very end. I'm ready to leave if you are." With his large arm around her waist, Joe forced a grin onto his parted lips.

"I'm ready, Joe, if you are."

Joe drove Sue out of Mendota, Illinois, the town in which they resided, and passed by the only nursing home in town. Joe's father lay there, brain damaged, a lifeless human being. The car radio played Laurie London's "He's Got the Whole World in His Hands."

Joe knew his mother was at the nursing home tonight, as she was every evening, until midnight. She still hoped her husband of over twenty years would come out of his coma. Sue squeezed Joe's cold hand. His eyes burned; the bile rose in his stomach. He rubbed his eyes with the palm of his hand. The powerful lightning strike, the enormous crash of thunder, and the smell of burnt flesh and hair would remain in Joe's mind forever. They rode in silence for several minutes.

Joe turned his Thunderbird south on U.S. Route 51 and pushed the accelerator to the speed limit of 65 miles per hour. They had only twelve miles to go to Samuel's Steak House, where they would dine by candlelight. Sue sat as close as she could without crushing her formal. She kissed Joe on his right cheek and whispered in his ear, "I love you very much." Her hand settled on his right thigh.

Joe swelled inside. "My love for you grows everyday." He kept his eyes focused on the two-lane, cement highway. Joe's favorite song, "All for the Love of a Girl," by Johnny Horton, began playing on the radio. The song was half-over when Joe gasped, "What the hell?" His grip tightened on the steering wheel, as he squinted into the glare.

A half-second passed. "Where is that car going?" Sue screamed. Her fingernails gripped Joe's leg.

Joe stared in panic at the out-of-control car's direction. Another split second, the car crossed into the Thunderbird's lane. Joe slammed his foot on the brake pedal. Time ran out.

Joe and Sue froze. The sound of the crunching metal filled their heads.

Joe saw his father smoldering, his Grandpa Clark on his death bed, Brownie lying in a wet ditch and Sue standing by her wall locker in eighth grade. He heard a scream from somewhere—SUE! As his T-Bird slammed into the car, he had no way of knowing how this impact would change his life.

The impact was so loud, so crushing, so deadly, and so useless. After hitting the car, the T-Bird ricocheted off and plowed head-on into an eighteen-inch diameter utility pole. Joe lost control of the car as the steering wheel disengaged from the tie rods.

The crash into the utility pole sent Sue to the roof of the T-Bird and then to the rear seat. Her body flew through the car like an angel in flight. Joe's hands remained frozen to the steering wheel.-His head struck the steering wheel with such force it imprinted his forehead. Blood splattered everywhere inside the car.

Brake lights, screeching tires, horns blaring, and crunching metal filled the night air. Joe's T-Bird forced the other car to roll over, sending it down in a ditch and through a four-foot, woven, wire fence.

Hot steam spewed from the T-Bird's busted radiator; its horn blared continuously. The engine rested against Joe's leg.

The smell of burnt oil, antifreeze and leaded gas filled the air. Murmurs of fire and explosion rippled through the crowd which had assembled. The doors of the Thunderbird were welded shut from the two impacts. The windshield shattered—broken glass strewn everywhere. The car hood landed on top of the roof, waxed side down. Sue's corsage showered the inside of the car.

Chapter 3

# DR. KNOWLES

Doctor Knowles' head remained clogged with the thought of having lost a patient that morning on the operating table. He questioned himself over and over again. He pictured the hurt in Ginny's, his nurse for over eight years, eyes. Doctor Knowles' eyes burned. He traveled alone in his Cadillac, heading south on U.S. 51 south of Mendota. The time: 11:50 PM. His body ached for sleep. He would be having breakfast early the next morning at Joey's restaurant in La Salle with an old med student he hadn't seen in ten years. Both of them would attend a meeting at County Hospital in La Salle right after. His speed exceeded the limit. With his jaw set tight, his hands gripped the wheel tighter than needed. His anger remained inside his body.

The car's brake lights in front of him came on. His Cadillac almost hit the car, but he managed to brake in time. "Oh! No! Jesus!" He slammed the brake pedal again, screeched to a stop, and parked his Cadillac on the shoulder. "My God, that car came out of nowhere." He shook his head. His heart began to race as he quickly climbed out of his car. He looked to his right to see where the other car had gone. He then ran toward the car with the blaring horn.

He tried to get the doors open. He could see two lifeless bodies in the crumpled car. Thoughts of his daughter's car accident flooded into his head. Murmurs of fire and explosion rippled through the crowd which had assembled a few feet from Joe's car. They seemed paralyzed with the fear that Joe and Sue could be badly hurt or worse.

"Get me a tire iron," the doctor screamed so he could be heard over the sound of the blaring horn. The steam from the crushed car moistened his face.

Several male students rushed toward their cars. Doc pulled on the door handle. He couldn't get it open. "Call an ambulance. Go to that farmer's house over there," he yelled. A student slapped a tire iron in

Doc's hand the way Ginny would pass him a surgical instrument. Three guys ran toward the farmer's house a quarter mile away.

He jammed the end of the tire iron between the door frame and the center post of the car, ripping the paint. After three tries and using his two hundred pounds of leverage, the door flew open. Throwing the tire iron on the ground, he shouted again, "Call an ambulance! Someone shut that blasted horn off!" Students stood in a panic; some crying; some praying; some so shocked they couldn't move, while others tried to help in anyway they could.

After what seemed like hours, one of the male students finally got the horn wires pulled. The silence of the horn brought on voices from onlookers. Girls cried and guys held back tears. Others spoke with startled tongues.

The doctor, using his finger tips on Joe's bloody neck, felt a weak pulse. "Did someone call an ambulance?" Doctor Knowles yelled while checking Joe's mangled and bloody right leg. No one answered the Doctor's call. Joe's navy suit, shirt and tie were drenched in blood. His unrecognizable face was splattered with small pieces of bloody glass embedded into his facial tissue. Joe's hands still gripped the steering wheel. The engine lay against his shattered right leg. His eyes were shut. He looked like a frozen, red, bath towel on a clothesline in January.

"Where's the ambulance?" Sweat, steam and blood dripped from the doctor's hands and face. He couldn't do anything more for Joe. The bleeding wasn't life threatening, but the head injury was. "Where's that ambulance? We need to get this man to the hospital." Doc knew he had to get into the back seat. He didn't want to lose another human being. He scrambled around to the front of the car, crawled over the hot engine and through the shattered windshield to the back seat.

The radio in Joe's car continued playing. "To Know Him Is to Love Him," by the Teddy Bears, filtered out the open door.

He felt her pulse, but found no signs of life from this beautiful girl whose body was still warm from the life she had loved. *Those bastards! I bet they were drunk. I'm sure there were at least two people in that car.* Moving Sue's head to the left, then to the right, Doc knew she had died from a broken neck. No visible marks could be seen.

The doctor crawled back out the same way he had crawled in. His hands, pants and shirt were smeared with blood.

The ambulance drivers laid Joe on a stretcher. A weak voice from the crowd flowed toward the doctor. "Is he alive?" One of the ambulance drivers asked the same question before Doctor Knowles could answer.

"Yes, he's alive. Take him to County Hospital. They have a trauma team there." They shoved the stretcher in the ambulance and shut the door. "As soon as you arrive at County Hospital, tell them they need to get a neurosurgeon immediately. I'm a doctor, a doctor from Rockford." They nodded in silence. Doctor Knowles watched the ambulance speed away into the night. "God help him," he whispered.

He walked toward the area where he thought the other vehicle may have ended up. Sue's best friend, Cindy Locklear, grabbed hold of the doctor's blood-covered arm, and asked with tears in her eyes, "Is Sue Ok?" Her voice cracked and her hands and lips trembled.

The doctor laid his arm on her shoulder. Tears ran down his cheeks. "I'm afraid she didn't make it." His daughter's body lying in the open coffin drifted into his mind. Cindy stared at him for a minute, mouth wide open, then collapsed in her boyfriend's open arms. The news echoed through the crowd. Shock, fear and anger reverberated in their whispers and shouts. Profanity filled the air.

"I'm sorry," the doctor said, running away from Cindy, "I need to locate the other car." He headed toward the ditch on the other side of the road. Leaving their dates behind, the male students, not knowing there had been another car, followed the doctor.

Chapter 4

# THE OTHER CAR

Reaching the other car, which landed over two hundred feet from the impact, they found it upside down with steam still rising from the radiator. Three men lay on the ground. The smell of liquor infiltrated the nostrils of the doctor and the students. Gasoline dripped from the fuel tank. The impact caused all of the doors of the car to open. All three men wore silk slacks, with one wearing a white sport coat—expensive, to say the least. The doctor didn't see any blood anywhere, or any obvious signs of injury, only two empty liquor bottles lying on the ground. A third liquor bottle appeared to be partially empty.

"You rotten bastards. How can you lay there and wallow in your liquor with one person dead and another person almost dead?" the doctor asked. His hands twitched as destructive thoughts entered his head. "If I weren't a doctor, I'd—" He looked toward the heavens. Hate filled his heart, leaving seconds later.

"Who are you?" one of the three men asked while looking around and seeing the students gathering. "Hell, let's have a party. The whole gang is here." The man with the white, silk sport coat asked, "You got any booze?"

The male students became enraged. Fists clenched, jaws tightened, and profanity spewed from their lips.

"You guys killed Sue!" Joe's friend, Larry Reynolds, blurted out. Tears ran down both his cheeks.

"I need—a-drink. Hey! Are there any-women around here?" Those last words were just too much for several of the students.

The first punch was thrown at the man who had opened his liquored-up mouth, followed by all of them getting beaten to a pulp. Tears continued to run from the eyes of the students as they punched and kicked them. Their cries for help vanished after the first blows.

"You bastards will die for this." The red lights from the ambulance that had picked up Sue's body flashed and reflected off the overturned car.

"They will pay for this."

"You drunken jerk. You killed my friend's girl." A student struck one of the drunken men's jaws again.

"You're dead meat." Another student slammed his foot into the side of one of the intoxicated men. A couple of the students dropped to their knees and vomited.

The sirens screamed from a distance and, as they came closer, they deafened those who had gathered. The punching and the kicking stopped, as the three men became lifeless, bloody and battered, but not dead.

The doctor stood there and watched the beating with concern. His heart raced. His blood-stained hands had dried. "Where the hell were the police?" Thoughts of his daughter as a baby flashed in his mind. He put his head in his hands. His emotions flowed from his eyes.

Three Ford Illinois State Police cars arrived on the scene. Two of the officers headed for Joe's car. The other officers came within ten feet of the three drunken men lying motionless on the ground. The students started tucking in their shirts and straightening their clothes. A loud, baritone voice boomed from one of the State policemen, Orville Summerville. "Who are these men on the ground? Call for an ambulance, Leroy," he instructed one of the other officers.

With his hands on his hips, one student shouted, "They killed Sue! Bastards killed Sue!"

Orville scoped out the men with his flashlight. "They must have been drinking. Smells like a bar around here."

"You guys get out of here. Hey, wait a cotton-pick-in' minute. These guys look like they've been beaten." Orville knelt on the ground near one of the three intoxicated men. He continued looking at the area with his flashlight.

Not one word was uttered by the students.

Orville stood up and repeated himself. "These guys look like someone beat the crap out of them. What are you going to tell me about this?" His voice canvassed the area. One hand rested on his revolver, a Colt 38 with a 6 inch barrel; the other hand tilted his trooper hat back on his head.

"They looked like that when we found them," one of the male

students blurted. All the students stared at the three men lying on the ground, never showing any signs of guilt. Some of the students headed back toward their cars.

"Hey, you boys, just wait a cotton pick-in' minute." The students turned around, but never moved toward the policemen. "You're telling me these men were beaten before the accident. I don't believe it for a minute." Orville looked at the three men and then at the students. He paused several seconds. "However, there isn't any reason to hold you since I have no proof. You best be getting out of here before I find some."

"These men sure are beat up. I guess I will write it up as, 'caused by accident, with possible lacerations before accident.' I wonder who the heck these guys are. Sure have nice clothes. They have a nice car, too." Minutes later, Trooper Summerville stammered as he stumbled backwards, "Oh, my God! These are the Capuanos. Holy Crap!" He knelt down to check their pulses. Summerville didn't want any dead mafia members in his jurisdiction, especially the Capuanos.

Still flabbergasted, Summerville tried to stand. "What the heck are they doing out here?" Summerville stood up and quickly turned toward his fellow officers. "Get me an ambulance—now. We need to get these men to a hospital. Howard, you and John follow the ambulance to the hospital and stand guard until your shift is over. These guys here on the ground are from Chicago and are members of the mafia. They are all Capuanos." Summerville wiped his chin. "We are in deep dog poop if anything happens to them. I knew these guys when I was a cop in Chicago." Summerville paced around the three men, shining his flashlight toward them. "The Capuanos are the most brutal organized crime family in America." The other officers stared warily at the three men, but never spoke.

# Chapter 5

# MOTHER ARRIVES

Helen Clark arrived at County Hospital an hour after her son had gone into surgery. She ran toward the first nurse she saw in the ER waiting room. Helen spoke frantically, "My son has been in a car accident. I need to know how he is doing. His name is Joseph Clark."

"You need to go over there," the nurse replied, pointing in the direction of SIGN IN, "and sign in and someone will be with you within the hour. We are very busy, as you can very well see." She never looked at Helen as she spoke and made smacking sounds as she chewed her gum.

Having worked in a hospital before, Helen knew the process and that meant waiting, and she had no intentions of waiting. Helen bolted for the door leading to the ER and said, in a somewhat hostile tone, to the first doctor she saw, "I'm Helen Clark. I'm a registered nurse. My son has been in a serious car accident and I want to know where he is."

"What is his name?" asked the doctor, who appeared to be in his late twenties.

"Joseph Earl Clark!" Helen's tone turned less boisterous.

"He is in surgery and you can wait out there," the doctor said, pointing in the direction of the door Helen had barged through earlier.

In a much softer voice, Helen asked, "How is he doing?"

"Not good, Mrs. Clark. He has several very serious injuries." The doctor's eyes dropped after he spoke.

The waiting room was partially filled with patients who needed emergency care and those who were waiting for patients being cared for. Helen found a chair to set her weary body in, when several of the students from Joe's high school came through the door.

"How's Joe, Mrs. Clark?" one male student asked.

"He's in surgery." She paused several seconds, looking at each of the students, thankful for their support. "He has several injuries." Her red eyes held no tears.

Helen knew what ER waiting rooms were like on a Saturday night after midnight. She worked enough of them after graduating from nurse's training. They are in total chaos and County Hospital appeared to be no exception—people screaming in pain; babies crying uncontrollably; people crying from the unknown condition of a loved one; people pacing the floor, praying, drinking coffee to stay awake. Some were dressed decently; yet, others wore salvageable clothing they had grabbed in a rush to get over here.

As she waited, Helen's mind rummaged through the past several years. She never guessed she'd be on this side of the fence again so quickly. It seemed like only yesterday that they had rushed her husband to the hospital. Her body ached, tired and totally drained. She took several deep breaths. It helped relieve the tension.

Helen sucked in the antiseptic aroma filtering in from the ER, body odors of people in the waiting room and the smell of bloody bandages. She saw the fear in the eyes of those waiting. She prayed for her son.

Helen opened her eyes and saw the students hugging, crying, pacing, praying, checking the clock every five minutes, and staring at her. She heard very few words spoken aloud and those that were supported her.

Several of the male students talked softly as if in a funeral home. They made statements like:

"Joe will survive this."

"Joe will be ok; he is as tough as they make 'um."

"I wouldn't want Joe mad at me."

"Joe's a survivor."

At three forty-five Sunday morning, all the students and Helen remained at the hospital waiting for news on Joe. The surgeon, Doctor Allen, who headed the trauma team, walked slowly through the door from the operating room. Doctor Richard Knowles followed him. Doctor Allen removed his surgical cap, his head damp with sweat, his surgical gown smeared with blood. He looked tired, drawn, and worried.

Doctor Knowles tried to smile, but it faded quickly.

"You must be Mrs. Clark. I'm Doctor Allen. This is Doctor Knowles. Doctor Knowles was at the scene of the accident. He assisted me in surgery." Helen was the only adult left in the waiting area.

Helen stared at both doctors. She hoped her prayers would be answered.

Helen tried to stand, but thought better of it. She felt dizzy and lightheaded. It's probably my blood pressure, she thought to herself. "How is he doing?" Helen managed to ask, fearing the answer. She clasped her hands together as if praying for the right answer. All the students' eyes focused on the doctors. Doctor Allen sat down next to Helen, while Doctor Knowles stood close by.

Doctor Allen spoke in a soft tone, almost a whisper. "Your son is a strong, young man and if he has the will to live, I think, unless some unforeseen circumstances arise, he will pull through." Helen heard the sighs from the students. An ounce of joy popped into her heart. The students huddled around the doctors and Mrs. Clark. Helen sat speechless, although her face showed a ray of hope.

"Is, is he awake?"

"No!" His voice became louder now. "It will take a lot of prayers on your part and all of his friends." His eyes surveyed the students quickly. "Joe will need lots of patience in order to get back on his feet." Helen knew her son's biggest weakness was patience.

"Will he be awake," her voice caught, "Will he be awake soon?" Her husband hadn't awakened since, since the tragedy.

"I don't believe so, Mrs. Clark. He will probably be in a coma for a few days and quite possibly longer. It is very difficult to tell with head injuries. Your son has a very hard skull. If he hadn't, he probably would not be here."

Helen's face turned pale. Her eyes pointed downward toward the tile floor. "His father has been in a coma for several years and the doctors thought he might come out of it." Helen's nose was as red as her dry eyes. Her jaw was set tight; her eyes were fixed, but saw nothing except her husband and son lying motionless in two different beds.

Doctor Allen rubbed his hands together, as if they were cramped. He looked lost for words. He was exhausted. "I'm really sorry, Mrs. Clark." He touched her moist hand and frowned.

Doctor Knowles put his large hand on Helen's shoulder and squatted by her side. "Mrs. Clark, I wish I'd had met you under different circumstances, but I want to assure you Doctor Allen is the best trauma surgeon in this State." He squeezed Helen's shoulder as he stood.

Helen nodded, but made no comment.

"You try and get some sleep. Your son will need you later." Doctor Allen smiled and held Helen's hand.

"I can't sleep and I won't sleep till my son wakes up. I want to see my son."

"Okay, I'll take you to him." Doctor Allen stood and helped Helen to her feet.

Helen thanked the students for being there. She received hugs of support from each one. She thanked Doctor Knowles for his assistance as she walked out of the waiting room with Doctor Allen. The waiting room stood empty.

# Chapter 6

## SUE'S MOTHER

Rene Andretti awaked the next morning with her heart filled with grief. She stared at the ceiling and realized she was alone—alone for the first time since her parents had adopted her. Her husband had been killed in the Korean War when Sue had just turned ten. Rene's adopted parents had been killed in a car accident a few years ago. Rene had no brothers or sisters.

Helen visited Rene late Sunday morning, the day after the accident. Helen found it most difficult to comfort her from her loss when she had two of her own lying in comas. Before she left for County Hospital, Helen called the minister of the Methodist Church to ask him to pay Rene a visit.

The first Thursday after the accident, Doctor Knowles' day off, he visited Rene and asked if he could deliver the eulogy. Sue would be laid to rest one week after her tragic death. He shared with Rene the tragedy of his own daughter's death. Doctor Knowles looked in on Joe that same day.

Due to the large crowd they expected, Sue Andretti's funeral took place at the high school football field. Most of the people who attended didn't even know her. They came to pay their respects to an innocent, lovely, young lady. The weather hovered around 70 degrees, with cloudy skies and a light drizzle.

# EULOGY
By
Doctor Richard Knowles

"This girl didn't deserve to die." He motioned toward Sue Andretti's coffin with his right hand as he spoke. "Her beau, Joe Clark, is lying in a coma at County Hospital," his left hand wiped his brow, "and will probably never walk again without a cane." His voice trailed off. Silence permeated the cloudy, cool, damp, spring air.

"Why? Why does God allow things like this to happen?" The question rang throughout the crowd, bouncing off the metal bleachers and floating into the afternoon sky. Doctor Knowles' eyes danced across the several hundred in attendance. "We don't know."

"My daughter's life was taken by someone who was driving while intoxicated. My life crumbled that day." Tears burned his eyes. "How many more lives have to be taken before the law protects the innocent?"

"Sue Andretti," he cleared his throat and fought back his emotion, "she was the only family her mother, Rene, had left. I didn't know Sue Andretti personally, but I know she shouldn't be lying here in front of us." His eyes focused on Rene, sitting not ten feet away, her head bowed. Tears poured from her eyes like water from a rose petal during a rainstorm. Her body shook uncontrollably. Rene's only child and last family member lay in the coffin, which would be lowered into the ground within the hour. None left, none left.

Doctor Knowles furrowed his brow grimly and considered the woman on Rene's left, Helen Clark. Her hands trembled, thoughts raced through her head. Her son was lying on a bed in a coma. Doctor Knowles suspected fear caused her trembling. Fear that, when and if Joe became able, he would try to get even with the men who took Sue away from him.

"It should never have happened!" The words shot through the air. The crowd reeled at the doctor's statement.

"Before I die, I will see these brutal men dead or imprisoned. They must be eradicated from our society." His voice grew in strength.

"I'm sure everyone here wishes those last precious seconds that this wonderful couple had could be blotted from this unpredictable world we live in. Live your life to its fullest. Share as much time as you can with those you love and fight for justice."


  Wondering if his words had helped, if he would live to see change in the world, Doctor Knowles stepped down off the podium.

  Ten days later, Helen, beyond exhaustion, received word that Joe's vital signs had improved. Doctor Allen informed Helen he might be in a coma for a while longer, but his progress looked very good, and he would probably regain consciousness.

  Rene had regained her composure, somewhat, but continued to experience a horrible time coping with the loss of her daughter. Ray Mathews, Rene's fiancé for the last year, had remained with her most of the time since the crash. Her doctor and the minister suggested she spend time at the hospital with Joe, since he was the closest person she had left for family, other than Ray and Helen. With encouragement from Ray, but with some hesitation, she decided to help. Within a few days, Helen and Rene were taking twelve-hour shifts at Joe's bed side. They wanted to be there when he awakened.

# Chapter 7

# THE CAPUANOS

Helen learned the three men that had turned this farm community upside down had been transferred to a hospital in Chicago. All three had improved, but would remain in the hospital for two more weeks. They all had the same last name, Capuano. Two of the three were brothers and the third, a first cousin.

The local paper reported the Capuanos were involved in prostitution, fraud, embezzlement, money laundering, illegal gambling, stealing, and several murders that could never be proven. The FBI had tried unsuccessfully for several years to nab these organized crime members. They would either buy their way out of it or the witnesses that could put them away would unexpectedly disappear, never to be found again. The Capuanos—that's who they were, and now they had killed a country boy's hopes and dreams. Chills ran wild through Helen's body after digesting the newspaper article.

The Capuanos were never charged with careless driving or intoxication on that Saturday night they took Sue Andretti's life. The Illinois State Police who investigated the accident said there wasn't enough evidence to press charges. The anger in and around Mendota began to stir quickly when the "No Charges" decision against the Capuanos came out. People discussed it everywhere—in grocery stores, gas stations, bars, and street corners. The farmers talked across line fences, in grain elevators, restaurants, coffee shops, and even before and after church.

After learning the Capuanos had gotten off the hook, Doctor Richard Knowles contacted his attorney to file manslaughter charges against the Capuanos. Three days after the charges were filed his home was torched and completely destroyed. It burned in the early night and went up like a dry Christmas tree. The Knowleses lived in an exclusive neighborhood in Rockford, Illinois. Fortunately, the doctor and his wife were not at home at the time. They got home later that night to find only ashes and a charred stone chimney.

They received threatening phone calls, as well as threatening notes posted on the doctor's office door daily. The people responsible for sending the notes and making the phone calls were never investigated, nor identified.

Doctor Knowles hired two former U.S. Marines as full-time bodyguards, one for him and one for his wife. The doctor purchased a Smith &Wesson 38 caliber, long nose hand gun. He frequented the indoor shooting range. The doctor knew he was up to his neck in mobster quicksand and the police would not protect him.

# THE DREAM

# Chapter 8

# SPRING 1947

"Help! Help! Help!" Five-year-old Joseph Clark had his pant leg caught in the gears of the fan blade up at the top of their windmill. He screamed at the top of his lungs. He sat 40 feet above the ground. Fortunately, it was late spring and the windows were open in the house.

Helen responded immediately. Racing out of the back porch, letting the screen door slam behind her, she scanned the property for her son. This was not the first time she had searched for the source of Joseph's cries. Yet, a chill of fear ran down her spine. "Now what?" Helen grumbled, trying to calm herself. "That kid is going to give me heart failure yet." Helen eyed the farm buildings.

"Help! Help!" screamed Joseph from top of the windmill, waving his right arm.

"Oh! My God. What are you doing up there?" said Helen, wondering how she would ever get him down. With panic written all over her face, she clutched her chest with her hands.

"Get me down. My leg is stuck in the gears," Joseph screamed, trying to yank himself clear.

Pushing back a bubble of hysteria, Helen struggled to get hold of herself. John and his Dad, Harry, were out in the field—too far away. Drawn by the ruckus, six year old Sarah, Joseph's sister, came outside, shading the sun with her two small hands. "What are you doing up there, dummy?"

"Get me down! My leg is hurting." The windmill had stopped running.

"Stay calm, Joseph. We'll get you down," said Helen, fidgeting, looking up, then down, then back up again, not sure yet what to do.

Just then, Peter Robinson, who lived south of the Clark farm, arrived in his Ford truck. Peter was the same age as Harry and in really good shape for his age, much like Harry. "Good morning, Mrs. Clark. I just came over to see if I could borrow a log chain for a bit?" Peter saw

Helen focusing on the top of the windmill. "How did he get up there?" Peter's voice sounded just like Pa Kettle from the movie, *The Kettles Down on the Farm.*

"I don't know, probably climbed up the outside ladder," Helen offered, with a frightened look on her face. "I told John to remove those ladder rungs."

"Well," said Peter, "I guess I better figure out a way to get him down." He frowned and furrowed his brow in thought.

"Are you sure you can get him down safely?" asked Helen, looking up at her son, her right hand shading the sun.

"If he doesn't fight me," Peter contemplated. "I think maybe, I think maybe I can get him down." An unconfident Peter looked up at Joseph and scratched the week's growth of grey beard on his chin.

Helen could not tear her eyes off her son. "Maybe you should go get John. He is out in the back forty planting corn," she almost pleaded.

Looking relieved, Peter climbed into his truck. "Back in a jiffy, Helen, Don't worry."

"Hurry!" said Helen, knowing Peter never moved very fast, even in his truck.

Peter headed for the back forty and pushed his Ford truck to forty-five. He had not had the truck over forty since buying it five years ago. He raced right across the planted field, dust flying, until he gained on the tractor John drove. He was heading away from Peter; his eyes following the planter marker. Peter pulled just ahead of John, stopped, and honked his horn to get John's attention.

"Come quick, John, it's your son."

John took in Peter's rushed voice and didn't even hesitate. He jumped off the tractor, leaving the engine running, and grabbed the door handle on Peter's truck. As the two climbed in and slammed their doors, he turned his white face toward Peter and asked "What's the matter with him?"

"Joseph," he paused several seconds, "he is on top of the windmill and got his leg caught in the gears."

"What? But he isn't big enough to climb up there. My God, he didn't go up that ladder did he?" He wiped his face with his hands. "Helen told me to get those ladder rungs off there."

"Yep, he did, John."

Peter came to an abrupt stop near the windmill, sliding the wheels on the Ford. John had the door open and jumped out of the truck before the Ford came to a stop.

"Take these scissors, John, to cut the pant leg. I told you to take those ladder rungs off that windmill last year." Helen's eyes pierced John before they again turned up to her son.

John knew he should have taken those ladder rungs off.

"Hey, Pa." Joseph waved like a man on a galloping horse. The imp looked like he was actually enjoying himself.

John went straight for the ladder, almost out of breath from panic, and began to climb the forty feet to rescue his son. "Hang on son, I'll be right there," said John, gasping for air halfway up. Those Camel cigarettes were starting to take their toll.

"I can't go anywhere, Pa. My leg is stuck in the gears," said Joseph, calmly, with a mischievous grin on his face. John shook his head in disbelief.

"I can't believe you climbed up here," said John, as he reached the top, sucking air from his toes. "How's your leg?"

"It's ok! Long as the wind doesn't blow." He was standing on a one-inch angle iron.

"How did you get up here?"

"It was easy, Pa. I came up the same way you did."

"I'm going to cut this pant leg so you're free from the gears." John caught his breath and, in a matter of seconds, snipped the scrap of fabric that had his son trapped and pulled him into his arms.

Joseph squirmed. "I can climb down by myself, Pa."

"No, you get on my back and hang onto my bib overalls."

"Come on, Pa! I'm not afraid."

"Get on my back and hang on tight," demanded John.

"OK!" Reluctantly, Joseph grabbed hold of his Dad's bibs and waved to his Mom, his sister, and Peter.

As they stepped off the ladder, Joseph dropped easily to the ground and smiled. "That was fun."

"John, you get those ladder rungs off that windmill before he tries to climb up there again," Helen said, sharply.

John looked at Helen and headed for the garage to fetch some wrenches.

Helen hugged her son, but he pushed her away. "Stop, Mom." He dropped his head and stuffed his hands in his pockets as he spoke.

"You could have fallen and might have been killed."

"I wouldn't have fallen. I like to climb," he said, squinting and rubbing his eye with his fist.

"You are going to give me grey hair before I'm forty."

John removed six ladder rungs from the windmill while Helen scolded him again, "I told you. You should have done that last year. If you had, your son wouldn't have climbed up there. He could have been killed." She stomped back toward the house. John had no reply. Peter hung his head.

Peter returned John to the back forty to finish planting. Harry was waiting and wondering where they had gone in such a hurry. "Everything okay?" Harry asked, trying to hide the urgency in his voice.

When John told his Dad what had happened, Harry could only smile. "That boy is not afraid of anybody or anything."

Chapter 9

# FIRST GRADE

The Clarks received *The Chicago Tribune* everyday by mail. When Jackie Robinson joined the Brooklyn Dodgers in the spring of 1947, it made headlines in the Tribune. Jackie was the first Negro to play major league baseball. Joseph saw the word "Dodgers" on the front page and asked, "What does Dodgers mean?"

"That's a baseball team. They're in the national league," his father replied, never looking at his son, focusing on the funnies.

That is when it all began. The paper always came a day late, but Joseph would get that sports page and look to see what his Dodgers did. By summer's end, he knew almost everyone in the starting line-up by heart. That's how Joseph learned how to print numbers and letters, by listing the players' names and their averages.

August 24th, 1948 came way too early for Joseph. It was his first day of school. The school sat three miles from the Clark farm. Helen had Sarah, along with a reluctant Joseph, in the car to make the journey to Snyder School. When they arrived at the school, he wouldn't get out of the car, nor obey his mother when she asked him to meet his teacher.

One look at the ugly, old teacher and Joseph lowered himself further down into the seat. Miss Stanley, an old maid school teacher, kept her graying hair tied up in a bun. Her face appeared to be twenty years ahead of her age. Sarah told her brother she smoked in the furnace room. A large, German woman, she could handle any male eighth-grader with ease, no matter how big. She spoke with a sharp voice and her lips didn't move much. Joseph wondered if she ever smiled. He thought if she did, her mouth would probably crack.

The one-room school house contained all eight grades in one large room. A wood and coal furnace provided heat to the school. The eighth grade boys, if there were any, kept the furnace full. They also carried out any ashes. If eighth graders weren't available, then seventh graders had to do the manly jobs. One thing for sure, no matter what, girls never participated in this sort of thing. They swept the floors and dusted the room.

The school had separate cloakrooms for boys and girls. Many mornings, the students had to leave their coats on until the furnace had put out enough heat to keep them warm. The cloakroom served other purposes, as well. It stored unused books, props for different skits the students would do, students' lunches, the rope for the school bell that hung down from the roof, and, sometimes, by an older boy and girl for kissing.

The first grade class consisted of just Joseph and Billy West. The teacher taught all students twice a day. First grade always went up front first. Students sat in straight back, hard, oak chairs near the teacher. While they were up front, the rest of the students had an assignment and were supposed to be busy studying, but most times they sat gawking at the students up front.

Joseph sat in the chair farthest from the teacher. Before sitting down, he would move the chair farther still. Joseph appeared to be almost twice as big as Billy. Joseph folded his arms, slouched in his chair and pouted.

"Do you boys know your ABCs ?" asked the teacher. Joseph cringed.

"Yes, I know mine," said Billy, quickly, with his hand waving above his head. Joseph remained speechless and stared at the floor as Billy rattled off the letters of the alphabet.

"That's great, Billy." Miss Stanley smiled quickly and turned her attention to Joseph.

"What about you, Joseph, can you say your ABCs?" she said sternly. Helen Clark had informed her that Joseph could be bullheaded.

With hesitation, Joseph responded, "I know what Duke Snider's batting average is. I can name all the Brooklyn Dodgers' players." He never looked at the teacher as he spoke.

"We don't care about baseball averages or names of players in here, Joseph Clark," said Miss Stanley, emphasizing Joseph's last name. Her teeth clenched as she stared Joseph down, not more than three feet from his face.

Joseph would not let this ugly, old teacher scare him, nor was he going to show any type of fear. Never changing his position, he continued to stare at the floor. Billy was scared to death and showed it with quivering lips and bulging eyes. Joseph thought about the Dodgers, climbing trees and, if he could, the windmill.

For the rest of the morning, all the eighth graders sat up front and none received the stern voice that Joseph had gotten. Joseph sat at his desk, right in front of the teacher's desk, not doing anything pertaining to the ABCs. He wrote down all the Dodger players he could remember and the positions they played, which was over ninety percent of them.

After lunch, all the students returned to the classroom and took their seats. Joseph came through the door last. As Joseph started to sit down, Miss Stanley demanded, "Joseph, you come right up here and sit by me. We will see if you can learn something worthwhile." Her voice was curt as she pointed her finger to the chair next to her desk.

Joseph, hanging his head and scuffing his feet, walked toward the desk. Before sitting in the chair next to Miss Stanley, he slid it about six inches away from where it was. Just before his weight hit the seat, Miss Stanley shoved him out of the way with her arm. She picked up the chair and slammed it down in its original position. She outweighed Joseph by over a hundred pounds.

"Don't you ever move that chair again, Joseph, or I'll take the stick to you. Do you understand?" she threatened through clenched teeth. Her eyes bored into Joseph, but he never blinked. The students fell silent; fear showed in their eyes. Joseph stared at her.

Joseph thought to himself that that would be the last time anybody pushed him and got away with it. He now hated her even more than the Yankees.

# Chapter 10

# NEWBORN CALF

While John wiped the newborn calf down, he said to Joseph, "Go to the house and get a bottle of warm milk. Tell your mother what has happened and she will prepare everything for you."

The heifer became a cow after giving birth to the bull calf. They both survived. On Sunday nights, the Clark family sat in the kitchen and listened to the Crosley Radio. The radio had two knobs—volume and tuner. In the fall of 1950 at 5:30 p.m., Joe's favorite program, "THE LONE RANGER," came on the radio. He liked it when the announcer, belted out "And a Hi-ho Silver. The Lone Ranger rides again." The whole family tilted their heads toward the radio to make sure they heard every word. "THE AMOS AND ANDY SHOW" followed. Everyone laughed at this show. The next program, "FIBBER MCGEE AND MOLLY," was another favorite show, especially for John. At 7:00 came "THE JACK BENNY SHOW," with Rochester; Helen loved this show. During the commercials, Joe would try to mimic Benny and Rochester. Helen laughed harder at her son than at the show itself. Joe loved seeing his Mom laugh.

Joe liked Sunday nights when the whole family would relax and sit around the kitchen table, laughing. They always had things on their minds the other nights. If Joe's parents had been upset with him during the week, come Sunday evenings all seemed to be forgotten. Joe figured they were less tired, or maybe because they had attended church.

The Clarks were progressing very well since the war had ended. The economy surged forward, making farm prices rise. Like most farmers, John wanted to expand his operation.

John Clark ventured into a new avenue of farming. With Helen's approval, they purchased ten registered Black Angus bred heifers. The Clarks only had low grade feeder cattle previously. The registered Angus would allow John to raise breeding stock. They also needed a bull for breeding, but that could wait till next year.

On a cold, rainy, Saturday morning as Joe helped his Pa with the morning chores feeding hay to the Angus heifers in the barn, John spotted the heifer having problems dropping her calf. "Joseph, go get a halter upstairs by the oat bin. Hurry, Joseph."

Joe ran up the ladder as fast as his legs would carry him. He grabbed the halter off a spike nailed to a beam and tore down the ladder, almost falling.

John stood beside the young heifer that lay stretched out flat on the manure-laden floor of the barn. "Bring me the halter."

Joe climbed over the hay manger, jumping down onto fresh, steaming manure and reached out with the halter toward where his Pa stood. Joe's eyes narrowed. "She isn't goin' to die, is she, Pa?"

John never answered.

The calf's hind legs were exiting first. John knew he didn't have time to have his wife help him. He had to act fast in order to save the calf. He quickly tied the rope halter on the calf's hind legs and began to pull. "Joseph, help me pull." Joe got in front of his Pa, grabbed hold of the halter rope, parked his feet firmly into the manure and tugged on the rope. The calf was half out of its mother's womb when both John and Joe slipped down into the manure. "Keep pulling, Joseph. Pull harder."

The calf plopped onto the manure floor wrapped up in its umbilical cord. John pulled a pocket knife from his bib overhauls and cut the cord. He picked the calf up, stood it on its legs and pulled the placenta from its mouth. The calf let out a small sound. "Joseph, run upstairs and fetch me an empty gunny sack to wipe this calf down."

Joe tore up the ladder, grabbed an empty gunny sack and, while hurrying to come down the ladder, fell into a heap at the bottom. He scrambled over the manure, handing the gunny sack to his Pa, rubbing his leg that had gotten caught in the rungs of the ladder.

# Chapter 11

# THE FAIR

The LaSalle County Fair took place in late August 1952. Joe turned ten and this would be his first year in 4-H. The Clarks entered two steers, Blackie and Oscar.

The temperature the day Joe and John hauled the two steers to the Fair in a borrowed truck reached a scorching 80 degrees at 10:00 a.m. John and Joe had to unload the steers from the truck and lead them down a chute to the barn. Joe led his steer first. When Joe and the steer arrived at the base of the chute, a couple of city boys set off several firecrackers. Oscar spooked and took off running, dragging Joe behind.

Joe would not let go of the rope. He dug his feet in and hollered at Oscar to try to get him to stop. But the steer kept running and dragged Joe across 100 feet of coal cinders, tearing up his belly, arms, hands and face. Joe finally let go. Oscar kept right on running, until several farmers corralled him into one of the barns.

Joe got up almost the instant he had let go of the rope, Oscar already forgotten. Where were those city kids? He wanted a piece of each of them. The voices of the farmers trying to calm his steer reminded him of his responsibility, though, so he headed over to claim Oscar.

By the time Joe got Oscar into the barn and tied up, half an hour had gone by. Oscar was in sorry shape. He had lost over a hundred pounds from running all around the fairgrounds in the hot weather. By this time, the temperature had climbed to the high 80's. He could have died from heat exhaustion. Joe wet Oscar down to cool him off, paying no attention to his own injuries. Joe looked like he'd been in a fight with a can of red paint.

"You need to get those cuts taken care of before you get an infection," said Helen, who had driven Sarah down in the car.

"I'll be okay! I just want to get my hands on those punks," said Joe, looking around to locate the jerks.

"You don't worry about those boys. You need to get to the infirmary and get those cuts bandaged up. You are bleeding all over the place," said Helen, her finger pointing in the direction of the infirmary.

"I can describe those jerks to a tee. When I get hold of them, they will pay for this," said Joe.

Helen said no more, except, "Your Dad will deal with those boys, not you."

"It's my steer and my cuts. And besides, he won't do anything to those punks."

"You won't either, Joseph, so get that through your head right now," said John, with firmness in his voice. Sweat dripped from his face. His blue denim shirt was soaked with perspiration. The air in the barn was as still as dry mud.

Joe hung his head and, reluctantly, let his mother drag him to the infirmary.

The infirmary doctor shook his head when Joe walked in, which immediately put him on the defensive. "I don't need any band-aids. My mother is a registered nurse and she can take care of me if I need anything." He turned as if to head back out the door.

"You will need more than bandages and band-aids. You need stitches in several places," said the doctor, as he prepared the cleaning solution.

"Now, I'm really mad at those punks," said Joe, with clenched teeth.

After twenty stitches in four different places, Joe looked like he had run through a plate glass window. Joe's pride hurt more than the stitches. 'They won't get away with it,' Joe promised himself. He remembered how old Miss Stanley had pushed him.

# Chapter 12

# GETTING EVEN

At 2:00 P.M. the next day, Joe and Sarah waited in the show ring for the judge's decision as to which of the eighteen steers he would select as the best five. They and the other contestants paraded their steers around the ring, keeping their eyes on the judge just in case he motioned for them to position their steer in the final five.

The judge picked the five steers and had them parade around the ring, while the others held their positions. The judge lined them up and grabbed the microphone and picked the fifth steer. Joe's heart pounded, as he searched the crowd for the two city punks, not paying any attention to the judge and what he had to say. "Those punks will get what's comin' to them." He missed Blackie's second placement and ignored Helen, John and Harry waving and clapping in the crowd.

The ribbons were handed out to each one that placed and pictures were taken before the steers were returned to the barn. The judge asked Joe, "How did you get all those stitches? Have you been in a fight?"

"Not yet, but if I catch them, I will," replied Joe, with a quick grin.

The next day Sarah and Joe entered the ring again, this time for showmanship. Sarah and Joe didn't have enough experience yet to place in the top five. A steer had to be groomed just right. The handler had to have complete control of the animal at all times. If the judge asked him to do certain stops and starts, they had to be able to do this without any hesitation on the steer's part. The contestant must look sharp—hair, smile, clothing, shoes or boots, and stride.

They were in the ring parading their steers around with the same judge as before when Joe spotted his targets out of the corner of his eye. He ground to a halt in the middle of the ring. "Hey! Pa! Look over there! Those are the two punks that shot those fireworks," Joe said, pointing in their direction. Everyone in the ring, along with the audience, heard Joe.

39

Their heads turned to see where he was pointing.

"Son, are you in this ring, or are you out?" the judge asked Joe.

Joe didn't hesitate a second. "I'm out!" Handing the halter strap to his sister, Joe jumped the fence, running after the two city boys. They had missed the commotion in the ring and were walking with their backs to Joe. The parade stopped as everyone in and around the ring turned for a better show.

Joe tackled the boys from behind and immediately landed on top of them. He slugged one, then the other, in the face and stomach. They were older than Joe, but Joe's strength appeared to be too much for them. Before John and a policeman arrived, Joe had busted them up pretty badly.

"Stop it, Joseph!" John said, pulling his son off the two battered boys.

"What is going on here?" asked the policeman.

"They shot firecrackers and spooked my steer," said a still-angry Joe, struggling to get back at the two boys.

"What about it, you two?" The policeman asked the two lying on the ground, bleeding from the nose and mouth. "We didn't shoot no fireworks," said one of the boys, holding his nose. The other boy cried.

"You sure did," said Joe, straining against his fathers arms, trying to take another swing. "You're a liar! I know it was you two." Joe's face turned as red as a ripe tomato.

"Do you have any witnesses?" asked the policeman, looking at Joe.

"I don't know," said Joe.

"Why don't we just let this lay? I think enough has been done already," John said, wiping sweat from his forehead with his forearm. "Gosh! It's hot."

"Okay with me," said the policeman. He raised his hat and wiped the perspiration off his forehead with a handkerchief.

John grabbed Joe by the shirt collar and led him to the ring. "You get your steer and get to the barn, now." Joe marched away with his head down until reaching his steer.

Joe walked quickly to the barn with his steer and tied him up, waiting for the others to return. He figured his Pa had gone to watch the judging, and then would come back to deal with him. He sat on a bale of straw, with a piece hanging from his mouth, lips mashed together, fists doubled up, and heart racing. He never saw his Pa so angry, not at him, ever. "I should've hit 'em harder." Joe slammed his fist in the other open palm.

"What on earth were you thinking, going after those two kids that way?" said John, his voice very loud. Joe looked at his Pa with glaring eyes.

"You embarrassed your sister and all of us. You should be ashamed of yourself," said Helen, her finger shaking in her son's face. People listened to Joe getting raked over the coals. He hated that.

"Your temper will get the best of you someday," John said, his face inches from his son's face.

Harry stood about ten feet away. He managed to catch Joseph's eye and smiled and winked. "You ought to let Joseph alone. I think I would have done the same thing," Harry said, half smiling at Joe.

Helen whirled around. "You stay out of this. He may be your grandson, but he's not your son." Harry's smile left his face as his eyes remained fixed on Helen's. John said nothing, just looked at his wife as she made her remark. Everyone was sweating from the scorching heat and high humidity. Tempers were short. Joe wanted to run away.

Harry looked at Joe, winked again, tilted his straw hat and left. Joe thought maybe Sunday, two days away, things would heal over. The Sunday evening radio programs would make them laugh.

# Chapter 13

# HOMER

Pheasant season had just opened on the Saturday before Thanksgiving, 1954. Homer hated pheasant season more than any living creature on earth. He hated guns even more. During the two week pheasant season, Homer always managed to stand on the rock garden every morning at sunrise and crow until his throat became raw, or at least it sounded that way. The Clarks had their farm posted with "NO HUNTING ALLOWED" signs every 300 feet on the perimeter of the 480 acres.

The Clark's minister, Reverend George Stanton, said to John the Sunday after the opening of pheasant season, "John, I would like to come out and hunt on your property this coming Saturday."

"I'm afraid not. I don't allow anyone to hunt on my property," John said, sternly.

"I know your land is posted. That's the reason I would like to hunt your land." He rubbed his fleshy hands together. "There should be lots of pheasants." John had heard comments and suspected Reverend Stanton had fished and hunted on posted ground before.

"The answer is NO!" John said, with fire in his eyes. He walked away from the conversation, cussing under his breath. The Reverend's look turned somber instantly.

At 8:00 a.m. Saturday morning, the start of the second week of hunting season, Reverend Stanton drove south toward the Clark farm and spotted Homer in the garden. He slammed on his brakes, got out of his car, opened the trunk and took a Winchester 20-gauge shotgun from its gun case. He loaded three number six shot, shotgun shells into the chamber. Stanton raised his shotgun to his shoulder and sighted Homer walking slowly across the garden. When Homer spotted the fat man by the car, he turned tail to the lilac bushes, which were less than twenty feet away. He lifted, spread his wings and stayed low, bright eyes focused on the lilacs just ahead.

One crack and the empty shell ejected. The sound echoed

throughout the house like thunder.

Joe, still upstairs in his bedroom, heard the boom, ran to the window, and screamed, "No! No! He shot Homer!" His fingers froze to the window pane.

Helen was downstairs when she heard the crack, but the ten foot high lilac bushes blocked her view out the north window. She just knew that Homer had been shot by someone. "OH, NO!" she yelled. Helen hated guns. Wiping her hands on her soiled apron, she headed for the back door.

"Mom, that damn minister shot Homer," Joe said, running down the stairs, four steps at a time.

"Don't use such language about our minister. And how do you know it was Reverend Stanton?"

"I saw him with my own eyes. I will kick his butt!" Joe said, running out the back door, slamming shut as he left.

Helen ran out the door after her son. When she reached Reverend Stanton, Joe already was standing in front of the preacher, grabbing the bloody Homer from the murderer. "You no good preacher, you killed our Homer," Joe said, eyes red, right fist clenched, ready to throw the first punch.

Stanton's smile faded quickly. "Why, Joseph, shame on you. The Lord doesn't like it when young boys talk like that."

Hearing these piercing words from her son, Helen, with hands waving, eyes burning, screamed, "No, Joseph! Wait! Wait!" She knew how much her son loved that pheasant. She knew he'd strike back. "Please, Joseph, No!" Thoughts of the county fair came rushing in.

Joe's uppercut hit Stanton right in the center of his already red, knurly, large nose, knocking him backward several steps. Blood gushed from his nose. Joe gently dropped Homer to the ground and threw a second punch, another uppercut, striking Stanton just below the ribs. His fist went deep. The two-hundred fifty pound preacher stumbled forward. Joe let him fall slowly into a fetal position in front of his shoes. The two punches took less than eight seconds. Moans came from Stanton's bloody mouth. The blood oozed from his stomach out his mouth. "Stop, Stop! Please Joe! Stop! You will kill him," Helen screamed.

"Bastard doesn't deserve to live."

"You have no right to do this, Joseph! You let the law handle this!

My, GOD, what am I going to do with you?" Helen said, tearfully, trembling all over.

"He killed Homer!" Joe said, kicking stones at the helpless man.

Joseph picked up the Winchester shotgun and took the remaining shells out of the chamber. He smashed the shotgun several times against the telephone pole, stinging his hands on impact, until only small pieces and a bent barrel remained. Joe took the pieces and the bent barrel and threw them in the trunk of Stanton's car, slamming the lid closed. Helen tended to the Reverend.

Reverend Stanton came to and mumbled, "You can't do this to me. I will see to it that you serve time for your actions. I have my rights. Why-Why, I'm a voice of God."

"Go to hell, you murderer," Joe said, ready to swing into action again.

"You can't talk to me like that." Joe lunged toward Stanton as he hurried toward the safety of his car.

"Joe! Please stop. Please!" Helen begged, now crying loudly. She knew she wasn't strong enough to stop her son.

"God will get you for this," Stanton shouted as he plopped his portly body in the driver's seat. Stanton started the car, glancing down at Homer before engaging the shifter into drive.

"Are you okay to drive? Shall I call an ambulance? Oh! Dear GOD!" Helen felt herself growing faint. "Oh, Joseph, Why, why couldn't you wait?"

Reverend Stanton raced the engine and disappeared down the dusty road.

Helen, feeling weak, turned stricken eyes toward her son. He stared back at her, jaw clenched. Nothing she could do would change him. She shook her head and turned to the house. Joe waited for his Mom to vanish from the scene before he turned and picked up the lifeless Homer, as if he were a baby.

Joe found a cardboard box in the garage and placed Homer in it. He buried him on the north side of the rock garden. He found a large stone by the fence in the orchard and carried it to Homer's grave. "This will keep any varmints from digging up the grave," he said. His Grandpa had taught him that. He wiped tears from his face with his fist as soon as they appeared. "That bastard, how could he? Why not shoot some other old pheasant?" Tears ran uncontrollably down Joe's face.

John arrived home 30 minutes after Joe had laid Homer to rest to find Helen crying upstairs on their bed. Helen told her husband what had happened, but couldn't bring herself to mention Joseph's actions just yet. She knew he would become very angry.

"I really can't believe Stanton shot Homer in our garden from the road. That is illegal. I just told him last Sunday he couldn't hunt out here." John paced the kitchen floor. "You can't be that close to a person's home and you can't be that close to the road while firing any kind of a gun." John slammed his flat hand on the table top.

"Wait, John. Before you do anything, there's more." Helen told John the rest of the story.

"My GOD! Oh, My God! What did he do that for? That is attempted murder! Oh, My GOD!" John continued pacing the kitchen floor, trying to walk off his anger.

"That boy has such a temper. What on earth are we going to do? I am just beside myself," Helen said, worry written all over her swollen face.

"We'll probably have to get an attorney," John responded. He scratched his chin and looked out the window, searching for answers.

Harry knew of a good attorney in Ottawa that might represent Joe. His name was Harold Bridges. He handled these types of cases. Harry was proud of his grandson. He figured this would cost the Clarks some money, but he would pay, if necessary.

George Stanton was hospitalized with a broken nose and severe stomach disorder. His heart, according to his wife, was beating too fast. The rumor in town was that Stanton had already contacted an attorney.

# Chapter 14

# THE VERDICT

Monday evening, the Chicago television station WBBM broadcast the latest on the bizarre shooting by Reverend George Stanton and the severe beating he had gotten from Joseph Clark. The TV station portrayed Joseph as a bully kid who couldn't hold his temper. They never mentioned the fact that Stanton had shot the Clark's pet pheasant from the road near the house. The Clarks watched with sunken hearts, except Joe. He sat upstairs in his room. Every few minutes he would look out his window, down at the rock garden where Homer had been put to rest. His eyes welled up.

Charges were filed against Joseph on December 1st for aggravated assault. The hearing for the case would be held in Ottawa on December 14th at 9:00 a.m. The presiding judge would be the strict Honorable Judge Hubert Horowitz. Judge Horowitz had been on the bench for more years than John had been farming.

Joe dressed in a navy suit, a white shirt, and a red and white striped tie. Joe, at twelve years old, looked old enough to be a junior in high school. At 8:59 a.m., Judge Hubert Horowitz entered the courtroom.

Harry and Gertrude sat with Helen and John. They all appeared to have aged twenty years in the last three weeks, especially Helen.

George Stanton remained in the hospital. The Clarks felt he used the hospital stay to make things tougher on Joseph.

"The court is now in session," the Judge barked, as he rapped the gavel on the bench. Joe stayed very calm and expressionless. The other Clarks showed their concern with their eyes, as they exchanged solemn looks.

Both Harold Bridges, Joe's attorney, and Robert Blackly, the prosecuting attorney, had already met with Judge Horowitz that morning. Joe's attorney had explained that he would try to avoid a trial, if possible. He knew, in a conservative community like LaSalle County, beating up a man, especially a man who served the Lord, was a serious offense. Joe's chances in trial were not good. Instead, Attorney Bridges attempted to convince the judge and the prosecution to give Joseph Clark six months at Sheridan Boy's School in Sheridan, Illinois.

"Will Joseph Earl Clark please rise," Judge Horowitz commanded in a gruff voice. Joe's eyes remained fixed on the judge, never blinking.

Joe, along with his attorney, rose from their seats. Joe stood very erect with his hands in front of him, one hand over the other. He stood several inches taller than his attorney.

"Joseph Clark, the court finds you guilty of aggravated assault. You are sentenced to serve six months in the Sheridan Boys' School in Sheridan, Illinois. Your sentence will start tomorrow morning at 9:00 a.m." The judge's gavel slammed down with a loud bang.

Joe blinked twice, never moved or said a word. Helen Clark wailed as loudly as if he had gotten a life sentence. A teary-eyed John bowed his head and prayed. Harry muttered under his breath, "Stanton will get his due." Gertrude, white as a ghost, started to pray. This would be the first time any Clark spent time in a prison.

The sheriff's deputy led Joe from the courtroom soon after getting hugs and support from his family. Joe said, "I'm sorry for all the trouble I have caused."

"Joseph, don't take any crap from those people over there," Harry whispered in Joe's ear.

"I won't." Joe had his arm around his Grandpa's shoulders, squeezing him with love.

The Clarks did not receive a fine for Joe's action. In fact, George Stanton had to pay his own medical bills, for which the church reimbursed him. The elders of the church, except John Clark, had approved it. The elders just wanted it to go away. John was furious.

# Chapter 15

# PRISON

The trip the next morning to Sheridan Boys' School took less than an hour—the longest hour of Joe's young life. It was cold, rainy and the sun hadn't shone in days. He thought of the mistakes he had made that had shamed his family. *Why did those boys have to shoot off those damn fireworks, anyway?* He stared out the side window of the sheriff's patrol car, seeing farmland, his Pa, his Grandpa and himself working the land. He visualized himself feeding the young, motherless calf. His eyes filled up. He rubbed them quickly so the two sheriff deputies wouldn't see. He had to be strong in mind and body. Grandpa had told him that this past October during harvest.

The orientation lasted one hour and, already, Joe hated the place. He received a set of clothes that included boxer shorts, which he had never worn before, a tee shirt, green pants, green long sleeve shirt, black shoes, white socks, baseball hat, winter jacket and gloves. All clothing bore the black stencil, "Sheridan Boys' School."

Joe was assigned to Cell Block B. The school consisted of three cell blocks. Each two story cell block held 84 boys. The cell blocks remained almost full year round. Two boys occupied each 8 ft. by 10 ft. cell. They had a small sink, cold water only, bunk beds, a toilet with no seat, one sheet per bed, two blankets per bed, a flat thin pillow per bed, a twelve inch square window that could not be opened or broken, and one roll of toilet paper. The steel entrance door had an eight-inch square opening with steel bars for stale air to enter. The interior walls were made of solid, 10-inch, unpainted concrete. Each boy could have a few personal items that couldn't cause any harm to anyone. These items included: Candy, toothpaste, a toothbrush, and pictures. No ballpoint pens, pencils, mirrors, or any other sharp objects were allowed. Letters were to be written in a designated location in the cell block with security guards watching.

Under the State Psychologists' ruling, no one could work in a department where they may have had previous experience. They figured if you were working in a field and were prosecuted during that time, it was best to be assigned to a totally different area. Joe got assigned to the shoe department. This department made every shoe worn by the inmates. The butchered steers on the farm supplied the leather.

Completely self-sufficient, the school had its own beef cattle, hogs, chickens for eggs and meat, a vegetable garden, and dairy cows. The inmates prepared all the food, supervised by chefs who worked for the State. Joe was upset that he couldn't work on the school's farm. He had more experience than probably anyone there.

A guard escorted Joe to his cell block and to his room on the lower level. As soon as Joe entered the room, the guard slammed the door behind him. The sound echoed through Joe's head. He shuddered and tears began to form in his eyes. He wiped them with his shirt sleeve.

He looked around the small room and saw a made-up bottom bunk. Joe threw his stuff on the top bunk. He saw a picture of a Negro family taped to the cement wall. Joe had never even been closer than one hundred feet from a Negro and that was the porter at the train station in Mendota. Joe shook inside. He tried to fight it off, but his whole body started to feel strange. *Don't be scared!* Grandpa reminded him.

# Chapter 16

# CELL MATE

The door opened and in walked a Negro about the same height and weight as Joe. The door slammed again. Joe cringed. They stared at one another for a few seconds before Joe said, "My name is Joe Clark." He couldn't keep the quiver from his voice and hoped the Negro boy hadn't noticed. The Negro boy looked at Joe's eyes, half-squinted, and said, softly, "Jimmy Robbins." Jimmy had never been around any white people, until he entered Sheridan Boys' School.

Two hours went by and neither boy spoke. Jimmy lay on his bunk staring at the bunk above him. Joe made his bed and put away a few personal items. Cell Block B got ready to go to lunch. Joe was as hungry as a bear. The doors all opened automatically. Jimmy moved out first, with Joe right behind him. "Hey, Jimmy, I see you have a Honky to play with," called one of the other Negro boys from a few cells down. Jimmy's eyes stayed straight ahead, not responding. Joe never looked at the Negro who had spoken.

Cell Block B marched to the dining room in columns of two. Each cell block went at different times. The dining hall had large, wooden, picnic-like tables. All trays were made of light-weight aluminum and the eating utensils consisted of aluminum spoons only. Several guards remained in the dining room to make sure everyone behaved. The guards did not carry any arms.

Boys aged eleven through seventeen made up the school's population. Boys who reached the age of eighteen and had not been released got transferred to the State penitentiary in Joliet, Illinois. The inmates consisted of mainly Negroes, mostly from the Chicago area. Their crimes ranged from minor infractions, like burglary, to murder, attempted murder, stealing, and rape.

Other inmates dished out the chow. Joe couldn't believe the size of the portions. *I'll starve in here.* "Is this all they give you?" Joe asked Jimmy.

"Yeah, man!"

It poured on the walk back to the cell block. It felt cold enough to snow, thought Joe.

"Where you from?" Joe asked Jimmy.

"Chicago."

"Wow! You ever go see the Cubs play?" Joe felt his heart lighten.

"Nah," his eyes lit up. "You like the Cubs?" Jimmy grinned quickly.

"I'm a Dodger fan."

"Yeah, Jackie Robinson plays for them." Jimmy's eyes opened wide.

"Yeah, third base."

"He's the first Negro to play in the big leagues."

"Yeah, I know. That's the reason I'm a Dodger fan. Well, not really." Joe told Jimmy about the Chicago Tribune's front page when Jackie Robinson signed up with the Dodgers.

They talked baseball until it was time to go to gym class. The rain had stopped and today they would be playing basketball on the outside courts. Jimmy and Joe were the tallest boys on the court. "You play basketball? Jimmy asked.

"No, I only played baseball."

"I'll help you. Watch that kid over there. He hates white people and he'll try some stuff with you." Joe was the only white boy on the concrete slab.

Joe looked at the kid and shrugged his shoulders. "Thanks!" Joe said, softly. The Negro boy glanced up and glared at Joe.

Each team consisted of five boys. When the kid Jimmy had told Joe about elbowed Joe in the throat, he let it go. When he hit Joe again, though, Joe was ready for it. He came back with an elbow to his throat and the kid fell in a heap. He tried to speak, but he could only rasp out his threat, "White boy, if I had a knife, you would be dead." Joe laid his size thirteen shoe on the Negro's chest.

"Don't ever hit me again." Joe applied more pressure to his chest. The other boys circled.

"You oughtn't have said that. Joe here has kilt several people," Jimmy said to the boy on the ground and loud enough for the rest of them to hear. Joe glanced at Jimmy with bewilderment.

The kid on the ground stood up. He came to Joe's shoulders, slapped Joe on the arm, and said, "Hey man, I didn't know," grinning as he spoke with a hoarse voice. Joe sensed some fear.

Joe glanced at Jimmy, then at the other boys and, saying nothing, just moved away.

The game continued without incident. Most of the guys tried to help Joe improve his basketball skills, even the kid who had elbowed Joe.

Later, when they were back in their cell, Joe asked Jimmy about the lie. "Why did you tell them about me killing people?"

"Look, man, they don't like no white folk on their court. I tell them that and they think you're a real bad man. They scared-a you now." Jimmy grinned.

"Ok!" Joe never had anyone lie for him. Surprised, but he thought he had made a friend, for at least his time at Sheridan.

# Chapter 17

# THE ADJUSTMENT

Jimmy had just turned thirteen and lived in Chicago, near Division Street. He was serving one year for stealing groceries for his mother and four brothers because they couldn't afford to buy any. His father had murdered one of his wife's lovers and had received a life sentence, currently being served in the State penitentiary in Joliet. His older sister, Geraldine, had a year left to serve in a school for girls, similar to Sheridan, for stealing cars for an organized crime group in Chicago. Jimmy thought they were mafia people, but couldn't be sure. "Mafia, what's that, Jimmy?"

"They are mean-ass Italians—organized crime. They will kill you for lookin' at them cross-eyed." His eyes dropped to the floor.

All ears, Joe couldn't believe some of the things Jimmy told him. He had never been to a large city before. "Wow! How did you survive, living like that?"

"You learn to be street smart. If you don't, you die, die young."

"You must be pretty smart, living up there."

Jimmy and Joe instantly became friends because they had to or they would have tried to kill each other. That's what prison life did to you. Some of the bigger Negro boys had smaller white boys for cell mates. They raped them until their anuses were torn up. Then, they would get another boy. The State of Illinois' Corrections Department tolerated this for years.

Joe learned a lot about inner-city people from Jimmy's nightly stories. Jimmy taught Joe how to street fight and how to protect himself from an opponent's knife. "Read their eyes, watch their hands," Jimmy would say. "The eyes will tell you plenty. Study them, know them and use them as your weapon against them."

"Thanks." Joe knew he had a lot to learn. He really liked Jimmy.

Jimmy's diction wasn't like most of the Negro boys. His grandma made sure he didn't use those slang phrases that accompanied the ghetto neighborhoods. Joe had a hard time understanding some of the Negro boys. They talked fast and their words rolled out of their mouths like stones off a shovel.

Everyday at Sheridan was about the same. They ate breakfast at the same time. An hour of detail time followed breakfast. Then, they went to work at their jobs. The job paid a dollar per hour and the prisoner got twenty cents of that to spend on miscellaneous items at the small prison store. They received the balance in cash when they were released. They ate lunch at 1:15 p.m.

Cell Block B had one hour of gym or exercise class. Most of the Negro boys played basketball, while most white boys played baseball. Joe chose to play basketball, but had a hard time competing since they could jump higher and move quicker than he could.

Dinner took place at 5:30 p.m. Joe never did get enough to eat. The food was the best he ever tasted, though. The State had nutritionists to make sure the prisoners were given the right balance of food. The State employed chefs to teach the inmates assigned to the kitchen how to cook. The prison guards always ate in the dining room mostly because of the free food. They couldn't get better food anywhere, not even at home.

There were plenty of fights at Sheridan, with several reported each day. Even more went unreported. Many boys, battling boredom and with low IQ's, would fight just to have something to do. Jimmy was not one of those boys. He didn't like to fight; but if he did fight, he always won. Jimmy was quicker than lightning. Any boy caught fighting, whether it was his fault or not, had an extra month added onto his sentence. Jimmy already had two extra months to serve. Several boys died each year at Sheridan, most of them from their cellmate beating them to death or raping them until they bled to death. The prison guards did very little to stop the barbaric actions. They rather enjoyed the bloodbath that took place. To many of the guards, prisoners were just lowlifes.

The Clarks would visit Joe every Sunday, the only day visitors were allowed.

Jimmy never saw anyone from his family. Helen would always fix some dessert or bake bread for Joe, which he would share with Jimmy. "Hey, Mom, how about bringing some extra food for Jimmy?"

"I'm not fixing any food to feed any Negroes. I'm not fixing this for you to share with him, either. I hate it that you have to share your room with a Negro. You understand, don't you? They wouldn't share

54

with you and you know it." Helen fumbled with the brown paper bag that contained homemade bread and a large apple pie, made with apples from the Clark's farm.

Mom's remarks devastated Joe. "You know, Jimmy is different. Nobody ever comes to visit him. He is a darn good friend. Probably a better friend than anyone I know."

"You don't want that kind for a friend, Joseph."

"I gotta go. Take this food and give it to the hogs. I don't want it." Joe got up and left the visiting room.

"Joseph! Joseph, I fixed this for you. Please take it."

Joe vanished through the door.

In shock, Helen's mouth gaped open in disbelief as her son left without taking the food. He never turned down food—never.

Jimmy seemed a little disappointed that Joe didn't have any home cooking with him when he returned. Jimmy liked Mrs. Clark's homemade cookies. His grandma could make good cookies, but Jimmy hadn't had any for a long time. Joe didn't tell him why he came back without any, but Jimmy sensed something was wrong. He kept his thoughts to himself.

The next week Helen came with John and brought enough food for six boys. "Thanks. When you meet Jimmy, and you will, you'll see what a great guy he is. Negroes are just like us. Their skin is different, but they bleed just like we do." Joe checked the two large brown bags of food.

Helen wasn't convinced, but she was glad that, at least this time, Joseph had accepted her home-cooked food.

# Chapter 18

# THE BRAWL

Joe had two more months to serve; Jimmy, three. As they sat down to eat in the dining room, a food fight began. Jimmy and Joe tried to stay out of it, but fists started flying and, before they knew it, they were in a life or death brawl. The prison guards just watched and laughed at what developed into the worst outbreak of violence in the history of the School.

After twenty minutes of battling, seventy-eight boys had shattered bones, internal injuries, and/or lost teeth and blood. The death count stood at twelve.

Jimmy and Joe walked away with some bruises and minor cuts, eyes almost swollen shut, and memories that would last a lifetime. Their friendship took a new road. Their protection of one another during that melee mirrored that of two brothers at war with a common enemy. Joe figured he wouldn't have survived if it hadn't been for Jimmy teaching him how to street fight and watching his back. Jimmy felt if it weren't for Joe's powerful strength protecting him, he wouldn't have survived. They made a promise to one another later that day that, no matter what, they would be there for each other.

The news media broadcast the story that night on Chicago television. The Clarks knew that Joe bunked in Cell Block B. "Oh, my God! John, we need to call. Where's the number?" Helen, already up, moved toward where she thought she might have the number to the School.

John recited a short prayer. "He is one tough kid and bigger than most I'd seen over there. Maybe he and Jimmy were together and made it through all right." John paced the kitchen floor.

Helen called that night and was told that no names were being released yet. It would probably be tomorrow sometime. They both had a sleepless night.

The Clarks waited four days before learning that Joseph was okay. Helen was aging fast.

The guards on duty in the dining room lost their jobs, as did the warden. They erected a small room, six foot by six foot, with a heavy, thick, glass window twenty four inches square, adjacent to the dining room. The bottom of the window had an opening to accommodate a gun barrel. A guard with a tear gas gun manned it during mealtime. The dining area had one guard for every ten boys.

Joe and Jimmy each received another month for their participation in the brawl. Of the twelve boys that died in the brawl, Joe and Jimmy never let on to anyone that their fists and hands had caused some of those deaths. It was kill or be killed.

The last two months of their sentences went by quickly. The School did not have one single reported fight during that time. The new warden enforced stricter rules for the guards and inmates. The new guards treated the prisoners with muted respect.

Jimmy and Joe parted company on a Saturday morning in July. They hugged one another, promising to write each other and to get together whenever they could. The eyes of both boys turned moist. Jimmy said, "Good luck with your Dodgers."

"You take care of those Cubs."

Joe's parents waited for him at the main gate. Joe wore the new Lee jeans, sport shirt and tennis shoes that his mother had brought to him the week before. When the gate guard handed Joe his prison earnings, Joe gave it back to him, making him promise to give it to Jimmy when he got released. He knew Jimmy would need that money.

The ride home was pleasant, but subdued. Joe asked a few questions and thought about Jimmy and where he would end up living in that inner city. Joe knew one thing—they would meet again someday.

Reverend George Stanton died of a massive heart attack the day after Joe arrived home from his stay at Sheridan. He had gone fishing on someone's private property without permission. Joe never made a comment to anyone about Stanton's death, but in his mind he thought, *"Good riddance to a rotten preacher."*

Chapter 19

# BROWNIE

The Clarks changed churches weeks after Joseph left for Sheridan Boys School since Reverend Stanton and John Clark were unable to resolve their differences. John opted to leave the church, rather than try to worship where he didn't respect the minister. The Clarks were getting ready to attend Church.

While looking out the window in his room upstairs, he saw what appeared to be a large, wet, brownish colored dog across the road in the ditch. It laid not fifteen feet from where Joe had beaten up old Stanton. Joe said nothing to his Mom or Dad. Dressed in his Sunday clothes, he crossed the road to check on this poor dog.

Approaching the dog, he said, "How are you boy? You are a boy, aren't you?" Joe knelt down, holding out his right hand. The rain began to come down harder. "Where did you come from? Do you have a name?" With every question, the dog moved its ears. The dog had short hair and a white stripe down the front of him. He or she was big enough, probably weighed around 90 pounds, thought Joe. "What a set of teeth you have. You have teeth like a small grizzly bear."

"Come here, boy" said Joe, reaching closer to the thin, drenched dog a few feet from his hand. The shy dog came to Joe, almost crawling, whimpering as if scared. Joe rubbed his fingers. "Come on boy. Let me look at you." The dog started to whine. Joe figured the dog was hungry and cold. Joe hadn't determined the sex yet. Its stomach looked gaunt, eyes hollow, and sported a cut on its face. "You look like you've been in a fight."

Joe picked up the dog, determined it was a male and said, "I'll take you in the house, feed you and get you dried off." The dog just looked up at Joe and whimpered.

By the time Joe and his new friend arrived back at the house, they were both soaked and muddy. The rain came down harder; the wind blew strongly out of the west.

Joe took the dog down to the basement and dried him off, then went upstairs and grabbed some food out of the refrigerator. He tracked mud all over the kitchen floor. "Ah, rump roast would be good." Joe grabbed the roast and got four slices of his mother's homemade bread and some left-over tuna salad. "Yeah, he'll like this." The Clarks' other dogs loved table scraps.

Upon returning to the downstairs, he found the dog upright, wagging his tail. Joe fed him a piece at a time. He never grabbed for the food, just sat and waited for Joe to feed him

"Joseph, where are you?" His mother hollered. "Wha-What is all this mud doing on the floor? I-I just scrubbed this yesterday. Joseph! Where are you?"

"I'm down in the basement." Joe cringed slightly, looking at his muddy shoes. The dog chomped away on the rump roast.

"What are you doing down there? Did you get all this mud on the kitchen floor?"

"I found a dog and I'm feeding him."

"You are doing what? Where did you get the dog? You're not getting dog hair on your Sunday clothes are you?" Helen said, hands on her hips, disgust in her voice. Looking outside, she saw the rain and grabbed a mop to clean up the mud. "You're not all wet and muddy are you?" She shook her head, knowing he probably was.

Joe glanced down, again, at his muddy shoes and pants. Didn't his mother ever ask one question at a time? He could hear his Mom's voice float down the stairs as she spoke to his Pa.

"Your son has a dog down in the basement and I'm sure he is all full of dog hair. It's raining out and he probably looks like he has been in the hog pen. Look at this floor, John." John sat in the kitchen, cleaning the dirt from his finger nails with a pocket knife.

"Where did he get the dog? What if it has rabies?" After a short pause, John continued, "What kind of dog is it?"

"Now my Dad is asking several questions in a row with no answer," Joe muttered to himself, just loud enough for him and the dog to hear.

"Joseph!" His Dad yelled, walking down to the basement.

"Look, Dad! I found this dog across the road." The wet mud now started to cake on his Sunday clothes.

"My God, don't let your mother see you like that. You're a mess."

"What do you think of my dog?"

"Well, he looks ok to me, maybe a little thin. I'll tell your mother you have to stay home with the dog, or I'll tell her you're not fit to go to church looking—oh, forget it, she'll be hollering at me all the way to church."

"I'll take care of the dog and have him all cleaned up before you get home." Joe looked happier to John than he had seen him look in a long time. The dog looked up at John with "I like it here eyes" and wagging tail.

"Ok, son!" John went up the stairs knowing his son may have found a real friend.

Helen waited at the top of the stairs. "Is he ready to go?"

"No, I think it best he stay home and tend to the dog."

"What?"

"Ever since Homer was shot, he seems almost lost. Maybe this is what he needs."

Helen mashed her lips, but didn't argue. Instead, she turned and hollered, "Sarah, are you ready to go?"

After Joe had changed from his muddy clothes to his farm clothes and had given his dog some more homemade bread, he took him for a grand tour of the farm. The rain had stopped and the sun was trying to shine. They headed for the barn first. The dog ran over the hay bales and then down to the ground level. The dog went straight down the ladder head first and never missed a step. "What a dog you are. Not one of our dogs ever did that."

Joe figured he better give the dog a name. "What's your name, boy? Well, you're brown like a paper bag and have some white markings." Joe pondered a minute. "How about I call you Brownie?" The dog responded as if that were his name by barking. "Ok, Brownie. That's it." Joe's heart allowed Brownie to slide in. He hugged his dog as Brownie licked his face.

Brownie and Joe spent the next hour checking out the cattle and the other livestock. "You can't chase the cows, hogs, sheep or the chickens. Do you understand?" Brownie wagged his tail and rubbed against Joe's pant leg. Joe rubbed Brownie's ears. "You're a smart dog." Betsy had died last year and Joe figured Brownie would be her replacement.

That night Brownie slept in the basement. Joe got up in the middle of the night and went to the basement to check on his new friend. Joe thought he looked lonely. "Come upstairs to my room." Brownie followed Joe all the way to his room. The dog acted like he understood every word Joe spoke.

Brownie slept the rest of the night in Joe's room. When Joe came downstairs to the kitchen the next morning, he had Brownie right behind him. John said, while sitting in the kitchen having his morning coffee, "What did that dog do, sleep with you all night?"

"Yeah Pa, Brownie is very smart."

"He must be housebroken if he stayed up there all night," John said, smiling at Brownie.

"I believe he is, Pa."

"You had better get him outside before your mother gets down here."

"Let's go, Brownie." And out the door they went.

Brownie was definitely housebroken and after a lot of complaining from Helen, he finally got to stay in Joe's room every night. The Clarks had never before let a dog in the house even for a few minutes, let alone for an entire night.

# Chapter 20

# FIRST DATE

It was two weeks before graduation when Sue Andretti approached Joe in the hall. "Joe, are you going to the eighth grade dance next Saturday night?" Her brown eyes looked up at him, as he stared, completely stunned.

Joe immediately started to sweat as he tried to find the words. Finally, he managed to shake his head once. "I-I don't dance." He looked down as the words came out of his mouth. Sure wished he knew how now. His face grew hot.

"I'll teach you if you ask me to the dance," Sue said, quickly. Eagerness covered her face, yet her composure erased her forwardness. Joe, completely in a fog by now, managed to stutter the words:" I would-love to-take you to-the dance, but I am afraid I will embarrass you in front of your friends."

"Then, it's a date. Don't worry. I won't ever get embarrassed being with you." Her smile broadened.

Joe's knees started to buckle. He never felt like this before. Until now, had he ever really known fear? "Sue, I want to take you to dance. I mean to the dance. I mean I want to take you to the dance."

Sue smiled, "Joe, I'm really happy you asked me."

"Me-me, too, Sue," Joe stammered, sweat pouring down his back.

Joe, still cloudy from Sue's words, pointed himself toward math class. His legs were so unstable he could hardly put one leg in front of the other. His math test proved to be a breeze and Joe walked out of the class singing to himself, smiling from ear to ear. As he walked down the hall, one of his classmates, a city boy, asked him how he got a date with Sue. *How did he find out?* "I just. I don't know. I wanted to go. She asked me," Joe managed, with a big grin on his face.

"I can't believe she would go out with an ex-convict like you."

Joe's eyes narrowed, jaw froze and, without thinking, he grabbed the guy and slammed him against the steel lockers. "I served my time and if it wasn't for that Stanton, I wouldn't have been in prison. Don't you ever bring it up again, or they'll have another reason to put me in there." The prison cell, Jimmy, and the brawl entered his head quickly. Joe knew he had to control his temper. He released the punk, letting him fall to the floor.

"I-I'm sorry Joe!" The shaken city boy didn't move, afraid Joe would start in on him if he did. But Joe's thoughts had already turned. His date with Sue washed away his memories of Sheridan. He walked away.

Joe couldn't wait to get home to tell Brownie and his parents about the big event. Sue Andretti was the best looking girl in school and she wanted to go to the dance with him. "Wow!"

Brownie met Joe as the bus's door opened and sensed Joe's happiness. "Hey!" reaching down and rubbing his head, "Hey, Brownie, guess what? I have a date with the best looking girl in school." They both ran toward the back door of the house.

John and Helen were in the kitchen drinking coffee when Joe came busting through the door. Brownie stood proudly with him as he announced, "I have a date with the best looking girl in school." Joe's eyes looked as if he were in la-la land.

"With who? What's her name?" demanded his mother.

"Sue Andretti! And her eyes are beautiful." Joe stared at the wall, but saw Sue's eyes when she had asked him. His smile widened.

"That's Rene's daughter." Helen gave her husband a meaningful look.

"You mean that woman that you said has been sleeping around?" John said, looking at Helen. Joe's eyes ricocheted from his Mom to his Pa.

"Yes, that's her and she is nothing but a tramp," Helen said, with fire in her eyes, arms folded across her breasts.

"I'm not taking her mother to the dance," Joe mumbled into his shirt.

"You're not taking her daughter to the dance, either. I won't have my son going out with any tramp's daughter."

Joe looked up quickly. "But I am going to the dance with her."

"I said, NO! Do I make myself clear?" Joe's heart crumbled and his body turned numb. He headed toward the door.

Joe ran outside. With Brownie right on his heels, they took off toward the barn. Joe sat in the hay mow with Brownie at his side. "How can she be so mean?" He picked at the hay. "I'm going to the dance. She's not stopping me. She doesn't like Jimmy, either."

Joe finally returned to the house after spending over an hour in the barn. He went straight to his room and changed clothes, then went back outside to help his Dad with the chores. He said nothing to his mother or his Dad. Sarah saw him and said, "Why didn't you pick someone nice?"

"Shut the hell up!" Hostility shot out of his mouth.

Joe refused to eat dinner. Instead, he went to his room with his schoolbooks and Brownie. He lay on his bed with Brownie beside him, trying to figure out what he needed to do. He said to Brownie, "Maybe we can go live with Sue." Brownie wagged his tail. Joe went to bed that night with his blue eyes wide open, thinking only of Sue.

The next morning, Joe came downstairs with Brownie to find his parents waiting for him in the kitchen. "We need to talk to you."

"I have nothing to say to you," Joe said, without making eye contact.

"Joseph, we are going to talk this over," Helen said, determinedly, with her fists mounted on her hips.

"We are only concerned about who you go out with, Joseph," John said, softly.

"You never listen to me. You hear crap and don't have a clue if it's true. You don't like Jimmy either." He bolted out the door with Brownie at his heels.

Helen paced the floor. Her heels dug into the linoleum floor. "I can't take much more of this. His temper flare ups and now these friends he chooses. I sure didn't raise him that way. This son of yours is going to be the death of me yet." John stood looking out the window, scratching his whiskered chin.

"Do we really know that this Rene is not a good person? Maybe she isn't as bad as they say." Their eyes met. Hers became wretched; his showed uncertainty. Helen hated to be questioned. Wrinkling her nose, she turned away from her husband.

"I heard it in the beauty shop. She has been a sleazy bitch. The way I hear it, she has broken up a few marriages along the way. She comes onto men and they become vulnerable," Helen said, with little room for doubt. "This town doesn't need her kind."

John waited before he asked anything more. "Do you know this woman? Have you ever met her? Where does she live?"

"I don't want to meet her and, no, I don't know her or care where she lives." Married women in Midwest farm communities were very protective of their husbands when it came to shapely women like Rene Andretti. Rene was built like a model compared to all the other women of the community. She made it worse by dressing revealingly—a little too revealingly for a Midwestern farm town.

John realized his wife had a bitter taste in her mouth about this woman. "I think we need to find out the facts here before we go by gossip heard in the beauty salon."

He knew the truth got stretched like a tight girdle in that beauty salon.

"I believe what I heard." She paused. "But we can try and find out the truth. I don't know how, though."

# Chapter 21

# THE DANCE

J oe's parents finally decided to allow him to take Sue to the eighth grade dance. Joe dressed in his Sunday best: a dark blue suit, a white shirt and black shoes. He polished his shoes until he could see his smile in the toes. He looked like he could be going to the high school prom, instead of the eighth grade school dance.

Joe's parents drove Joe to Sue's house, which was a nice two bedroom in the newer part of town.

Joe knocked on the door of the Andretti's house at 6:48 p.m., exactly two minutes early. Rene answered. His legs shook. He just couldn't get those legs to stop shaking once they started. When the door opened and Joe laid eyes on Mrs. Andretti, he could feel his face turning red. "Hi! I'm Joe."

"Hi! Joe. I'm Sue's mother and am delighted to meet you. Sue has spoken of you often the past two months. Please, come in. Sue will be ready in a moment." Sue had told her mother about Joe being at Sheridan and Reverend Stanton and everything she had heard about Joe. She shared things with her mother that most sisters wouldn't tell one another.

Rene wore a skin-tight, bright red dress. She had short black hair. Her face was beautiful, almost flawless. Every curve in her body showed in that dress. No wonder the women in this town started rumors about her. They were all jealous as hell, thought Joe.

"Please sit down, Joe. Sue will be down in a minute."

"Thank you, Mrs. Andretti," Joe said, still beaming at this gorgeous lady. *Why couldn't my mother be like her? She sure seems nice to me.* Joe sat down.

Sue appeared in a red dress, white shoes, and a necklace that her Dad had given her to wear when she attended her first dance. With her long black hair and brown eyes, she looked fantastic. Joe rose up out of his seat, with wobbly legs and dampness running down his back. "You look fantastic."

"Hi, Joe, you look great!" Sue smiled shyly.

"You kids have a great time. And, Joe, you take care of my baby. She is all I have." Rene's eyes watered slightly as she slid her arm around Sue's waist.

"I will, Mrs. Andretti." Joe could hardly move. Now, he had to face his parents with his first date.

The walk to the car went much too fast for Joe. The temperature outside was in the high 50's. Joe felt like he needed another bath. He hoped his Mom would be nice to Sue, but he had his doubts. He looked into the car. His mother's eyes were fixed on Sue like a cat ready to pounce on a mouse. His clammy body turned cold.

Joe opened the rear car door for Sue. He then rushed around the back of the car with his heart pounding so hard it felt as though it would pop out of his shirt. Joe quickly opened the door and sat down, hoping his mother hadn't been rude to Sue. "This is Sue Andretti. I told you she was the best looking girl in school. Her mother is really nice. Sue looks just like her mother. Their house is really clean." Joe talked as much as he could so his mother wouldn't have time to say anything bad.

Helen turned her head and said, curtly, "Nice to meet you," then turned toward the front of the car.

"Hi, Sue! You better be careful this guy doesn't step on your feet while you're dancing," John said, with a friendly smile on his face.

"I'm really glad to meet you both. Joe has told me so much about you and how proud he is to be a farmer's son," Sue said, sincerely.

Joe looked at her in admiration. She was so mature. Not like other girls her age.

"Have you ever been on a farm, Sue?" asked John, glowing from her words.

"No! But I'd love to someday."

"You will have to come over sometime. Joe can show you around." Helen threw daggers at her husband. How could he invite this little miss prissy to their farm?

Joe started to relax somewhat, even though his mother was as cold as frost on steel. Maybe Pa could keep her in check.

Sue stretched her arm across the seat to clasp Joe's hand. Joe sensed his mother's disapproval. He thought at times that she must have eyes in the back of her head. Joe didn't want to talk to Sue because he knew his parents, especially his mother, would capture every word spoken. The ride to the dance took only eight minutes, but seemed like an eternity.

"What time do we need to pick you up?" asked John.

"Eleven, Pa!"

"You don't need to be out that late. You be out here at 10:00. Do you hear me?"
Helen blurted. Joe's heart almost stopped. Sue quickly glanced at Joe.

"We will be here at 10:50, Joe," John said, firmly. He looked at his son and winked. Sue smiled.

"It was nice to have met you both," Sue said, as she got out of the car.

"It was nice to have met you, Sue. Have a good time and watch his big feet." Helen said nothing and that was just fine with Joe.

# Chapter 22

# TWO PUNCHES

Joe and Sue had a great time at the dance. Joe had stepped on Sue's feet only twice. Joe learned quickly from Sue how to do the two-step. Sue's mother had taught her how to dance. No more sweat to worry about. He seemed very relaxed now.

Sue excused herself and went to the girls' bathroom. Joe stood at one end of the gym waiting for his first date to return. Three boys from Joe's class came over to Joe. Joe knew them and didn't care for them, but really couldn't explain why.

Johnny Bracket was the school bully, or at least he thought he was, until Joe came around. Accompanied by two buddies, he felt he could give Joe a hard time.

"Hey! Farm Boy! What you doing? Waiting for your honey to come out of the john?" Joe clenched his fists; he knew he would have to take care of these three city punks. Memories of the county fair, his Pa screaming at him in the barn afterward, clouded his head. The last fight Joe had had taken place in Sheridan. From what Jimmy had taught him about street fighting, he felt prepared.

"I hear your honey's mother is a real looker and has the body of Marilyn Monroe. I also hear she goes to bed with any Tom, Dick or Harry she ca---." Joe lashed out—Johnny Bracket hit the gym floor like a sack of hog feed falling from a wagon. Joe only had to hit him once in the jaw, but he gave him a right upper cut to the belly on his way down, just to be sure. Johnny's two buddies backed away in shock at how fast Joe had put their friend on the floor.

Within seconds, everyone in the place, except Sue and a couple of other girls who were in the bathroom, had heard about the punches thrown by Joe. Two male chaperones at the dance appeared almost immediately. "What is going on here?" one teacher asked.

"Joe punched my buddy for no reason at all," Jerry Blandgaurd said.

"That's not right!" said one of the boys who saw the fight and

69

heard the taunting words from Johnny.

"I'll call an ambulance!" said the other teacher. Blood trickled from Bracket's mouth. The teachers had neither seen nor heard anything. They gave Joe a hard look.

It was now 10:30. Joe guessed he should have listened to his mother and left at 10:00. Thoughts that he might have to go back to Sheridan entered his mind.

What about Sue? How could he survive back at Sheridan without Jimmy? Joe wanted to run, but knew he had to wait for Sue. He glanced off in the direction she had gone, hands on his hips.

"Joe, what happened?" said Sue, touching his arm, looking down at a lifeless Johnny Bracket.

"He had to open his big mouth. He insulted your mother," Joe said, staring at the floor.

"Joe did what anyone would do, Sue," said David Carney, a good friend of Joe's.

"Oh! Joe! I wish we hadn't come," Sue said, with tears flowing down her cheeks.

The sweat began running down Joe's back again, but his legs weren't shaking. He was mad at himself, but really angry at Johnny for ruining his first date and first dance. Joe knew he shouldn't have hit him so hard.

They loaded Johnny into the ambulance. His two buddies approached Joe and said, "We will finish this some other time."

"Whenever!" Joe said, without thinking.

Joe's parents picked Joe and Sue up at 10:50. Joe's mother was very pleasant, to say the least. Both Sue and Joe worried about the consequences of tonight's fight.

Joe walked Sue to the door. They stepped inside, closing the door softly. They held each other for what seemed like ten minutes, without speaking. "I am really sorry about this," Joe said, his voice cracking.

"Joe, I know you did this for me. Now, I'm scared for you." She didn't want him going back to prison. "It's my fault." Tears trickled down her unblemished cheeks.

"No!" Joe shook his head. He kissed her moist cheek. "Bracket is to blame, nobody else." Sue gave a half smile, put her fingers on his lips and then touched her own.

"I'll call you tomorrow, Sue."

"Good night, Joe." Sue kissed Joe on the lips.

"Good night, Sue." Joe returned her kiss and squeezed her hand.

The ride home was very quiet and Joe preferred it that way. The repercussions could wait until tomorrow. Joe did not want to bring it up tonight or tomorrow, knowing it wouldn't pass without yelling and screaming from his mother. He felt his lips where Sue had kissed him. It helped quicken the ride. His throat burned slightly. Saliva vanished from his mouth, and he tried to swallow. His jaw tightened as he wished he'd left things alone.

Chapter 23

# 2:35 A.M.

The telephone rang at the Clark's home at 2:35 a.m. Helen heard it first and poked her husband. The Clarks only had one phone, which hung on the kitchen wall. By the time John got himself out of bed and downstairs to the kitchen, the loud ringing had awakened Joe. He knew it could be about only one thing. He rose from his warm bed and tried to listen to the conversation. Joe hoped Johnny didn't die. "If he is dead, I'm leaving immediately." Brownie, also awake, lay on top of the bed right next to Joe.

His father talked too low. Joe couldn't hear the conversation. Joe sat on the edge of the bed and waited while his father came back upstairs.

"Who called us in the middle of the night?" Helen asked, as John returned to their bedroom. She felt her heart pounding.

"Harold Bracket," John said, sitting on the edge of the bed, staring at the dark wall.

"Who is Harold Bracket?" demanded Helen.

John didn't want to tell his wife that Joseph had beaten up Bracket's son, who was now lying in the hospital with a busted jaw and severe intestinal injuries. He didn't want to tell his wife that Bracket would be getting a lawyer Monday morning and suing them for all he could get. John knew his wife would explode and then cry. He just wanted to wait till morning. He hesitated.

"Will you tell me what's going on? I have a right to know why he called." Helen sat up in bed and looked at John, her brown eyes piercing a hole through the back of her husband's skull. She was thinking fast. Bracket, I don't know any Bracket.

"Joseph beat the crap out of this Bracket's son at the dance and he is in the hospital. The old man is getting a lawyer and going to sue us for everything we have." John never looked at his wife. He stared at the dark wall, hoping what he had heard on the phone was a dream.

"Your son did what?" Helen sprang out of bed. With his hands holding his head, elbows resting on his knees, John continued staring a hole through the dark wall. "I can't believe this boy. His temper will put me in my grave. We need to get him up now and get to the bottom of this," Helen said, with grim determination in her voice. She touched her husband's head and pulled him toward her warm body.

"I think we need to wait till morning," said John, knowing his wife would rant and rave till daylight. Helen, ignoring her husband's plea, headed for Joe's room.

"Joseph! Joseph! You wake up right now and tell us what you did tonight at the dance," Helen hollered. She didn't wait for her husband. She wanted answers now.

Joe, straining, had heard the conversation. When she entered the room, Brownie could sense trouble for Joe. He began to growl low, so only Joe could hear. Joe put his arm around his best friend, but the growling continued. Helen flipped the light on.

"I will tell you what happened. Just quit your damn yelling," Joe said, looking straight into his mother's eyes that were close to shedding tears. Helen flinched as though he had slapped her. They all went downstairs to the kitchen, the room where all discussions took place.

Helen, John, and Joe sat at the kitchen table trying to discuss the happenings at the eighth grade dance. Brownie sat on the floor by Joe's chair.

"Alright, you tell us your side of the story, Joseph," John said, with sleepy eyes and a mouth that felt like it was full of cotton. He heated yesterday morning's coffee.

Joe stood up. He felt better discussing the episode on his feet. His chest ached. He needed to unload. He ran a glass of water and swigged it down his dry throat. Leaning against the kitchen sink, he folded his arms in front of his chest. Brownie kept his head erect so he could keep his eyes on Joe's mother.

"Johnny Bracket is a low-life. He came up to me with two of his low-life buddies while Sue was in the bathroom. He said some really bad things about Sue's mother so I hit him in the jaw. She is very nice, even though you don't think so. I didn't mean to hit him so hard, but he really made me mad. Then, he doubled over and I hit him again in the stomach. His stomach felt like a bale of sheep wool. I thought he was in better shape than that. I'm sorry!" Joe looked at Brownie. "I'm sorry that I have caused you all this grief. I will pay all the darn lawyer bills. If that Bracket

73

sues us, I will pay that too."

"With what? You don't have any money! The last lawyer we had to get for your temper cost us $5000. You've already caused us a lot of grief, son, and now this!" John said, speaking more clearly now that he had taken several sips of the dark, strong coffee.

"If it takes me forever, I will pay it. If that isn't good enough, I will pack my clothes now and get out of here." Joe shoved his hands in his jean pockets.

Helen started to cry. John put his face in his hands. Joe's face turned grim. He decided it was time to take a walk. Brownie and Joe left the kitchen and headed toward the barn.

They got to the barn, climbed to the top of the hay loft and sat down. Joe wrapped his arms around his best friend. "I really messed up this time." Tears started to well up in his eyes. Brownie licked his face to let him know he was there for him, no matter what.

Joe faced his dog. "You don't have a temper, do you boy? Maybe I need to have you with me all the time, so I don't lose mine." Joe stroked Brownie's back. "You're the best friend anyone could ask for, you know that? We need to figure a way out of this mess. You got any suggestions? I sure don't. If it weren't for Sue, we could just run away." The scent of Sue filtered through the air. Joe laid down, Brownie beside him.

Joe and Brownie lay up in the hay loft for the remainder of the night, neither one getting much sleep. Helen and John went back to bed. Helen cried herself back to sleep, while John prayed himself to sleep.

# Chapter 24

# SUNDAY

Sunday morning came way too fast for the Clarks. Joe awoke first and he and Brownie started doing chores. John came out later, but Joe and his father never spoke a word. Both of them were exhausted from lack of sleep. Neither knew what to say to the other, anyway.

Helen prepared the usual Sunday morning breakfast: pancakes and sausage or bacon. Sarah had missed all the excitement. She had stayed in town with a girlfriend.

Finally, Helen broke the silence. "John, why don't you take Joseph and go see this Bracket fellow so Joseph can explain his side of the story. Maybe he will understand and we can stay away from any lawsuit."

John, searching for answers, scratched his head with both hands. His facial expression remained gloomy. "I reckon that's the thing to do. I sure hope he doesn't sue us."

"I will pay all expenses, no matter what, but that Johnny Bracket will apologize to Sue's mother," Joe said hurriedly. Helen turned away from her son and shook her head.

That evening, Joe and his father drove into town to speak with Harold Bracket. Joe thought all the way into town, *What will I do?* He remembered what Jimmy had told him: Watch the eyes, watch the hands, stay calm. Let your opponent think you're not scared and keep your backside to a wall. Joe tried to pull up every memory of Jimmy's lessons. What was he forgetting? Oh yeah! Don't get mad, or you will lose.

Harold opened the door of the rundown, old, unpainted house that sat near the railroad tracks. Joe and his Pa smelled the cigarettes and booze immediately. "What do you want?" Harold asked, not knowing who stood before him. He wore an old torn shirt and frayed pants and no shoes. His tangled hair was turning grey and he had about two weeks' growth on his face. The remaining teeth in his mouth were tobacco stained. His finger nails were dirty and long. Tattoos covered both arms.

"Hi! I'm John Clark." Bracket's mouth dropped open and his eyes swelled.

"Get the hell away from my house you no good dirt farmer" Harold said, spitting as he talked.

It took Joe only seconds to digest Bracket's words. "Nobody's going to call my Pa a no good dirt farmer and get away with it." The words came out sharp and fast. Don't get mad! His body tensed. He reminded himself to stay calm. His lips tightened.

"Don't you talk to my Pa that way or I'll kick your butt from here to the hospital where your no good son is."

With fear in his eyes and enough booze in him to flunk a sobriety test, Bracket said, "You don't talk to me that way, you piece of sh--"

Joe, without saying another word, grabbed Harold by his dirty shirt, dragged the liquored-up Bracket outside and slammed him up against an old ash tree in the front yard. Bracket's juices leaped out of his foul mouth. His body went limp from his bonding with the oak tree. "You don't talk that way to me or my Pa. We came here to apologize. We don't need any of your crap."

Harold's eyes bulged—he looked terrified. John couldn't believe how quickly his son reacted and how strong he was. Bracket probably weighed over two hundred pounds. John froze, petrified that his son would beat the shit out of the man.

"I am sor- sorry, I accept your apology and I won't sue you. My son probably had it coming to him." He paused, rubbing the back of his head where it had connected with the bark of the tree. "His momma ran away some time ago. Please don't hurt me," Harold pleaded. Joe still had him by his scruffy, old, smelly shirt.

"Your son will apologize to Mrs. Andretti as soon as he gets his no good ass out of the hospital. I want you to put it in writing that you won't sue me or my family for what happened last night. Now get in that house and start writing."

Joe and his Pa headed home with two letters signed by Harold Bracket. The silence lasted a few blocks. Joe thought the gate had closed on this Bracket thing.

"Where did you learn to be so quick, and how did you become so strong for a boy your age? And, how did you know Bracket wouldn't beat the daylights out of you?"

"Pa, Grandpa told me a while back: Don't take any crap from anyone. My friend, Jimmy, taught me at Sheridan to read the guy's eyes. From that, you can tell what the guy will do. I got stronger by lifting weights at Sheridan."

"Which Grandpa are we talking about?" thinking it couldn't be his father.

"Your Pa told me."

"My Dad told you that?"

"Yep!"

"You know, son, you got to be careful hitting people. Someday, you will hit someone and you may kill them. You will go to prison for the rest of your life."

"I'll be careful." Joe thought about the dining room at Sheridan.

Joe said nothing to his mother when he got into the house. His Pa could tell her what he wanted her to hear. John reported, "We got it resolved and he apologized to us for what his son said." John never looked at his wife as he spoke. Joe looked at his mother's eyes and could tell she believed him and that she was relieved. Joe let out a long, silent sigh.

Chapter 25

# THE MEETING

The phone rang at the Clark's home Monday morning at 9:00. Helen, the only one home, was baking bread. She wiped her floured hands and answered, "Hello."

"Hi! This is Rene Andretti, Sue's mother. I would like to have lunch with you someday this week at your convenience."

Helen stood speechless. What did her son do now? How can I have lunch with a tramp? "I don't know. I am fairly busy this week." She didn't want to ask what it might be about.

"We need to sit down and talk about our children."

"What about our children?" Helen quickly responded. Her heart climbed to her throat.

"Please! We just need to make sure they are doing the right thing and we both agree."

Helen pondered, wondering how to answer. "I guess-I guess I can." Her breaths became shorter. *"Why am I doing this?"* "Where would-when would you like to meet?"

"Josephine's on Wednesday, at, say, 11:30 a.m.," Rene answered, without hesitation.

"Ok, I-I will be there." Helen's mouth felt dry; her hands became slightly moist.

"Thank you! Bye!"

"Bye!"

Helen told John about the meeting. He remarked, "It sure was nice of her to call you and invite you to lunch."

"I don't know if I want to be seen with her in town or not."

"You should go and see if she isn't a lot better woman than what they say about her at the salon," John said, with a grin that didn't show.

"I guess. She caught me by surprise when she called." Helen turned her head so John wouldn't see her face redden.

Wednesday came and Helen dressed carefully in her navy blue dress and red shoes. Could she really go through with this? What would people say? Still, she knew she had to find out what Mrs. Andretti had to say about their children. So, she resolved herself to do her duty and headed to Josephine's.

Helen was taken aback by Rene's beauty. Rene wore a conservative, but form-fitting, cranberry dress, with white shoes. She could be a movie star. Rene spoke first, putting her right hand out. Her smile reached to her eyes. "Hi! I am Rene Andretti. You must be Helen Clark. I'm so glad you could meet me today."

Helen seemed surprised at how pleasant she appeared to be. She didn't act phony, either.

"Hi!" Helen's heart raced. "I'm Helen Clark." Helen began to wonder if she had overreacted about Rene. Bewildered, she felt the blood flow to her head.

They sat down across from each other at a small table. Helen noticed, with some relief, that the lunch rush hadn't yet started and they were practically alone. Still, she didn't know what to say. Fortunately, Rene started the conversation. They made small talk about various things, other than their children. Helen began to feel she was wrong for accusing this nice lady of being a tramp. Rene told Helen about the death of her husband and the death of her parents, who were killed in a car accident. Then, she mentioned how she thought Joe and Sue made such a great couple.

"I really don't want my son getting too involved at such an early age."

"I don't think that is good either, generally, but I believe very strongly they are very good for each other at this time in their lives. Since Sue lost her father, she needs someone to look up to. And Joe is certainly someone to look up to." Her smile showed sincerity. "I think Sue will help Joe become better at understanding people. Sue has told me all about Joe and what Reverend Stanton did." She sipped on a glass of cream soda. "Maybe Joe went too far, but I believe what he did was surely justified."

Helen hoped someone would be able to help her son understand people better. He certainly needed to learn how to control his temper. Surprised that another woman seemed to understand her son's needs as well as she did, she had trouble responding. "Why don't we watch them closely and see how things go," Helen said, trying to force a smile.

Rene looked down at the tablecloth, then up at Helen. She parted her lips and waited a few seconds. "I would like to talk to you about my personal life and how the rumors have run rampant in this town. I'm trying to find a man and, believe me, it's not easy with a teenage girl, especially in a small town."

"Maybe you ought to try going to church and see what you can find," Helen expelled rapidly. Helen knew she shouldn't have blurted that out. She took a sip of coffee. "You have a church you go to?"

"No." Rene shook her head and looked down at her soda. "I don't. We are Protestant or, I should say, my husband was, even though he was Italian. We used to attend church regularly." She looked away and then turned back toward Helen. "Since he was killed, I guess I just feel unattached."

"Why don't you and your daughter attend church with us on Sunday at the Methodist Church?" "*What did I say? People will talk.*" Still, she knew deep down it was the decent thing to do.

Rene's eyes sparkled and her lips formed a smile. "I would love to."

"We will meet you in the vestibule at 10:50 a.m. this Sunday. We attend the Methodist Church here in town."

"I look forward to it, and I know Sue will."

John sat in the kitchen having a cup of coffee and a sugar cookie when Helen came into the house, all smiles. John hadn't seen his wife smile much lately.

"What are you so happy about?"

Helen dropped the smile instantly. "I never said I was happy." She couldn't stand it when he gloated.

"You look happier now than when you left." John could see a little sparkle in her eyes.

"Rene and I had a nice lunch at Josephine's."

"So, what kind of woman is she?"

Helen turned around and busied herself putting away the breakfast dishes.

John guessed things had gone quite well. "Well, tell me about her. Is she what you thought she was?" His ears reached for her answer.

"No, no, I don't think so. She has had a lot of tragedy in her life." Avoiding her husband's gaze, Helen removed a frozen chicken from the freezer for tomorrow's dinner.

"So, I take it you're going to let our son see this woman's daughter on occasion."

"Ah, maybe, we will have to see."

John leaned back in his chair and put his hands behind his head. Smiling, he thought if his son could see her eyes, he would know what she was thinking.

Later that same afternoon, Sue found Joe by his locker. She walked up behind him and wrapped her arms around him. "Joe, you won't believe what we are doing Sunday."

Struck dumb by the sensation of Sue's feminine form pressed against his back, Joe could only stutter. "Wha-what are w- we doing Sunday?"

"Your mother had lunch with my mother today and she invited my mother and me to attend church with you and your parents." Sue was ecstatic. Joe quickly turned toward Sue.

"What? I don't believe it. Not my mother. You sure?"

"Oh, Joe, I can't wait. Isn't it wonderful?"

Joe gave Sue a quick hug. "My mother must have had a change of heart. How did you find this out?"

"My Mom just called me and told me. I had to go to the office to get the call." Joe grinned.

"Great!" Joe left for his next class feeling good inside for the first time since Sue had approached him about the dance. His mother didn't hate Sue anymore and Johnny Bracket was improving. The doctor said he would be home by the weekend.

Sunday morning didn't come too soon for Sue and Joe. Everyone met in the vestibule at 10:50 a.m. Joe and Sue grinned from ear to ear while introductions were made. John was almost speechless when he laid eyes on Rene. She wore a light blue dress that revealed her shapely curves, with short-heeled, white shoes. Helen suggested, "Why don't we all sit together?"

Joe and Sue took the lead, with Sarah, Rene, Helen and John following. The service began with a song sung by the congregation. Rene's voice sounded as if she could be a professional singer. John was the only Clark that could carry a tune. He stopped singing to listen to Rene. Helen remarked to Rene after the song ended, "You have a wonderful voice."

"Thank you. I love to sing."

John leaned in front of Helen. "You have a great voice, Rene. You need to sing in the choir."

Rene smiled. "Thank you. You are both very kind."

Joe proposed after church that they all go out for lunch at Josephine's.

Everyone looked at each other. John answered, "That sounds like a great idea."

"Would that be ok with you, Rene?" asked Helen.

"Yes!" She looked at Sue, who was all smiles. Joe's heart was about to explode with happiness.

The rest of the summer went well for the Clarks, especially Joe. He talked to Sue on the phone as often as his parents let him. They saw each other Saturday nights at a movie or student function, and Sunday mornings at church.

The Dodgers played the damn Yankees, again, in the World Series in the fall of 1955. The Dodgers won the series and Joe was happier than any other kid in school. He put a banner up in his room that read "Dodgers, World Series Champions."

# Chapter 26

# May 1957

At 5:00 a.m., Tuesday morning, John hollered, "Get up, Joseph. We have a long day ahead of us." Joe already knew he wouldn't be going to school that day. He had to help his Pa plant corn on the back forty. Joe still did not like school, so this was a plus, even though he wasn't going to see Sue. Joe's feet hit the floor seconds after his Pa's bark made its way up the stairs.

After an hour of doing chores and having a large breakfast, Joe filled the gas tank up on the 1954 International M. Joe would be doing around 6 miles per hour while disking. Joe would disk the ground ahead of his Pa, who would plant the corn behind him. Thundershowers were in the forecast for the evening.

Helen fixed an early lunch for Harry and John before they left for the field. "I hope we get this corn planted before it rains tonight," John said, while eating his lunch.

"I believe we'll get rain earlier than the weatherman predicted," Harry remarked.

"Well, when it starts to lightning, I want you all to get to the house. If you don't get all the corn planted, it can wait," Helen advised, knowing her husband would try and get the last acre planted before the rains came. Helen said this every time she knew a storm was brewing. She put three pieces of homemade apple pie, John's favorite, on the table. And Harry never turned away any piece of pie.

"I believe we can get her all planted before it rains, if the planter doesn't break," John said, as he put the last piece of apple pie in his mouth.

"If it starts lightning, you get to the house. That lightning scares me," Helen repeated, while gathering up the dirty dishes from the table. "A minute ago Paul Harvey, on his news show, said that severe storms are possible later today." Neither Harry nor John commented, as they both headed for the door.

John kissed his wife before he left. "You need to get some lunch out to Joseph. I want him to disk the other field when he is finished with the back forty." Every field had to be disked twice before getting planted. "Dad is taking out fuel for the M with him, so Joseph doesn't have to unhook and come back to the house."

"See you about five. You can bring out supper to us," John said, with a big grin on his face and patting his wife's behind as he left. Helen sighed. She kept her fear corralled inside her.

Joe had lunch brought out to him by his mother, who stayed with him until he finished eating.

"I just want to tell you how proud we are of you, Joseph. You work like you owned this farm. Your father is thinking about buying the Carlson farm so you both can farm together when you finish high school."

"Wow! I didn't know that." Joe could already picture him and Sue on the Carlson farm.

"He was going to talk to you about it tonight after you came in from the fields."

"That sounds really great. Maybe I can skip school more if we buy that farm."

"You keep your grades up, you probably can." She pictured her son and John farming together for years to come. Her eyes focused on the planted field.

"Sue will help me with my grades," Joe said, staring off into space, seeing Sue's smiling face.

Joe gave Brownie part of his roast beef sandwich and a very small piece from each of the two pieces of apple pie.

Helen said before she left, "You watch those clouds this afternoon." She looked up at the sky, seeing only scattered clouds. The fear of thunderstorms crept under her skin.

Brownie stayed with Joe all day, either riding on the tractor or running beside him, just in case he spotted something to chase.

The corn planter worked like a sewing machine and Joe had already finished disking the back forty. Joe thought about his Pa buying the Carlson farm and he and Sue getting married and living on the farm. The Carlson home needed to be remodeled, but that wouldn't be a problem for the Clarks since Joe's uncle worked as a carpenter.

Joe had stayed in touch with Jimmy Robbins since their time at

Sheridan. They hadn't seen each other, but had corresponded several times. Jimmy continued to have problems with trying to support his mother and his two younger brothers. She still slept with any male she could get into bed. Jimmy hated it, especially for his younger brothers. Joe wanted him to come out and stay on the farm. His Mom had said NO too many times, so Joe stopped asking. He knew someday they would be together again, maybe when he lived at the Carlson place.

By 2:35 p.m., the clouds almost completely blocked the warm sun. Harry figured the rain would be pelting down on the Clark farm within two hours. Joe was disking the 50-acre field for the first time. John was about two hours from finishing the back forty.

The wind picked up to over 30 miles per hour. The clouds rolled faster and faster into black storm clouds. John had another three rounds to go before finishing the back forty. Harry gave John enough corn to finish the field and went to the house. Harry left the bags of seed corn lay at the end of the field. The blowing dust and dirt in the field caused trouble for John in locating the marker track left by the planter. In order to get the corn rows straight, this marker needed to be followed.

# Chapter 27

# A BOLT OF LIGHTNING

Joe had stopped disking and unhooked the tractor from the disk, when the first streak of lightning flashed in the black sky. He headed towards his Pa, two fields away. Brownie jumped up on the tractor with Joe with his back to the wind.

Joe met his Pa at the end of the back forty, where he had one more round to go. "Do you think you can finish before the rain comes?"

"Yeah! You wait here and I'll ride back to the house with you." A long streak of lightning flashed just then. A loud crash of thunder came within a second of the lightning. The lightning was less than a mile away.

If the storm moved 30 miles per hour, they had plenty of time to finish the field and get to the house before it rained. They new most thunderstorms in the Midwest travel at that speed.

"You better get moving Pa, before it rains on us," Joe said, as he filled the last planter box with corn. He waved to his Pa.

John put the Oliver in gear and headed for the other end of the field. He pulled his hat down so the wind wouldn't blow it away. The wind blew even stronger than before and, within less than a minute, John had disappeared from Joe's sight.

Joe and Brownie waited and watched the storm move rapidly toward them. They were less than a mile from the house. With the M at full speed, they should be able to reach the house in six to seven minutes.

Lightning appeared everywhere, but Joe's Pa was nowhere in sight. The wind gusted at around 60 miles per hour and Joe couldn't see ten feet in front of the tractor. Joe finally heard the Oliver coming. The wind had died down a little, but the lightning and thunder remained. The streaks became more visible and the crashes of thunder deafening. The cold rain drops pierced his skin like hail. He knew this couldn't be a tornado because the rain comes after the tornado, not before. He learned that from his Grandpa.

Joe had the M running and Brownie aboard. John parked the Oliver, got off the tractor and ran toward Joe. "Pa, you need to put a can on the exhaust pipe." They used an empty Del Monte green bean can. John ran back to the Oliver, got on the tractor and reached for the can, which sat on the power take-off lever. He stretched out to put the can on top of the hot exhaust pipe that extended 30 inches above the engine.

At that moment, a long streak of lightning flashed, striking John on the top of his head. An explosion-like crash of thunder followed. Joe couldn't speak—Brownie let out a whine. The sulfur smell, similar to rotten eggs, sickened Joe's nostrils. Joe couldn't move. Frozen, he watched his Pa's smoking head and smoldering shoes.

John collapsed across the front of the steering wheel. The rain pelted down so hard now, Joe could hardly even see the Oliver. The wind blew harder than ever and the lightning and thunder were constant. Joe, shattered, hollered, "Pa! OH MY GOD! Pa!" Tears formed in his eyes only to be washed away by the torrential, blowing rain.

Joe got off the M and ran toward the Oliver. Lightning hit an old, sixty-foot oak twenty feet from the Oliver splitting the tree right down the middle. The crack of the splitting tree rang through his ears, but his eyes remained fixed on his Pa. He had eaten lunch several times with his Pa under that tree. He had had lunch under that same tree less than three hours ago with his Mom. As the splintered tree fell, one of its pieces hit the Oliver within inches of John's motionless body. It broke the Oliver in half right behind the fuel tank in front of John's smoldering head. Another piece landed between Joe and the M. The rain continued to pound against their skin.

His Pa was pinned between the fallen oak tree and the rear half of the tractor. Joe tried to get him free, but couldn't because of the weight of the tree and the tractor. The smell from the broken fuel tank entered Joe's nostrils. Joe knew he had to work fast or the leaking fuel would explode if it got close to the hot engine. Farmers usually carried a log chain on the rear of the tractor in case they got stuck or needed to pull another tractor. The Clarks had a log chain on the M.

Joe got back on the M and backed it up to the front half of the Oliver, hooking the chain around the front wheels. Joe pulled the Oliver a few feet to free his Pa. He went back to his Pa and threw his motionless, limp, wet, smoldering body over his shoulder and got back onto the M. John's head sat in front of Joe as he put the M in gear and headed for the house. Brownie stayed on the ground. As Joe drove the M toward the house as fast as he could go, the Oliver exploded behind him.

Joe feared the worst. He began to cry, asking for God's help. Something he hadn't done much of recently. Joe's only direction came from Brownie's barking, who couldn't be seen because of the driving rain.

When Joe got the M on the dirt road that went to the house, he put her in high gear and pulled the throttle back all the way. He knew if he held the steering wheel straight he would be ok.

Joe managed to get to the house and dismounted from the M with his Pa still on his shoulder. Joe, speechless, carried his father into the house.

"Oh! My God! What happened?" Helen said when she saw Joseph carrying her husband. Harry stood in the kitchen looking out the window, watching the storm. He turned quickly.

"Mom, we need to get Pa to the hospital. He got struck by lightning."

The smell of burnt flesh and hair permeated the kitchen. "Get him into the car. I'll be right there," Helen said, with a painful expression on her face.

Helen grabbed her purse and headed for the garage to get into the Chrysler.

Harry, stunned at seeing his son in such a lifeless state, said nothing. He sat down and began to pray.

The storm would not let up. Joe drove as fast as his eyes could make out the way on the dirt road to town. Helen repeated, "I told him and you to get to the house before the storm came." She cried uncontrollably in the back seat of the Chrysler, holding her husband's burnt head in her hands. His pulse was very slow.

Joe drove his mother and father to the hospital in silence. Being only fifteen, he had no driver's license. He wished he wouldn't have told his Pa to put that damn bean can on the exhaust pipe. He didn't want to tell his mother. He might never tell anyone. He knew his Pa was in bad shape and probably wouldn't live. The Carlson farm would never be his. He needed Sue to comfort him. No one else could make him forget like she could. Joe began to cry like he had never cried before. Brownie stood on the front seat watching out the front window. The wipers tried to wash away the water.

They arrived at the hospital and rushed into the emergency room. Joe carried his Pa in his arms. He laid him on a bed in the emergency room. The doctor began to check his vitals. Helen and Joe were asked to wait in the waiting room.

Joe shuddered when he realized he was to blame. The bean can. Damn it! He laid his big arms on the wall and put his head against them. The tears ran down his already wet face. He couldn't tell his Mom.

Helen sat and prayed out loud. Her eyes remained wet, but the crying had stopped for now. After what seemed like hours, Doctor Langhorn came and spoke to Helen and Joe about John's condition.

"John is unconscious and probably will be in a coma for awhile. Then again, he may never come out of this unconscious state. We never know about these kinds of injuries. He must have had the Lord on his side. He should have been dead." Joe cringed. His body shook under his soaked clothes. That damn bean can.

Joe and Helen could say nothing for a few minutes. Finally, Joe said, in a trembling voice, "He was on a tractor when it happened."

"That's what saved him—the rubber tires," replied Doctor Langhorn.

John had serious burns on his feet and head. He had a slow heart beat. The doctor thought he may have suffered heart damage from the lightning strike. Helen remained speechless. Joe grabbed his Mom's arm and led her to the car.

Joe drove his distraught mother back home. The ride back was slower; the storm was now just a light rain. "Mother, I'll get the corn planted. Don't worry. I'll do the farming until Pa gets better." His last statement contained little hope. His dreams were crushed, and it was entirely his fault.

Helen did not respond, but just put her hand on Joseph's shoulder, the shoulder that had carried her husband to safety, and patted it. Joe looked over at his Mom. He saw her weary body and reflected on it being his fault that she had become this way.

Sarah, attending a class trip to the Museum of Science and History in Chicago, was unaware of the tragedy that had occurred.

The next morning, after an almost sleepless night, Joe arose at 6:00 to do chores. He was eating breakfast when his Grandpa drove into the yard at 7:00. Harry entered the kitchen and said, "Let's all kneel and pray for John."

It took several days before the fields dried up enough for Joe to finish planting the last fifty acres. He had never planted a hill of corn prior to that day. He worked fourteen-hour days and only attended school when the weather wouldn't allow him to work outside. The crops seemed to be doing well and school would be out next week. Sue helped Joe with his lessons. He needed a lot of help.

Midsummer passed and John's condition hadn't changed. Helen moved him to the only nursing home in town. The doctor gave John very little hope of ever recovering.

Joe saw Sue whenever she came out to the farm. She would ride out with Harry in the morning and stay all day. Joe never said anything about the damn bean can. He just couldn't say anything, not yet anyway. Sue sensed something was wrong. Joe wasn't himself.

Sue drove the M and pulled the hay bailer behind. When they got to the end, Joe would jump off the wagon behind the bailer and line the bailer up to the next windrow. Brownie was always on the ground or on the wagon with Joe. Harry raked the hay to put into the windrow ahead of the bailer.

While on the farm, Sue wore as little clothing as possible so she could tan her beautiful body. She never minded getting dirty. Joe thought what a great farmer's wife she would make someday. *What am I saying? There won't be any farm!* Joe never wore a shirt or gloves. His chest and hands were cut and scratched from the hay stubble. Joe had grown another inch during the summer and had gained another ten pounds. His arms were like fence posts; his hands like bear claws. The hopes, smiles, grins and laughter, however, did not existent on the Clark farm, not even on Sundays.

Chapter 28

# GRANDPA

Summer ended and school had begun. Joe would attend classes three days a week until harvest time. Joe had never run a corn picker, one of the most dangerous machines on the farm. His mother had a fit, but he didn't listen to her. She wanted to hire someone else to pick the corn. Joe read the manual and knew he could figure it out with his Grandpa's help.

His Grandpa had changed. He had become quiet and reserved. He seemed tired and had slowed considerably since the bolt of lightning had struck his son.

Joe installed the mounted-type corn picker on the M. It could pick two rows at a time. A box wagon sat behind the tractor. When he drove between two rows of corn, the picker would snap the ears of corn off the stalks and send them up an elevator into the wagon.

Harry pulled the loaded wagons to the corn crib with the LA Case and unloaded them. The Clarks had 150 acres of corn to pick. With the weather not cooperating and Harry moving slower than he had been, it took Joe a month to get all the corn picked and put into the crib.

The corn yield turned out to be the best the Clarks had ever had, and the best throughout the Midwest, as well. This caused a drop in the price of corn.

Joe returned to school full time after he finished harvesting. He would have rather been on the farm, provided he could still farm with his Pa and Grandpa. Joe and Sue didn't see each other much during the winter, except during school. Sometimes he would get dropped off at Sue's house on Helen's way to visit John. John's condition hadn't changed.

Helen had aged another twenty years since that terrifying May afternoon. Her hair had turned snow white and she had just reached the age of thirty-nine. She hadn't laughed or smiled since last spring.

In April, 1958, an ambulance rushed Harry to the hospital. Joe never had another conversation with his Grandpa. He died the next day of a heart attack, with Joe by his side. Joe walked out of the room with the emptiest feeling in his heart. He headed directly to Sue's house, twenty blocks away, running most of the way, crying, wondering when the nightmare would end.

When Sue saw him, she knew he had lost the man he admired most. She hugged and kissed him on his sweaty cheek. "Joe, I'm so sorry," Sue said, with tears already running from her brown eyes. Joe shook.

He cried for several minutes. "If it weren't for that damn bean can, none of this would have happened."

"Joe, what are you talking about? What bean can?" Sue said, with her hands on his shoulders, looking into his wet, blue eyes.

Joe stared straight ahead, eyes frozen, heart racing, a cold chill throughout. His thoughts of that dreadful day were right there in the room. *I can't tell her. I can't tell anyone.* He turned away, clenched his fist and smashed the wall. His hand broke through the plaster, dust flew and blood splattered. He gazed at his bloody hand. "I got to go." He grabbed the door knob, flinging the door open. Sue reached for his shirt, tears flowing, her heart aching.

"Joe! Please! Please tell me. You have to tell someone. I want to help." She held her grip on his shirt, her knuckles turning white.

Joe wanted to leave, but his heart screamed at him, telling him to talk about the bean can. He took a deep breath, letting it all out. "Ok! I-I'll tell you." He sat with her on the davenport and told her. Sniffling on every few words and fighting back tears, he finally broke into a weak cry. He jumped up from the sofa and quickly moved to the other room, avoiding Sue.

Sue waited several seconds before she spoke. "Joe, Joe you will never forget that day. You need to stop blaming yourself, though. It was God's will and not your fault." Sue had never been this forceful.

"I can't help it, Sue. That extra minute might have made the difference. My Pa would have been ok and Grandpa would be alive." He burst into loud crying, burying his head in a pillow. She kissed him several times, wiping the tears and stroking his back. "Why did it have to happen?" he sobbed.

She kissed Joe on the mouth and held him tight and whispered in his ear, "I love you. We will get through this together. When my father was killed, I hated our government for a long time. The North Koreans killed my father, not our government. You can't keep on hating, Joe."

Joe held Sue for a long time. "I need to go home, do chores."

"My Mom will be here shortly. She can take you over to the nursing home to meet your Mom." Their lips met again. She felt Joe's trembling body. "Joe, maybe you should get some professional help."

Joe pulled away and looked at Sue with wild eyes. "I don't need any damn shrink telling me what to do." He broke away from her, ran out the door and headed for the nursing home. Sue sat stunned. She had never seen Joe so upset. She ran to her room and cried.

When Sue called Joe that night, he apologized right away, but remained very sad. "Please don't tell anyone I cried. I don't want anyone to know."

"I would never tell anyone, Joe." She knew she probably would tell her mother, but that would be all.

"Thanks. I love you." His voice trailed off.

"I love you, too, Joe. I'll call you tomorrow," Sue said, anguish running from her head to her heart.

That spring the farm sold, along with all the cattle and machinery. It had been Joe's idea to sell the farm. He couldn't bear to be there without his Pa and Grandpa. Helen never blinked. She just sold it quickly to a neighbor.

# Chapter 29

## THE MOVE

Helen bought a three bedroom home in a nice neighborhood in town. The home had a large backyard for Brownie and a two-car garage. Living in town would make it a lot easier for Helen to get to the nursing home everyday. Joe didn't like becoming a city boy.

After the farm, machinery, and all the livestock were sold, Helen had enough money to pay cash for the house and bank the rest. She still had bills to pay—the loans on the farm and the machinery. She gave Joe $10,000 for all his efforts over the past few years, along with the F200 Ford truck.

Joe traded the pickup and bought a polar white, V-8 automatic 1959 Ford Thunderbird two-door hard top, with black leather seats. Joe still had several thousand to put in the bank after his big purchase.

Joe took a job at the local bowling alley as a pin setter. He worked 20 hours a week and made $.75 per hour. He would have rather worked on a farm, but gradually adjusted to city life. Sue and Joe spent a lot more time together. Joe was starting to come out of his depression, in large part due to the support of Sue and Brownie. She encouraged him and her smile would make him melt almost every time. He seldom visited his Pa in the nursing home. The thought of his burnt hair and flesh made him sick.

Sue had a job at one of the local grocery stores as a cashier. Sue and Joe worked almost the same hours. Brownie remained a constant companion, whether at Sue's or Joe's home, or in the T-Bird.

# RECOVERY

# Chapter 30

# JOE WAKES UP

Two months, three days and eleven hours from the time of the crash, Joe opened his eyes for the first time. He gazed at the ceiling, his blue eyes wide open, and realized he was lying in a strange room. Since birth, he had awakened in three different rooms and this, definitely, did not appear to be one of them.

Joe glanced to his right to see Rene sitting in a chair reading a yellowed page copy of *Gone with the Wind*. He had been in Sue's room once, but this looked different. He saw the IV in his arm, the curtain and rails on the side of his bed. The medicine smell brought back memories of his Grandpa lying on his death bed. Where the hell was he? His heart began to pump and he feared he was dying, but from what? He couldn't be dying, he was famished, he thought, as he lay there motionless.

He looked at Rene again. She seemed twenty years older. Her beautiful, dark hair had grey streaks running through it. She wore glasses and her eyes remained fixed on the large book. He had never seen her with glasses before. Her face looked paler, thinner, and her hair, her hair was not neatly combed. The glow he remembered had disappeared.

Joe's mouth felt extremely dry. He tried to speak, but he couldn't get any sound to come out. The saliva formed slowly, allowing him to speak softly.

"Mrs. Andretti, what…I'm hungry." Joe fell back to sleep.

"Joe! Joe!" The book dropped to the floor. "Oh, Joe, I am so glad you are awake. You're ok!" Rene said, stroking Joe's right arm, which had atrophied since the crash.

Joe didn't answer. His chest rose and fell in sleep. Rene's heart raced. She showed a quick smile and touched the bed with her fingers. She then ran to the floor desk and interrupted the two young nurses who were deep in chatter about their boyfriends. "He's awake! He spoke to me!" Rene said, in a panic.

The two nurses appeared disgusted that they had been interrupted. One of them finally responded, "He will wake up and go back to sleep several times." "Just go back to the room and don't bother us unless it is an emergency," the other nurse said, not even looking at Rene. Rene, mashing her lips together, turned abruptly and left.

She hurried back to Joe's room. He was still asleep. Breathing fast, she ran down two flights of stairs to the pay phone on the first floor. Almost tripping in her heels, she grabbed the railing to square herself. She had to call Helen—hungry, he said he was hungry. He was alright! Thoughts of her daughter entered her head as she reached the first floor. *"It's not fair. Oh, God, why did she have to die?"* Rene shook her head, fought off the tears and dialed Helen.

# Chapter 31

# HELEN NOTIFIED

Helen stood in the bathroom brushing her white hair when the phone rang in the kitchen. "Hello!"

"Helen! Joe woke up and said he was hungry!"

Helen's heart skipped a beat. "Oh! God! Oh, Lord. Thank you, Lord." She put her left hand on her face, forgetting about the brush, which pressed into her makeup.

"He went back to sleep. The nurses said he will do that. I don't like those nurses.
I think I should call his doctor. What do you think?"

"Yes! Call him and I will be there as soon as I go to the bank. I'll be right there. I'll hurry. Rene—Rene, thanks for calling."

"Ok, bye."

"Bye!" Helen returned to the bathroom to touch up her make up, smudged from the hair brush and the tears. Brushing her hair a few more strokes helped calm her, then out the door she flew.

# Chapter 32

# JOE'S ROOM

Helen arrived at Joe's room at 12:45 p.m. to find him asleep. Rene greeted her with, "Joe woke again for just a few seconds, but didn't say anything. The doctor will be here at 1:00."

"I know we will have a problem when he wakes up and Sue isn't here. Joe has such a temper. He will just explode when he finds out. I hope the doctor will have an answer for us when he gets here," Helen said, with her hand on Rene's arm.

The admiration that had grown between Helen and Rene held them together now—a complex, tightly-wrapped sisterhood.

Rene, hearing this, started to shed tears and Helen, also crying, embraced her. Joe interrupted them. "Is there any food? I'm hungry! Hey, why are you two crying?"

"Oh, Joseph!" Helen said, and kissed her son on his right cheek.

Joe fell asleep again, but seemed to have a smile on his face. "Maybe he will wake up soon," Rene said, her hands clutched to her chest. Helen touched her elbow gently.

Doctor Allen knocked before entering the room. "I hear our young man has opened his eyes a few times."

"Yes! He just said, 'I'm hungry'," Helen answered, trying to smile through burning eyes.

"Great! He should come out of his coma soon; hopefully today, maybe tomorrow," Doctor Allen said, as he placed one hand on each of Helen's and Rene's shoulders. "I have wished that John would wake up someday from his coma." Helen visualized John embracing her. She closed her eyes for a moment, then opened them, blinking.

"Doctor Allen, I'm afraid when Joseph wakes up and finds out about Sue, he will just go—I'm afraid he will have such an intense reaction it may damage his recovery. He loved Sue more than anyone can imagine."

"We'll sedate him so he'll sleep. When he wakes up again, he'll be sedated again, if necessary. Let's get him to wake up first, then we can handle Joe accordingly," Doctor Allen said, with a smile on his face.

# Chapter 33

# JOE'S CUSSING

Joe opened his glazed eyes again around 2:30 p.m., screaming, cussing and head pulsating. Startled, Rene and Helen jumped from their seats and stared at him with concern. After several minutes, Joe quieted, his eyes rapidly moving around the room. His silence urged Helen and Rene to say something. Their mouths were ready to speak when Joe said, "Am I ever going to get some damn food? I am really hungry." A grin appeared on his face.

Helen tried to smile, but her mouth wouldn't widen. Puzzled, she said, "Yes Joseph! I-I will get you some food. What, what would you like?" fearing the next question he might ask.

Rene ran quickly to the nurse's desk and blurted out, "Joe is awake and he wants to eat. Can you send someone down to the kitchen and get him some food?"

"He will eat when dinner is served," said Nurse Barker, without looking up. She wore her hair up in a bun and appeared to be in her fifties. Her uniform looked soiled, like it had just been taken out of the laundry basket. She weighed as much as a hog ready for market.

"I will get him some food. Where is the kitchen?" Rene said, firmly.

"I said he will eat when everyone else eats. This is not a restaurant," Barker insisted.

"You are extremely rude." Rene glared at her. "So help me, if I could, I would fire you on the spot!" Barker shot her a glance.

"I've been here for over twenty-five years and no bimbo like you will get me fired," Barker said, her smile not matching her eyes.

Rene went back to Joe's room in a huff. "Where's Sue, Mrs. Andretti.?" Joe asked, angrily. "My mother won't tell me. Where is Brownie?" Rene said nothing, reached for her face with both hands and began to cry.

"Joe, you need to listen and not get upset," Helen said, with her face turning white from fear of how her son would react. Helen had more courage now that Rene was there for support.

Joe tried to sit up, but his head felt like it weighed eighty pounds. The pressure was tremendous. Joe felt the bandages on his head. "What the hell is wrong with my head?" His voice turned loud. He moved his right leg, and winced. "Oh, my God!! What did they do to my leg?" He screamed, in pain. Profanity filled the room.

Helen spoke to Rene softly, "Go get a nurse. We need to get him quiet."

"Quiet, hell! I want to know what's going on."

"Ok!" said Rene, and ran out of the room.

"Joseph, please try and stay calm. You have been in a car accident and in a coma for over two months. You have a severe head injury and your leg was broken in three places."

"Where is Sue?" His head turned back and forth. "Why can't you tell me? I want to know!" His eyes swept everything in the room. "I want my dog. What car accident?" He looked up at the ceiling. Then, Joe quietly said, "my car." His eyes closed. His breathing slowed.

Nurse Barker barged into the room. "I am going to give you a shot to quiet you down, sonny." She attempted to push Joe's hospital gown sleeve up.

Joe's eyes flew open and he shot her a dirty look. "Get your fat ass away from me. I want my questions answered first." Joe's head throbbed and he felt nauseated. He needed to throw up, but wanted answers first.

"Joe, please, you can't get all upset. Your head won't—your head—you must stay calm." "*I have to tell him'*" "I'm sorry, Joseph. Sue died in the car accident." Helen's voice broke on the word accident. Her hand trembled, resting on Joe's arm.

Joe just looked at his mother, then at Rene, then his mother again. His mouth moved, but no sound could be heard. A moment passed before anyone spoke, and in that moment, Joe saw a white figure in front of his bed. His heart jolted. He realized it was Sue. She smiled.

"Joe, you got into an accident on prom night. It wasn't your fault," Helen said, knowing Joseph would lose control.

"I don't believe this. Why are you playing with my head? Sue can't be dead. Why are you—I don't feel well," Joe said, as he fell back to sleep. Rene pictured Sue's coffin being lowered into the grave. Her crying grew louder.

Rene couldn't control her emotions any longer. Helen tried to comfort her. They held each other while Nurse Barker jammed the needle into Joe's arm. "He won't call me a fat ass anymore today." Pushing the sleeves up on her stubby arms, she walked out the door. Helen watched her leave, her mouth dry, throat burning from a milky hate.

Exhausted, Rene decided to go home.

# Chapter 34

# FIVE HOURS LATER

"When can I have some food?" Joe opened his eyes wide, staring holes in the ceiling.

"I'll go out and get you something. What do you want?" Helen said, with eyes half-shut from just waking up.

"Just some food, I don't care. How's Brownie?" Joe's eyes appeared to be less glassy.

"Brownie misses you something awful." Her voice quivered. "He hardly eats and paces the floor. Every time the door opens, he runs to meet you, but when he sees you're not there, he goes back up to your room and lies on your bed." She could see the pain in her son's eyes. "I'll be back soon."

"Bring Brownie back with you."

"Joseph, they won't allow dogs in the hospital."

"Brownie is more human than that damn fat Nurse Barker," he snarled.

"I'll see what I can do. I wish you wouldn't swear so much, Joseph." She held her right hand to her mouth. She was afraid to tell Joseph he was in LaSalle.

When Helen returned, Joe had fallen asleep again. Helen set the Steak and Shake burgers and fries on the table next to his bed. She also brought him a large chocolate milk shake. Joe loved their burgers.

Within ten minutes from the time Helen had set the food on the table, Joe's nostrils got a whiff of the grease and he opened his eyes. He looked around the room, not finding anyone, except Barker walking through the door. "What is it I smell in here? It sure smells like french fries to me." She crossed the floor with her chunky legs and a hungry grin on her chubby face.

Angry at himself for not hiding them under the covers, he just knew she would take his food and devour it in less time than a hog would eat an ear of corn: *Sooey! Soooey!* He thought to himself.

"You can't be having that kind of food. You will eat what the hospital gives you, not restaurant food," Barker said, smiling, shaking her head as she grabbed the fries, two burgers and the large milk shake from Joe's tray.

"Hey! That's my damn food. Bring that back. Ouch!" Joe said, trying to get out of bed, but the pain wouldn't allow him to move more than a few inches. "Ouch! Damn it!" Joe shut his eyes, but the vision of Sue made them open quickly.

Helen returned to Joe's room, miffed at Nurse Barker for taking Joe's food.

"I want to see Sue. Where is she? Why hasn't she been here? What did Barker do with my food?"

"Oh, Joseph, I don't know what to tell you. Please try and be calm."

"Just tell me what the hell is going on."

"Joseph, Sue was killed in the car accident." Helen knew, even in his weakened state, if he tried to get out of bed, she was not strong enough to stop him.

"*What?*" He glared at his mother. Anger set in. "***Why?*** Why didn't you tell me this before?"

"I tried to, but you went back to sleep again. You must have forgotten."

Joe's eyes became wet. "How did it happen? Where did it happen?"

"Joe, we don't know." "*How am I going to tell him?*" "You were in the wrong place at the wrong time. A car went out of control, you hit the car, and then you hit a utility pole. It happened the night of the prom. Joe, I'm so sorry. You've been in a coma for over two months," Helen said, with tears coming down her cheeks.

"Two months!" He stared into space. "I wouldn't do anything to harm Sue. I promised Mrs. Andretti I would take care of her. Why can't I remember this?" Several heartbeats later, he began feeling dizzy. "I need my dog," Joe said, looking everywhere but at his mother. His body hurt in so many places he couldn't tell what had been damaged until he moved. He touched the deep scars on his face. He was afraid to pull the covers back and look at his leg, which burned like hot coals.

"It wasn't your fault, Joseph. There were three men in another car that went out of control and you hit them," Helen said, knowing the worst was yet to come.

His eyes turned cold. "They better be dead," Joe snapped, looking directly at his mother, waiting for an answer. She shuddered.

She had to change the subject, at least for now. "Joseph, I believe Nurse Barker has left for today. Would you like for me to get you another order from Steak and Shake?"

He gave a quick half-grin, "Yeah! Thanks." She took her purse and headed for the door. "Wait! What are their names?"

"I-I can't remember. I-I think they said their names were Capenno, or something like that, but I don't know." Her breath lodged in her throat. Before she continued, she remembered Doctor Knowles saying, *"Before I die I will see these brutal men die or be put into prison."*

"Joseph, you need not worry about those men. The law will handle them." She knew that that probably would not happen. She left the room quickly, hating the fact that there would be no help from the law and her son would want revenge.

Joe just stared at the ceiling, imagining Sue and how beautiful she was. He remembered running his fingers through her black, soft, silky hair. The back of his eyes burned. *"Those no-good-sons-of-bitches."* Joe's jaw tightened. Brownie and I will kill those bastards. "I want my dog! Brownie! Oh, my God!"

"Who is Brownie?" Doctor Allen asked, grinning as he entered the room. Joe turned his head quickly.

"It's my dog! Who the hell are you?"

"I'm Doctor Allen." He ignored the second comment. "What kind of dog is he or is it a she?" the doctor asked, sitting on the edge of Joe's bed. He placed his stethoscope on Joe's hairy chest.

After a moment, Joe closed his eyes. "He's mostly German Shepherd and Red Bone Hound. The rest is just dog. He has short hair. I want him in my room. He's housebroken and a whole lot better to have around than that Barker nurse."

"You have your mother bring Brownie here tomorrow and he can stay in your room. I think he would be the best medicine for you. I have a Golden Retriever and I think a dog is the best thing a person can have to share his problems with. Your heart seems to be good. We will get you started on rehabilitation probably next week, if you continue your progress. How big is Brownie?"

"About ninety-eight pounds." Doctor Allen didn't respond, just smiled at Joe.

"When will I get out of here?"

"That depends on you and Brownie. It will take some time. You'll have to learn to walk again and you'll need to regain your strength. I know Brownie will be your best guide and get you back to almost full recovery very soon."

Helen returned with his food.

Doctor Allen's face lit up. "Hello, Mrs. Clark. I just told Joe he could have Brownie stay in the room with him. Dogs are great to have around." Helen nodded her head and flashed a quick smile.

"You talk to that Barker nurse and tell her about Brownie. I don't want her coming in here and giving me any grief," Joe said, somewhat happier now.

"Joseph, please don't talk that way," Helen said.

"She won't be bothering you or anyone else for some time. She is leaving this hospital. Today was her last day."

Joe's eyes showed signs of happiness. "Thanks, Doctor, for letting Brownie stay with me. I'll be out of here soon."

"I believe you will be," Doctor Allen said, as he left the room.

"I'll bring Brownie tomorrow."

"Why not today?"

"Joseph, you're in LaSalle. I'll bring him down with me tomorrow."

"How's Pa?" Joe asked, finishing his last bite of burger.

"Your father's the same."

"What about sis? Where is she?"

"She's in Kentucky. She got a job with a beverage company." She didn't like her daughter being so far away.

Joe twisted his mouth. "Kentucky?"

"Tell Brownie I miss him. Don't forget his water and food dishes." Joe daydreamed for a moment. "Don't forget his food."

"I will bring it all tomorrow when I come down." "*Joseph will get his strength back, now that he is eating real food. He will be alright. He is his father's son.*" She turned away for a moment, blinking back some tears.

Chapter 35

# THE TRUTH IS TOLD

Sometimes a dog is the most reliable friend in an unreliable world. Brownie had proven this to Joe many times.

Happy to see Joe, Brownie leapt on his bed and began licking his face.

"How you doin', old boy? I sure missed you, boy." Joe rubbed Brownie's ears and hugged his best friend, elated to have him with him.

"We will never be a part again, old boy." Brownie looked at Joe and gave a half bark and licked Joe's face to let Joe know he approved.

"Does Jimmy know I'm in the hospital?"

"Yes, he has written several times. I have his letters here in my purse. I sent him a short note."

"I'm going to need some writing paper, pen and envelopes so I can write him back.

"I have writing paper in the car and some envelopes. I'll go get them now."

Joe and Brownie talked and horsed around on the bed for several minutes while Helen went to the car.

Helen walked back into the room out of breath. "Hey, I need for you to get me—no, go to the lumber yard and get me a hickory stick. I need it to be 4 inches by 4 inches by 40 inches long. Make sure it doesn't have any knots in it. I need Grandpa's Bowie knife, too. Make sure it's really sharp. Sloan's hardware will sharpen it for you. Where is my Thunderbird anyway?"

Helen looked startled. "What are you going to do with a hickory stick and what on earth do you need that Bowie knife for?" She clutched her hands to her breasts.

"I am going bonkers in here. Doc told me I'd be here at least two more months. I want to whittle out a baseball bat."

"Where's the Bowie knife?"

"In my room, in the chest of drawers, second drawer down, under my underwear."

"How long have you had that knife?" Helen hated knives, except for use in the kitchen.

"Grandpa gave it to me before we sold the farm." A quick-second flash of him lying on his death bed brought a slight burn to his eyes.

"Tell me about these men that caused the accident." Joe rubbed Brownie's ears. His Mom sat in the chair in front of the bed, watching. Her face dropped.

"Did they go to jail? Did they get hurt? Tell me!"

"I'm afraid they aren't dead and they didn't get any jail time."

*"He's going to explode. I just know it."*

"What? The bastards are out on the street?" Joe's eyes grew wider. He tried to raise himself, but the pain forced him back.

"They're from Chicago and are believed to be associated with the Mafia. Joe, you can't do anything about these people. They will kill you and, possibly, me and your sister. You must try and forget and get on with your life." She knew he would never listen to her or anyone else. Her hands trembled.

Joe stared at the ceiling. His lips mashed together.

Joe looked at Jimmy's unread letters. He thought of the cafeteria at Sheridan. He looked at Brownie and imagined his dog man-handling an olive-skinned, dark-haired man. He assumed all Mafia people to be Italian. His fist clenched and his fragile body stiffened. The silence scared Helen. Tears engulfed his eyes. *"I can't let on to anyone. Don't get mad."* He had to keep those thoughts to himself. Jimmy taught him that. "Mom!" Her head swung up quickly. "Mom, I need you to bring me all the papers on the Capuanos and the accident.

"I-I don't know about the papers. It-it's been almost three months." She didn't want him to know about those men.

"Go to the damn library," he growled, teeth clenched. "If they don't have them, call the newspaper. They'll have them" He looked at his mother with stern eyes.

"Joseph!" She shook her head. "Joseph, I realize you don't like it here and you are in a lot of pain, but try and be a little more sensitive when you talk to me. Your tone of voice is threatening."

He stared at his Mom. "I'm sorry, Mom! I just can't stand it anymore. I need to get out of here." He stored thoughts of revenge in his head. Several moments passed. Helen remained motionless.

"Where's my T-Bird?"

"Your car is at the Ford garage."

"How bad is it?" Joe's eyes had a frozen look; his hand rested on Brownie's front legs.

"They-The insurance company totaled it. I'm sorry, Joseph."

"Joseph, would you like me to get you another order from the Steak and Shake?" Helen kept her voice calm. She had to get that look off his face. She last saw that when Stanton shot Homer.

Joe's stomach churned, his head cluttered with blame. "No! I'm not hungry."

# Chapter 36

# JIMMY'S LETTERS

Joe opened one of Jimmy's letters.

> *Joe,*
> *I hope you are doin' much better. Your mama told me you had an accident. She never tells me how it happen. I real sorry to hear your girlfriend got killed. Things aren't good up here, Joe. My mama got herself killed by some spic from Mexico. His name's Javier. He just got out of Joliet State Prison. This man Javier slashed my mama's throat while she was making whoopie with some no-account guy. The guy was cut real bad. He lived long enough to tell who done it. My younger brothers were asleep in another room. Word from Joliet is Pa had her killed. She probably better off dead, Joe. She never was a good mama. I goin' to live with my aunt. My little brothers go to an orphanage. Sis is gettin' out of prison soon. Tells me she has to stay with the mafia or they will kill her. This mafia is some real bad asses Joe. She steals cars for them. Let me know how's you doin'. I weighs 225 pounds now. I six feet-four inches. I work at an old boxin' gym. I try to get job at Ford garage detailing new and used cars.*
> *Jimmy*

Joe read all of Jimmy's letters and wondered if Jimmy would help him kick the shit out of those bastards—no, kill those sons-of-bitches who killed Sue. Joe bet he would. Joe just knew that between Jimmy and him, they could destroy anybody who stood in their way. *"I just need to get my ass out of this damn hospital. I will never let anyone know what I'm doing. I must stay calm. I must never reveal my intentions to anyone, except Jimmy."* His mother interrupted his daydreaming, "Joseph, you look like you're in deep thought." She feared that look.

"Just thinking of Jimmy and how hard it's been for him."

"You had better think about yourself, not some colored boy in Chicago."

Joe cringed at her remark. His face darkened. "He is a Negro and he is my best friend. Don't ever forget I wouldn't be here if it weren't for Jimmy. He saved my ass in that dining room at Sheridan." Helen's face turned white. The memory of waiting to hear about her son back then made her heart skip a couple of beats.

"Joseph, I just wish you had better friends."

"Mom, if you don't like my friends, get the hell out of my room." They both waited for the other to speak. Helen's face froze; her mouth dropped open.

"I think you need to leave me alone, Mom. I need my rest and have a lot of thinking to do. Don't make comments about Jimmy unless you know him."

"Joseph, I know you're upset, but please don't take it out on me."

Joe sighed. "I'm sorry Mom. I just need to be alone with Brownie."

Helen, distraught, hesitated, "Do you want me to bring you supper again tonight or do you want to eat that hospital food?" Thinking about the Steak and Shake, Joe thought he better say something other than "no." He'd been eating the hospital food, even though he didn't like it.

"Yes, I'd like a repeat order of last night."

Joe ate all his hospital food, all of what his mother brought him and could still have eaten more. Joe thought he must be healing fast since he was so hungry. Even so, he shared some of his fries with Brownie. "Remember the pot roast, old boy. That's been awhile, huh?"

# Chapter 37

# THE PHYSICAL THERAPIST

The following week Joe tried to get out of bed for the first time since the car accident. The pain would really start with rehabilitation. His therapist, Joan, was a very pretty woman, short, with dark hair and dark eyes. Italian, thought Joe. "Hi, Joseph."

"My name is Joe, Joe Clark."

"Ok, Joe." She smiled. Her scent was sweet, but didn't make his eyes water. She wore a white uniform that hung below the knee. Joe blushed for an instant when she appeared. He thought of Sue, in his arms. His body stiffened and his thoughts vanished.

She helped him sit up in bed. Joe had never felt such pain before and never knew you could experience such pain. Joan was gentle. Joe would not utter a sound to show his discomfort, only allowed himself a grimace and some teeth gritting. When he managed to swing his legs off the bed, Joe thought they dangled like wet noodles. He felt as weak as a newborn calf. He felt foggy and his head pounded like a hammer on an anvil. His ears rang. *"How am I ever going to get back to where I was?"* He suddenly filled with anger. Fear crept up on him with the thought of never being the same. Brownie squirmed anxiously at his feet. Joan spoke, very softly, "Joe, I want you to just sit there and think about eating your favorite food."

Joe thought for a minute—*warm Rhubarb pie with vanilla ice cream.* He gave a faint smile.

"I want you to eat that food very slowly and savor every bite until it is all gone."

Joe began to feel better, even though the pain remained. His head seemed less foggy, but still throbbed. The numbness in his left leg faded, but his right leg hurt like hell. He could stand the pain, he thought, as long as he continued to eat that rhubarb pie. Joe continued to sit there. The pain in his right leg began to change from hurting like hell to hurting like someone had stuck a rusty knife into it and twisted it around. He kept thinking about the ice cream on the warm pie going into his mouth.

"Joe, I want you sit there and try moving your left leg straight out. Do it very slowly," Joan instructed, with her left hand on Joe's right shoulder.

"My leg feels like it's in a bucket of sand."

"Good! That is what we want. It will feel like it is in a bucket of water in a couple of months." Joe's face turned sour with those words. *"Two more months! No way."*

"I want to be out of here in a couple of weeks," Joe said, forgetting about the pie. *No way was he getting out of here in less than two months*, she thought.

Joan's warm smile directed at Joe's eyes softened his feelings. "Joe, we will get you where you want to be. You have to believe me. You will have lots of pain before we get there. You must have patience and don't get down on yourself. Brownie and I will be here everyday until you walk out of here on your own. We are a team." Brownie whimpered and rubbed his head against Joe's left leg.

Joe knew he had to grit his teeth and deal with the pain so he could get out of there. They needed to be taught a lesson. Joe began to move his left leg faster. Joan reached down and put her hand on his leg just above the knee. "Slower, Joe, we can't rush this. You will do more damage to yourself if you go too fast. Trust me, Joe." She now had her hand on the back of his neck. It felt warm and soft radiating down his back.

Joe slowed down, hating the fact that he was so weak and useless. He just wanted to cry. Brownie put his front legs on the bed and laid his head on Joe's right leg above the crushed and shattered bones. Joe reached down and petted his dog and continued the slow motion with his left leg, grimacing the entire time.

After one hour with Joan, Joe, completely exhausted, was relieved to lie down. He felt like he had just moved a hundred bales of hay in the barn with temperatures in the high 90's. He was sweating and sucking air.

"You did great today, Joe. You're a great guy and you have what it takes to get where we want to go. I will be here tomorrow at the same time," Joan said, with her hand on Joe's chest.

"Thanks!"

"You're welcome, Joe. Bye! And bye to you too, Brownie." She gently stroked Brownie's back. Brownie panted graciously.

"Bye," said Joe, watching her stroke Brownie. The last person to do that was Sue.

# Chapter 38

## RENE'S VISIT

The floor nurse entered as Joe sat up in bed eating his breakfast. "Joseph, you have a guest waiting downstairs in the lobby. Her name is Rene Andretti."

"Tell her to come right up," Joe answered, with oatmeal dripping from his mouth.

Joe finished his oatmeal and second slice of toast before Rene walked into the room. "Hi! Joe. I sure missed seeing you! You are looking good!" Rene found it hard to smile.

She brought a basket of homemade food for Joe. Rene wore a yellow dress with white, low-heeled shoes. Her hair was not as silky as before; her skin had less color and her hands looked older. Her face appeared drawn.

"Hi, Mrs. Andretti, it sure is great to see you," Joe said, never taking his eyes off her. She looked tired, he thought. Sue floated through his throbbing head.

"I brought you some homemade goodies I thought you might like."

"Gee, thanks, I could use some homemade food. This hospital food stinks." He wondered what the basket contained.

Rene reached over Joe's tray and kissed him on the right cheek. "Your mother said she will be down later this afternoon."

Joe looked up at Rene; his heart ached for Sue. "Mrs. Andretti," he swallowed, "Could I hold you? You are as close as I can get to Sue." The tears began to well up in Joe's eyes.

Rene removed Joe's tray from his bed and set it down by the door. She came back, with tears in her eyes, and wrapped her arms around Joe. Hugging each other, they both cried loudly. "Please don't tell anyone I cried."

"Sue told me you had cried. It takes a real man to cry, Joe."

"I'm so sorry. I didn't protect her like I said I would. I just can't believe she isn't here." The loss they shared and the rage they felt increased the guilt that Joe wouldn't release.

"Joe, we must go on. It will be hard for both of us. You and Ray are all I have left, Joe."

"I wish I could make this all up to you," Joe said, burying his head in her shoulder.

"You can, Joe! Just be yourself and love me as Sue's mother. That's all I ask."

"I will do that, for sure." The sniffling continued for several more minutes.

Rene and Joe talked for several hours, about Sue mostly. "Joe, I believe this is good for both of us," her voice raspy from tears. "We need to get it out." Rene sat on Joe's bed, holding his big paw in her slender hand, her face as red as a rose. She smiled slightly every once in a while.

"Yes, I guess, but it sure isn't right what we're going through."

"Joe, would you like to sample some of my homemade goodies?" Rene said, picking up the basket from the chair and putting it front of Joe.

"Yeah, what do you have in here?"

"I hope you like everything. I didn't really know what you liked."

"If you fixed it, I'll eat it," Joe said, as he pulled a large piece of German chocolate cake from the basket. His red eyes fixed on the piece of cake.

"I'll see if I can get you some milk to have with your cake."

"Hey, Brownie, this tastes great. How about a bite?"

The basket contained several large pieces of the German chocolate cake, a small loaf of homemade bread, several dozen sugar cookies, several kinds of fresh fruit, a pound of homemade fudge, six Hershey bars, six packages of Wrigley's Juicy Fruit Gum, and, at the bottom, a picture. Joe's eyes focused on the picture. The picture had been taken on prom night at Rene's house. Joe and Sue stood together. *"She was so beautiful! I loved her so much."* He placed the picture on his cluttered bed table.

"I got you some really cold milk."

"God, she looked beautiful that night," Joe said, looking at the picture, his eyes filling up once again with tears.

"Yes, Joe. You were such a great looking couple," Rene said, biting her lower lip before the tears flowed down both cheeks.

Before Rene left, she gave Joe a big hug and kissed him several times, once on the lips. "Bye! And, thanks again." He grinned. She waved once.

Helen brought the newspapers at 2:10 that afternoon and laid them on the chair. Brownie slept next to Joe on the bed, but opened one eye to check out who had come in. "Hi! You must have been tired. Did you have a nice visit with Rene?"

"Yeah!" His eyes focused on the newspapers.

Chapter 39

# DR. KNOWLES' VISIT

Joe had three more days to go before he would go home. The floor nurse came into the room. "You have a Doctor Knowles down in the lobby wanting to see you." Joe's heart leapt; his mouth went dry. His eyes shot to the door. He didn't believe it—the doctor in the news! Joe thought for a second, and then responded, "Yes! Send him up." Joe decided he would keep his rage to himself and not discuss it with the doctor.

"*What if this Doctor Knowles wanted revenge? What if this doctor, Jimmy and me took on this mafia? How should I react?*"

The man walked confidently into the room. "Hi, Joseph, I'm Doctor Richard Knowles. I've been following your recovery everyday since you entered this hospital." Doctor Knowles walked over to Joe and shook his hand.

"Hi, I'm Joe Clark." Doctor Knowles was not as big as Joe, maybe two inches shorter and probably lighter. "*I wonder if he knows how to fight? His hands look big, but soft.*"

The doctor crossed in front of the bed with one hand bedded in his pant pocket. He stopped and looked directly at Joe. "I was driving behind you when those Capuanos came across our lane. I saw the whole thing." Joe read a thirst for revenge against the three men in the car—the doctor's eyes told him. Thanks to Jimmy, Joe thought, he could read every wrinkle of the human face. It amazed him.

The doctor paced the floor. He peered out the door to see if anyone was nearby. "Joe, when you get yourself healthy enough, I would like to talk to you about these men who took Sue's life and messed up yours." Looking nervous, he walked toward the door again and glanced down the hallway. He turned quickly. "Those Capuanos have to be stopped. The law won't touch them." Joe took in every word, but held his feelings back. "I know you must hate those bastards." The doctor ended the conversation with "Joe, I will stay in touch. I know where you live and have your phone number. Here's my phone number. Call me anytime and I'll get back to you."

Joe's eyes danced up and down the Doctor's body. Joe thought for a minute. "We can get together maybe in a couple weeks. I need to get myself home and back into shape. I should be out of here in a couple a days."

The doctor put on a large, friendly smile. "I'll call you, Joe."

"Thanks for coming to see me, Doctor Knowles."

# Chapter 40

# GOING HOME

The last day at LaSalle County Hospital for Joe Clark consisted of the same grueling routine. Although not easy, Joe sailed through therapy without complaint. Joan worked Joe as hard as she could without doing any damage. Joan seemed to be more touchy-feely than before. She placed her hands where she had never put them before.

Joan gave Joe a hug and kissed him on the right cheek, pressing her breasts against his chest. They both pushed away. "Joe, I know you will work very hard to recover, but make sure you don't overdo it." Her hands stroked his upper arms. A chill went through Joe like a shot. "I wouldn't want to see you back in here, even though I will miss you when you leave today."

Joe, stunned by her remark, managed to respond after several seconds. "I really appreciate everything you have done for me. I know I wouldn't be leaving here this soon if it weren't for you." He forced back a tear he felt forming in his right eye.

Joan kissed Joe on the lips passionately and reached into her uniform pocket. She pulled out a folded piece of paper and placed it into Joe's hand before running from him.

Joe stared at the door for several minutes before opening the note, which read:

*Joe, these past two months have been very difficult for me. I have never let myself get emotionally involved with any patient. You are so different. I can't help myself. I wanted to tell you in person, but thought it better to write it down. I know we are nine years apart, but I want to see you again. I am giving you my telephone number. I won't come and see you until you are well enough to drive. Please call me, Joe.*

*Joan Amato*

Joe's heart raced; his head began to spin. She had never given him any indication she liked him that way. He wasn't interested. She probably had a great body, but then it was all covered up in that uniform. She seemed kind. When she touched him, it felt good. He liked her voice. He had too much to do—he had to get those bastards in Chicago. He couldn't. Sue is all he had ever wanted. Brownie sensed his master's dilemma and inched his nose against Joe's leg.

Joe's hands sweated as he stared at the wall. He placed Joan's note into his shoe box saved for personal items. He sat on the edge of the bed, seeing Sue, then Joan. It made him crazy. His thoughts turned sharply to his Dodgers. Joe picked up the *Chicago Tribune* his mother had brought down.

The Dodgers had moved to Los Angeles, California. They were in fourth place and it didn't look like a good year, as it was already almost September. Reading still made Joe dizzy, if doing so for too long. The doctors told him that would last for several months yet.

*"Last day! I'm going home!"* The floor nurse, Bell, brought a wheel chair for the ride down the elevator and out to Helen's car. "What's this for?" asked Joe, rudely.

"Joe, I know you want to walk out of this hospital on your own, but we can't let you do it. It's hospital policy. I'll let you wheel yourself out, though. I promise." Nurse Bell held the wheel chair for Joe to set his 200 pounds in.

"I want to talk to Doc! I'm not letting anyone push me out of here. I can walk and that is what I intend to do." Joe moved slowly toward the door.

"I'm sorry. The doctor is in surgery and your therapist went home." Her voice got louder.

"I'm walking. You can push my Mom in that chair. I don't care." Joe proceeded toward the door and started down the hall carrying his hickory bat. Brownie trotted at his heels.

"You're too stubborn. If you go that way, you won't find the elevator." Nurse Bell said, standing in the hall, hands on her wide hips.

Joe turned around. "I'll follow you, then!"

Helen just shook her head and followed Joe, Brownie and Nurse Bell, who pushed the empty wheel chair.

Joe hadn't smelled outside air since he had walked with Sue to his car after the prom. Taking a deep breath at the exit door, he almost passed out. He grabbed hold of the door frame to steady himself, not wanting to show any weakness to Nurse Bell or his mother. *"I'm not goin' back in there.*"

Helen opened the front passenger door of the car. "It feels great to get the hell out of that hospital." He thought he would throw up his three pounds of Steak and Shake any minute. Sweat ran down his face. He wiped it off best he could, before anyone would catch on. He closed the car door after Brownie had jumped in the back seat and licked his face.

"You look a little pale. Are you ok? Maybe you should have stayed another day or so," Helen said, as she left the hospital driveway.

"I'm fine, Mom! It's the fresh air. I'm ok," Joe said, with his face still sweaty and his hands moist. He laid his head back on the headrest and closed his eyes.

He saw Sue, dressed in white, smiling at him. She glowed; her hair flowed behind her; her hands extended out. She was beautiful. Joe reached out, eyes still closed. His fingers hit the windshield. His eyes popped open; fingers sprang back.

They came upon the crash scene. Helen never uttered a word. Joe kept his eyes closed, except when Helen applied pressure to the brake peddle. His stomach told him to remain quiet and still.

When they got home, Joe managed to get himself to the front porch swing. Helen brought Joe's personal things from the car and went inside. "Joe, do you want anything, maybe some Kool-aid, ice tea, or soda?"

"Nothing, Mom!" He didn't feel real good and he couldn't figure out why. He felt very weak, almost helpless. He realized he was not in very good shape and it pissed him off. How long will it take him to get back to his normal self? The rage began to build up inside him. He knew he had to hide it.

"I'll call Rene, maybe she can come over," Helen suggested. "*It might make him feel better.*" Joe didn't answer. "Joseph, did you hear me?"

"Yeah, Mom, that's fine." He felt nauseous. His head throbbed. "*Damn it.*"

Rene arrived an hour later. "Hi! Joe!"

"Hi! Mrs. Andretti! Come in." He tried to stand up from the sofa, not sure if he wanted any company.

"Joe, I bet you're happy to be home."

"Yeah!" He felt dizzy. "*I can't stand up that quick.*" "How is Mr.

123

Mathews?"

Rene hugged Joe and kissed him on the cheek. "You look great, Joe! It'll take sometime to heal, but when you do, you'll feel much better." She set a container on the table. "Ray is doing great. I don't know where I'd be without him. I think he hangs around just for my homemade cookies. I brought you some cookies. I hope you like them. They're something new. They're called chocolate chip supreme. They have raisins in them."

"That's great, Mrs. Andretti! Please, sit down." Joe started to feel better.

They talked for several hours and Joe felt more like himself again. He ate a half dozen of Rene's cookies and chased them down with a glass of cold milk. The combination of the cookies and Rene did the trick. Sue could always make Joe feel better. Rene remained his only link to Sue.

# Chapter 41

# A FEW WEEKS LATER

While driving down the street toward his house, Joe spotted a dark blue, 4-door Ford sedan parked in front. Joe noticed a man standing on the porch dressed in a tan sport coat, navy slacks, penny loafers and open collared shirt. He stood maybe six feet tall, with an average build.

"Who the hell is that?" Joe asked Brownie, who had put his head out the window of Helen's car, showed his teeth and made a suggestive growl. Joe parked the New Yorker in the driveway and got out as quickly as his leg and throbbing head would allow. The man stepped off the porch with a small grin.

"You must be Joe Clark?" the man said, pleasantly.

"Who wants to know?" Brownie growled softly.

"My name is Jerry Moore. I am an investigative reporter for the *"Tribune."* Jerry stopped ten feet from Joe.

*"The Chicago Tribune?"*

"That's right. I'd like to talk to you if you have some time." He reached out to shake hands with Joe.

"I guess! What is it you want to talk about?" Joe said, taking the guy's hand, without taking his eyes off him. Brownie showed teeth and sniffed the man's pant leg, silently.

"I have some information about the Capuanos."

Joe's heart opened wide. "Let's talk!" Joe replied, moving toward the porch swing to set his tired body down. He limped slightly; head pulsated with each step.

Jerry sat down in the other chair on the porch. "The Capuanos are the meanest people on the face of this earth. They are much worse than Capone and his people ever were. They are the most ruthless, immoral, vindictive, lawless, hateful, murderous men on this planet. Yet, they are very giving to the church, many charities, even the Chicago Police Benevolent Association. They buy their way into and out of anything they want and when they want. They are into prostitution, illegal

125

gambling, illegal betting, corrupt boxing in several states, fraud, and embezzlement. They control several unions and own every cigarette that comes into this corrupt state."

"The Chicago police are damn near as crooked as they are. Don't get me wrong, there are a few good cops left in Chicago, but most are on the take from the Capuanos, including the Illinois State Police. I have proof that several judges, Federal, County and State, have been paid off by these lowlifes. I, also, have very good information that the FBI is on the take in Chicago." Jerry now stood and paced in front of Joe. "I'm not sure, but I believe the FBI is running an internal investigation on the Chicago Division." Joe listened, but said nothing.

"You can't trust too many people. I'm telling you this because— because I think, God knows, and I don't blame you one bit, you will try and kill these bastards." Jerry's eyes stabbed a hole through Joe's eyes. Joe did not flinch, nor blink. "I have checked you out. I know you won't back down from anyone or anybody. But, you don't know a damn thing about them." He pointed his finger towards Joe's nose. Joe blinked once. Jerry sat down with a thud. "They will try and kill you before you kill them."

"I have talked to Doctor Richard Knowles in Rockford." Joe looked at him with hard eyes. "I told him the same thing I've told you. You, or any army you employ, will not destroy these people. The only way they will ever be destroyed is if the FBI does it. Then, maybe, just maybe, we will see the destruction of the Capuanos." Jerry stood yet again and leaned against the porch rail.

Joe thought about his plans to kill the Capuanos, but wasn't sure he wanted to convey this to the stranger on the porch. He remembered his Grandpa telling him: *If you don't know them, don't tell them nothing you don't want them to know.* "I haven't given much thought to these men," Joe said, looking down at the porch floor as he spoke.

"Bullshit, Joe Clark!" Jerry roared. "You have it on your mind morning, noon and night. You hate the Capuanos. You are going to try and kill them. Don't tell me you're not." Jerry shifted his weight from one foot to the other as he spoke. Brownie showed his teeth and growled, softly

"You get your ass off my porch. I don't need you or anyone else telling me what I'm thinking and what I'm not." Joe's head now throbbed twice every second. His stomach threatened to revolt.

126

"Joe, I am just warning you. I know these people. You must trust me. You can't win this war. They will destroy you for just thinking about it. They will get the doctor in Rockford. Not today, maybe not tomorrow, but they will get him. They will rape his wife and torture her until she begs them to kill her."

"Go back to Chicago, where the rest of the scum live."

"I'll stay in touch, Joe. If you decide you want to pursue this, please contact me at this number." Jerry placed his card on the porch rail.

Joe took the card after Jerry walked off, his hand shaking and his head banging.

Jerry sat in his car, window rolled down. "I will try to get as much information on these bastards as I can. Please call me before you proceed." Jerry drove away slowly.

Joe didn't know what to do or say. He sat down in the porch swing and began to swing. He stared out toward the street at nothing. Brownie put his head on Joe's sore leg above his knee and looked at Joe with big, sad eyes.

The mailman arrived a few minutes later. "Hi! Cliff."

"Hi, Joe. How are you doing?" Cliff had the Clark's mail all sorted and ready to give to Joe.

"Great!" The pain shot down his leg as he reached for the mail.

"You have a letter in there for you, Joe." Cliff turned and grabbed another bundle of mail from his leather bag.

"Thanks, Cliff! You have a great day." Joe flipped through the mail, looking to see who had sent him a letter.

"You do the same." He waved.

It was a letter from Jimmy. Joe tore it open and began to read it.

*Joe,*

*I got my ass tore up, Joe. My sister got the shit beat out of her by the mafia men. When she tell me, I went after their sorry asses and they beat me to a pulp. I have broken jaw, broken nose and three missing teeth. They came at me with six men. I got in some good licks but I was no match for all them. They say they will kill me next time. They told me they would beat my aunt up and burn her place to the ground. I wished you been with me Joe. We would've kicked their asses. They from the Capuano mob. I hear*

*they control everything in Chicago. Maybe when you get to feeling*
*better and the swelling goes down, we'll pay these bastards a visit. I*
*can get some help. Now I have better reason. Let me know ok.*

*Your buddy*
*Jimmy*


Joe read the letter three times before he sat back down. "Damn!"
Joe looked at his leg. The adrenaline rushed through his weak body. He
slammed his open palm on the porch railing. "Now they beat up my best
friend. This is too damn much. I got to get myself back into shape. I can't
sit around here and wait for this damn leg to heal. In the morning, my
training will start," Joe said, loud enough for anyone within thirty feet to
hear.

The phone rang. Joe jumped up, almost running to the phone.
The pain was brutal, but he gritted his teeth and answered, "Hello! What
the hell do you want?" The rage surrounded Joe.

"Joe, this is Doctor Knowles."

"Hi, Doctor Knowles! I'm sorry." Joe's voice became much
softer.

"How are you doing, Joe?"

"Ok, I guess."

"I would like to see you this week, Thursday afternoon, if you
can. I thought maybe we could meet at the city park in Rochelle."
Rochelle sat between Rockford and Mendota. "Are you able to drive?"

"Yeah, I'll be there, Doctor Knowles. What time?" The pain
rushed down Joe's leg.

"Let's say 1:00 p.m."

"I'll see you then!"

"Thanks, Joe"

"No. Thank you, Doc. I mean Doctor Knowles."

"Joe, just call me Doc."

Chapter 42

# THE NEXT MORNING

Joe headed for the high school track field with Brownie before
sun up. The track measured 440 yards, or ¼ mile. Determined,
Joe set a goal of running the ¼ mile in less than a minute
before March 1st. He had four months to do it.

He looked at his watch. With the second hand on 12, he began
his ¼ mile walk. The pain nearly stopped him before he got 100 yards.
He gritted his teeth and drove his 6 foot 4 1/2 inch lean body, now
weighing 204 pounds, till the tears rolled down his face. He had less then
100 yards remaining when he felt as if he would collapse from
exhaustion. "No! No! I have to finish! I can't quit!" His legs wobbled; the
right one dragged. "Those bastards!" Joe imagined Sue in her prom dress.
The picture Rene had given him remained on his night table. Brownie ran
ahead, then looked back, barking, cheering Joe on to finish.

As he crossed the finish line, he looked at his watch. It read 15
minutes and 38 seconds. "Shit!" How am I going to do this? Damn it!"
His eyes fogged. He threw up and collapsed on the cinder track. He laid
there until Henry Winters came by for his three-mile run. "Hey! You ok?"
Henry said, reaching down to feel Joe's pulse. Brownie let out a slight
growl.

"Yeah, I'm ok!" Joe tried to get up, but his body said no. He tried
again and, finally, with Henry's help, he managed to stand up.

"You'd better sit down over here." Henry started to lead Joe over
to the bleachers.

"I'm ok!" Joe judged he would pass out again.

"You better sit here a minute before you drive home."

Henry started his three-mile run. Joe made it to the car. He still
felt faint and had blurry vision. He managed to get home without hitting
anything. He thought the pain in his leg didn't seem any worse than when
he walked. He reached the kitchen refrigerator just as his mother came
down the stairs.

"Well, good morning, Joe. Are you hungry, this morning? How

about I fix you ham and eggs with homemade bread I baked yesterday?"

"Ok, Mom!" Between the throbbing in his head and the pain in his leg, Joe could hardly speak. His throat filled with bile. He grabbed a jug of orange juice and took a big swig to wash it down.

"Don't drink out of that jug. Let me get you a glass. You don't look too good, Joseph. What on earth did you do to your pant leg? It's torn and it looks like you're bleeding. Let me look at it." Helen reached down to pull up Joe's pant leg.

"I went to the track and fell down. I'll be ok," Joe replied, trying to correct any weakness he may be showing.

"What on earth were you doing at the track this early?" Helen asked, while getting a rag and some hydrogen peroxide to clean the cuts.

"I am trying to get back into shape," Joe muttered, as his mother cleaned him up.

Helen turned the other way. "I don't want you to overdo it, Joseph."

"No problem!" Joe said, sitting down on the kitchen chair with a thud.

Joe devoured four eggs, four pieces of ham and three pieces of homemade bread, with strawberry jam piled ½ inch thick on each slice.

"That was great, Mom!" said Joe, rubbing his slim tummy. He felt stronger; his spirits lifted. Soon he'd kick the Capuanos all over Chicago.

# Chapter 43

# PHONE CALL

The phone rang. "Hello!" Joe answered, knowing he wouldn't last long in this conversation since his bowels were calling.

"Hi, Joe, this is Joan! How are you doing?"

*"Dang it! Not now!"* "Hey! Can I call you back? You caught me at a bad time." Joe hadn't called Joan since he had gotten home.

"Sure, I'm home today! You have my number?"

"Yeah!"

"Bye!"

"Bye!"

He got Joan's phone number out, but couldn't decide if he wanted to return the call. He mashed the paper up in his sweaty palm. A lump grew in his throat as thoughts of Sue penetrated his head. He sat down and waited. Almost an hour had passed when the phone rang again. After four rings, he answered. "Hello!" He was sure now that he didn't want to talk to Joan.

"Joe, are you able to talk now?"

"Yeah," his voice trailed.

"I haven't heard from you. I thought I would see how you were doing."

"Great!" *"Go away."*

"I would like to see you this weekend. Maybe we can go to a movie. I'll come up."

"I don't think so. I just ain't in the mood," Joe said, with little enthusiasm in his voice.

"I'll cheer you up, Joe, I promise. I'll get you to take your mind off your pain and everything else that is bothering you," Joan pleaded. Joe started feeling helpless.

Joe's loins tightened. He thought for a minute and responded, "Ok! Do you know where I live?" The picture on his night table entered his handcuffed brain. *"Why am I doing this?"*

"Yes, Joe! I drove past your place a couple of times since you went home. I wanted to stop, but was afraid to. I miss you, Joe."

"Maybe we better wait."

"No!" she rebuked, quickly. "I need you," she offered, softly. Joe's loins took over.

"What time?"

"7:00 p.m., this Saturday, ok?"

"Yeah, that'll be great!" Sweat crept out from his fragile body.

"See you then, Joe!"

"Ok!"

Joe hung up the phone and sat down on the living room sofa. "What? What the hell am I doing? I still love Sue. I can't be going out with someone nine years older than me. My body can't take it yet, anyway. I'll call her back and tell her I can't make it. Besides, I feel like I'm just half a man. This damn leg and my head beat like a drum. Shit!" Brownie looked at him strangely.

# Chapter 44

# THURSDAY AFTERNOON

Joe arrived at the city park in Rochelle before 1:00 p.m. He sat on the park bench with Brownie at his side, watching an old lady one hundred yards away feed a half dozen pigeons. No one else appeared to be in the park. Doctor Knowles arrived at 1:20. "I'm sorry I'm late, Joe. I had an emergency surgery to perform early this morning and it took much longer than anticipated." Doc reached out to shake hands with Joe.

*"For a surgeon, this guy sure has a strong hand shake."* "It's such a nice day, I didn't mind waiting," Joe said, as he sat down again on the park bench. Joe looked him over. He seemed bigger than what he remembered when he had seen him in the hospital.

"Joe, I don't have a lot of time so I will get right to the point." He stood in front of Joe, hands clasped behind his back. "I want to see these men dead for this awful crime they've committed. I don't know how, but I will get it done someway. I have the money to hire someone. I would rather be involved myself, but I need to think of my career. I can't afford to get my hands busted up." His pupils danced as he spoke. Doc looked at his hands. "These hands are my life. Without them, I have nothing. Do you understand, Joe?"

Joe nodded.

Doctor Knowles' face turned almost grey. "I don't know how you feel towards these people, but I want revenge." Moisture gathered in his eyes. He looked down at the ground. "They deserve nothing better than to die for their actions. Jail is too damn good for them. Then we'd have to feed the bastards until they died." Joe could feel the rage in this man; it almost matched his own. Joe stood, fire in his eyes.

"I will kill these men if it is the last thing I do." His heart skipped a beat. He spoke before he realized what he had said. He stared at the doctor. Oh well, the cat is out of the bag now, thought Joe. Joe had read in the paper about Doc's daughter being killed.

"I had a feeling that is how you would feel. I talked to Jerry

Moore from the *Tribune* the other day. I believe he can help us. He has a lot of inside information." Doc sat on the edge of the park bench and rested his elbows on his knees. Joe sat down beside him.

"Yeah, I talked to him, too. He gave me his card. I told him to get the hell off my porch." Joe stood, the pain shot down his right leg. He gritted his teeth and sat down again. "I guess I shouldn't have been so hard on him. I'm not sure I can trust him, though."

"I think we need to trust someone. We don't have the knowledge this man has about these people."

"I have a friend in Chicago who can read a man's eyes and tell if he's lying or not. He'll help me kill these bastards." Joe told Doc what had happened to Jimmy. Joe thought he read fear in Doc's eyes, but only Jimmy would know for sure. "We need to have a meeting with these guys soon."

"Sounds ok to me."

"Great! I'll call Jerry. How about three weeks from today? I am usually off on Thursdays. That will give you and Jimmy time to heal up some." Doc paced in front of Joe.

"I don't have a car yet."

"I'll pick you up, Joe. I know a restaurant in Downers Grove where we can meet. I'll have Jerry pick Jimmy up in Chicago. That way everyone will get there without any problems," Doc said, as he continued to pace.

"Yeah, that way Jimmy can feel Jerry out before we meet." He knew Jimmy would be able to tell if the man were honest.

Doc looked skeptical. "I'll stay in touch, Joe."

"Ok, Doctor Knowles." Joe's emotion remained hidden by the pain in his leg.

He checked his watch, "I better get moving."

# Chapter 45

# SATURDAY

The day arrived too fast for Joe. He never called Joan. His manhood told him he wanted to see her, but his heart told him he didn't want any part of her, or anyone else. His head appeared to be winning the battle. Joe looked at the clock in the kitchen. It was already 6:05 p.m. She was picking him up at 7:00 p.m. Joe went up the stairs, got undressed and got into the shower. As he thought of Joan, his loins ached.

When the door bell rang, Joe rose from the kitchen chair and walked as fast as his legs would carry him. Joan looked intensely eager. She wore a short, red skirt just above the knee, and a form fitting, white, long sleeve sweater. Her lips, covered with bright red lipstick, were full. "Hi! Joe. I am so glad to see you." Her breasts stretched the woven white sweater. Her black hair fell on her shoulders.

"H-Hi, Joan, you look great!" Joe said, peering at her chest.

Joan put her arms around Joe's large frame and planted a wet, passionate kiss on Joe's parted, dry lips. Joe felt his eagerness within seconds as her body pressed firmly against his. "I thought about you everyday, Joe." She kissed him again, pushing her tongue into his still dry mouth. Brownie let out a faint disapproving growl. Her lips parted. She glanced at Brownie, gave a short smile, and nibbled on Joe's ear and whispered, "I need you, Joe. I have wanted you for over two months now." Brownie gave another faint growl.

Joe grew uneasy. "W-We ne-need to go," he said, as he moved toward the open door. "Bye, Brownie."

Joe got into Joan's red, 1960 Chevy Impala, two-door coupe. "Nice car you have here," Joe said, as he made himself comfortable on the white leather seats. Her skirt crawled up her thigh. She had her knees spread at least 8 inches, maybe 10 inches, thought Joe. The view from Joe's perspective reduced the pain in his right leg considerably and brought a small grin.

"Where would you like to go, Joe?"

Joe's heart rate elevated drastically. "Maybe we should just go for a ride. I know, how about out to our old farm." Her scent, her breasts and the short skirt derailed all Joe's hopes of self control.

# Chapter 46

# THE OFFER

The still-warm air acted as their invitation. Joan impressed him as being more than willing.

Joan sat on a fallen, barkless tree; her knees slightly spread. "Come here, Joe!" She parted her moist lips. A full moon lit up the area.

Joe's legs went numb, frozen. He moved toward her, head not listening. He felt uneasy signs of dizziness. His mouth dried up.

He stood in front of her sensuous body. She put her arms around him and pulled him closer. Joe trembled slightly. Her hot breath pushed him to the edge of control. Moments later they were both naked and ecstasy rang out.

They dressed and walked to the car. Joe felt as weak as a newborn colt. His legs barely held him up. Images of Sue entered his foggy head. He managed to get into the front seat of the car. *"Why did I do this?"* She entered the car and slammed the door. Joe turned to look at her, not sure what to say next, when her distraught look stopped him. She sat there gaping out the front windshield. Joe's head throbbed. He wished he were home.

Joan's face reddened, eyes became wide. Joe sensed her mood, but couldn't see her clearly. Her fingers tapped the steering wheel. "Joe, Joe, I can—I can get you all the information you need on the Capuanos: Where they live; what kind of cars they drive; where they eat; and how they make their money." She took a deep breath, exhaling quickly. "I know who their bodyguards are, who their hit men are and where they live." Her voice cracked on every word. Joe took it all in. He did not respond.

"I can get you all the facts—for a price." She glanced at Joe, who peered into the darkness ahead of the car. "$250,000" She sucked in more air and blew it out, slowly, between her smudged lips. "I need half upfront." Joe didn't answer, didn't move his aching body. Silence took over. "Come on, Joe. I know you want to kill those Capuanos." Her voice rose. Joe looked at her, a rush of hate exploding inside him. His silence provoked Joan. "Hey, hey you stupid, crippled farm boy, how do you think you will ever kill those Capuanos? You need me. I can help." Joe's head spun.

He slammed his fist on the dash. "How much did they pay you to get information on me?" Joe shot back.

Joan looked at him, anger in her eyes. "*Voi sbagliato! Buratt!*"

"What the hell did you say?" Joe's rage began to get the best of him. That must be Italian, he thought. "*Stay calm, Joe.*" The car engine roared. Joan dropped the gear shift into low and punched the accelerator down. The car spun around the green pasture twice before she pointed it toward the dirt road. Her speed terrified Joe.

They were within a block of Joe's place when she said, "Think about it, Joe. I know you want to kill the Capuanos. I can help you! You will die without the information. They know every move you make. You have until Saturday to let me know. If not, they will kill you. I don't know when, where, or how, but they will do it. You are in their way and they don't want anyone in their way. They will get that dumb-ass Doctor Knowles, too."

Joe shook his head and shut the car door. As he walked slowly to the porch, he heard her tires squealing for half a block. He knew that would awaken old Mrs. Larson down the block. Brownie met Joe at the door. They went to the kitchen to get some much-needed food. He had worked off the food he had eaten over three hours ago.

"I have to be the dumbest jerk in the world. How could this sweet therapist become some sort of an evil, money hungry, conniving bitch? She set the whole thing up. She must be a damn slut." Brownie sat on his hind legs, taking in every word, as if he understood. "I can't believe I am so stupid. How could I not see this before? My head really must be messed up. I know I would have smelled a rat before now. You tried to tell me. I heard you growling, but I never listened." Joe sat on the porch eating two ham and cheese sandwiches, potato chips and a bottle of Coke. It was after 2:00 a.m. by the time Joe crawled into bed, Brownie curled up at his feet.

# Chapter 47

# THE NEXT MORNING

After going to the track and eating breakfast, Joe headed for the Ford dealer in town. He had yet to see his Thunderbird. The insurance company had given Joe a check for his car. He got almost what he had paid for it.

"Good morning, Joe!" Harry Smith, the sales manager, greeted Joe as he entered the showroom. Harry knew everyone in town, especially the young guys. They were all future customers to him.

"Good morning!" said Joe, waving toward Mr. Smith.

"What we lookin' at this mornin'?" A big grin spread over his rugged face.

"I don't know!" said Joe, thumbs in his front jean pockets, wandering over toward a new red Ford F-100, with all the goodies and a big V-8 under the hood.

"That's a great truck, Joe. You want to take her for a spin?" Harry said, scratching his chin with one hand, with the other hand in his pant pocket playing with loose change.

"Nah!" What else you got outside?" Joe did not want red after being with Joan.

"Come right this way, son. I have a whole lot full of those great trucks."

Joe followed him out the door and thought about when he had bought his T-Bird.

This same Harry Smith had given Joe the BS on his Thunderbird. Joe let most of it go in one ear and out the other. Joe's Grandpa had told him about car salesmen.

"What color you want, Joe? I have white ones, red ones, blue ones and black ones." Harry moved fast. He wanted to make a deal and get on to the next sucker who walked in.

"Black."

"Here's one right here, Joe." He pointed in the direction of the only black F-100 in the lot.

"I'd like to drive this one!" Joe said, walking around the truck and checking it out. It also had a V-8 and all the goodies.

"Sure thing, I'll get the keys." Harry ran toward the shop.

"Let me start her up for you, Joe!" He returned, out of breath from the Camels he'd smoked during the past twenty-five years.

Harry opened the hood and that big V-8 rumbled, sounding powerful to Joe's ears.

Joe got in the driver's side and took her for a spin, while Harry rattled on about the features and benefits and all the reasons why he should buy a Ford rather than a Chevy or Dodge.

They returned to the shop and Joe said, "I want to talk to your service department."

"Sure, Joe! Is there anything I didn't answer?" A worried look appeared on Harry's face, as he motioned toward the service department.

"Nah!"

"Sid, this is Joe Clark. He wants to ask you a couple of questions. Joe, Sid is our service manager."

"Hi, Joe."

"Hi! I want to know how much it would cost to have that engine in that new black F-100 boosted up to maybe 50 more horse power, or more if you can do it." Harry's eyes widened and his mouth fell open.

"I would have to call the factory, Joe. That truck out there has a 292 horse power rating. I believe we can have that punched up to 345. That would make it a really fast truck." Joe grinned. "I could have your answer this afternoon. Maybe the factory can build you what you want cheaper than I can, Joe."

"Yeah, Joe!" Harry nodded his head. He didn't get any commission on anything done in-house.

"Ok, I'll stop back this afternoon, say about 3:00."

"I'll have you an answer then."

At 3:15 that afternoon Joe returned to the service department.

"Joe, I can get you a 345 horse power. It will be a bigger engine block and the pistons will be larger. There won't be a soul in this State that could ever catch you, son." He winked at Joe. "The factory will do it for $565.00. They have to change the transmission also, but that's included in the price.

"Thanks, I'll order it."

"You can do it in black, flare sides and get all the goodies," Harry remarked as Joe entered the show room. He had a big, old grin on his face and already had the commission check counted.

"How long will it take?"

"Thirty days, max."

"Let's order it! I also want an all-chrome grill in front of the existing bumper and up to the top of the hood." Joe had seen one on *M-Squad*, a TV cop show.

"Great, Joe! Let's get her drawn up."

Joe headed for the track and walked it in under 14 minutes. He needed to get much stronger. He wouldn't stop now for anything, especially a sleaze like Joan. The thought of her made his stomach move to his throat.

# CHAPTER 48

# THE REFUSAL

The telephone rang right after Joe had finished his breakfast and his Mom had gone upstairs to change her clothes. "Hello!"

"Joe, this is Joan! What is your answer?" *"What the hell! I plum forgot she wanted that answer today. Maybe I should just hang up on this sleaze bag."* Joe tried to decide what to tell her. A smile came over his face. "Come on country boy give me an answer. I have to go."

"Take your offer and shove it where the sun doesn't shine, you sleaze bag." Joe's head throbbed and the chiseling started to erupt in his leg. The thought of her warm body next to him gave him cold chills.

*"Voi beledo! Voi merdu! Voi burati!"* She blasted through the phone.

She sounded angry. Joe laughed and laughed! "You are messing with the wrong guy, you two-timing bitch."

*"A'mbola!"* The slamming of the phone rang in Joe's ear.

Joe slammed the phone down and put her on his hate list, along with the Yankees. He hit the wall—the wall shook.

"Joseph, did I hear you call someone a bitch?" his mother asked, with her hands to her hips.

"Nah!"

"It sure sounded like it to me."

Later that morning, Joe received a letter from Jimmy Robbins.

Joe,

*"I met Jerry Moore and I like him. He seems straight to me. I believe he can help us. I never said nothin' about the Capuanos. He brought it up and I told him I don't know nothin' about any Italians, except the ones that beat the shit out of me. I think we can trust him. I sure will be glad to see you. It has been a long time.*

*Your Buddy*
*Jimmy R.*

Joe was glad to hear Jimmy trusted Jerry. He read the letter four times to make sure he had read it right. "Next week, Thursday, we sit down and try and figure some things out. I wonder if I should mention Joan or not? Maybe I will ask Jerry if the name "Amato" rings a bell. You know what, Brownie, those scum bags that killed Sue were coming from LaSalle and heading north. They were probably headed for Highway 34 East toward Chicago. Why didn't I think of that before?"

# THE PLAN

# CHAPTER 49

# MEET THE CAPUANOS

Marco Capuano had led the Chicago mafia for fifteen years. Marco's father, Vito Capuano, had headed the mafia in Sicily for thirty years. Marco came to the United States by boat at the age of thirty with an older brother, Alex. Vito Capuano, the eldest brother, stayed in Sicily to help his father run the mafia there. Marco and Alex settled in New Orleans. They got involved mostly with smuggling small gems and jewels that could be brought in easily from South American countries.

Alex got mixed up in prostitution in and around the ports. One of his two dozen prostitutes, a French Cajun prostitute named Carmen, made Alex very good money. When she decided she wanted more than Alex allowed, she tried to cheat Alex out of some money she had earned. Alex beat her so badly she never worked again. She had been beautiful, but when Alex had finished with her, she carried nothing but scars. Her nose was smashed and cut so badly she had to have eighty percent of it removed, which made her horribly disfigured.

Three of Carmen's brothers, who were not much better company than Alex, found him and castrated him. They hung him naked by his arms in a tree in the Cajun swamps and left him there to die a slow death. It took place in late July and the mosquitoes swarmed like flies on road kill. They say it took seven days for Alex to die, only because the three brothers had kept enough food and water in him. Additionally, the daily rains in the swamps kept him from cooking in the sun. Marco identified the body.

Marco immediately closed his business in New Orleans and moved to St. Louis, after sending his brother's remains, minus his testicles, back to Sicily. He opened up a nightclub in the heart of St. Louis called "Marco's." He had live music and it brought in good money. He later bought a bigger building and made it into a restaurant and night club. The name, "Marco's," remained.

Members of the St. Louis mafia paid him a visit one day. They wanted thirty percent of his gross or they would blow his place to bits. Thinking of his brother and what had been done to him, Marco gave them thirty percent without a fight. He did this for more than a year before he sold the place to another Italian, Tony Torletto, for a huge profit. He neglected to mention the thirty percent.

Marco left for Chicago with Maria, the sweetheart he had met in St. Louis. She, also Italian, had grown up in St. Louis. Marco took the money he made and bought another nightclub on Rush Street in Chicago's old downtown. The club, "Marco's," did great and no one had approached him about getting any percentage. The mafia in Chicago wasn't very well controlled at the time. Marco saw an opportunity and hired some strong arms to put pressure on different businesses. He decided he would only take ten percent, but then increase it every other year.

After one year, Maria became pregnant with Marco's first son, Alex, named after his brother. Marco got involved in cigarette vending machines, setting them up everywhere cigarettes were smoked or sold. Within a year, he had three thousand of them in Chicago alone. Within two years, he controlled the entire cigarette market in Chicago.

Jimmy Capuano arrived when Alex was two. The Capuanos lived on the south side of Chicago in an exclusive Italian neighborhood, with their house being one of the best in the neighborhood. The house, a two-story, all brick home built by an Italian contractor, had large rooms with high ceilings and oak, hardwood floors throughout. It sat on over an acre of lawn, trees and shrubs, with a large front yard and a swimming pool in the back. Marco paid the contractor very well and also covered the higher education tuition costs of his six children.

For many years, Marco donated twenty percent of his earnings to Saint Vincent's Catholic Church. Ten percent went to various charities and political affiliates. Those charities included: the Boys' Club of Chicago, Policeman's Ball, several hospitals and many politicians that would help Marco in his businesses. Many saw him as a hero and most parishioners at Saint Vincent's loved him.

By 1945, Marco had gained control of the Chicago mafia. He owned many businesses and controlled the labor unions that had started up right after the war. He seemed to be in the right place at the right time. So well-liked, he could have run for mayor of Chicago and won by a landslide. Hardly anyone knew how corrupt he really was, and those who had any idea were either paid off or fished out of the Chicago River. Several were buried alive in the concrete roads in and around Chicago.

Marco gave generously to those in need, and he made sure the newspapers reported it on the front page. Marco's name or picture appeared, both in the *Tribune* and the *Sun Times,* almost everyday for some great thing he had paid for, or deed that had been completed with the help of his employees.

Alex and Jimmy attended Catholic school. By the time Jimmy was in the fifth grade, they had a money-making business selling candy from their father's vending operation to other students. They made 200 percent profit on the candy sales. You couldn't buy a candy bar at their school, except through them. The sisters and the priest even bought from them.

Four years later, they had four more businesses. They sold cigarettes, chewing gum and soda pop. They loaned money to students at a rate of twenty-five percent. Borrow $10.00, pay back $12.50, provided you paid it back by the end of the week. If not, it increased to $15.00, or you got the tar kicked out of you and they still got their money, or they threatened to kill you. They had strong-arms—big black boys paid peanuts to do their dirty work.

While in high school, a very good Catholic school, they started a prostitution ring. They had non-Catholic, less affluent girls, mostly teenagers and black, as their prostitutes. They would pimp them for $20.00 per lay and $10.00 per blow job. More adults paid them than students. After two years, the Capuano boys had twenty young prostitutes working for them.

Before the two brothers left high school, they had ten different businesses, taking in over $750,000 per year, tax free. They ran a stolen car ring. Again, they would use black kids to steal the cars, which they would then sell to used car dealers in and around Chicago.

When a problem arose with the law, their father would step in and either pay off the judges or the cops, or someone would just disappear, never to be found again.

Alex, the first to marry, wed a former classmate, an Italian woman from a very good family, named Margo. She was beautiful and worshipped the ground Alex walked on. She had no clue about his corrupt businesses or his father's operation. They had two children, both boys, Marco and Vito.

Eddie Capuano, the son of Marco's brother who had stayed in Sicily, arrived in Chicago when Alex and Jimmy were in their early twenties. He could speak English fairly well. Marco took him into the business as if he were his own. The main office for the Capuanos remained on Rush Street above Marco's restaurant and night club. "Marco's" now had illegal gambling going on in the basement.

Eddie wasn't married; neither was Jimmy. They both screwed anything they wanted when they wanted. If the ladies resisted, they were beaten up and threatened.

Marco hired thugs from all over, some even from foreign countries; such as, Greece, Italy and Spain. Marco paid his people well, providing they did the job right. The chain of command for the Chicago mafia was simple: Marco sat at the top, then Alex, Jimmy, Eddie, and finally, Johnny Amato, who had been with Marco for fifteen years. He would kill you for just looking at him cross-eyed. As Marco's main hit man, he either killed or had killed over one hundred fifty people over the last fifteen years.

The last Saturday in April 1960, the Capuanos, Alex, Jimmy and Eddie, attended a high school graduation party in LaSalle, Illinois, for their cousin, Vince Amato, brother of Joan Amato and nephew of Johnny Amato. He had graduated from Saint Bede Catholic High School. The party started right after 2:00 p.m. and went till 11:00 p.m. Alex drove, with Jimmy passed out in the back seat. Eddie sat in the front seat with Alex. All three were drunk as skunks when they left the party.

# CHAPTER 50

# MEETING WITH "THE BOSS"

When the three Capuanos left the hospital, Marco called a meeting at his office on Rush Street. When Marco spoke, everyone listened, or suffered the consequences. Marco lit a hand-rolled, Cuban cigar and leaned back in his high-back, leather chair. The smoke appeared in several circles as he blew it out of his punchy lips. "What the hell? I try to be a good citizen. I give to the church. I donate thousands of dollars to charities and you three guys try and screw my ass up in ten seconds." Those listening looked at Marco, never blinking. Fear crawled through their spines. "You kill an innocent, young lady, Italian at that, and messed up some farm boy for life." The silence in the room became deadly.

"If you weren't family, I'd kill you myself. The damn papers have been murdering me over this shit. It will take me years to earn back what you dumb idiots destroyed in ten seconds. Alex, you are supposed to be my number one man. You drove the car." Marco drew on his Cuban cigar as he spoke. His exhaled smoke filtered around the room.

"I'm sorry, father. We were really messed up. I wish we could erase it all," Alex said, with eyes dancing around the room.

"You can't erase it, dip shit," Marco screamed. He stood as he spoke. Alex hung his head, along with the other two.

"That country boy lives, and he may, he might cause us problems. They may not be real smart, those farm boys," Marco paced the hardwood floor, "but if they get on your trail, they stay on your trail. They are like bloodhounds chasing a fox." Thoughts of New Orleans and his brother entered his head.

"Have Johnny take him out," Jimmy Capuano suggested, with a twisted grin on his face.

"You kill that farm boy and you'll have the whole country against us. This shit hit every paper in the country. You guys think like a sheep herder in a meadow. You think with your penises." Cigar smoke continued to fill the air in the small room. The younger Capuanos started coughing.

"That Doctor, what the hell is his name?"

"Knowles," Eddie answered.

"Yeah, we already hit his house. Hopefully, that will shut him up. If not, Johnny will shut him up for good."

"We'll keep an eye on this farm boy. I believe his name is Joe. Johnny's niece was this farm boy's therapist." Marco paused a few seconds and laughed. The others in the smoke-filled room joined him. They all knew Johnny Amato could kill anyone, anytime, any place. "Now, get the hell out of here and make the organization some money."

# Chapter 51

# THE BROTHERHOOD

The next day, at noon, Jimmy, Jerry, Doc Knowles and Joe met in a private room at Fredrick's Steak House in Downers Grove. Joe and Jimmy took several minutes to reminisce about their days at Sheridan. They engaged in several hugs, handshakes, slaps on the back and a little sparring. They both stood 6 feet 5 inches, with Jimmy outweighing Joe by 10 pounds, tipping the scale at 230 pounds. His arms appeared to be twice the size they were when he lived at Sheridan. He had virtually no body fat and still had three front teeth missing. Joe knew he needed to work like the devil to get himself prepared for what lay ahead. Seeing Jimmy's build made Joe even more determined to be the best he could be, no matter what.

Doctor Knowles spoke first. "I'll finance this whole operation starting today and until we complete our mission of ridding Chicago and all of Illinois of the Capuanos, including any of their killers, rapists, thieves, or others who have to do with the destruction of innocent people. Jerry, I know you have a tremendous amount of information on the Capuanos, but I believe we need at least three, possibly four more investigators we can trust. I'll pay them whatever it takes to gather the information we need."

"I know a very good investigator in St. Louis," Jerry offered, looking directly at Doc.

"Great! We need two more. I want to know everything about these bastards. I want to know who they pay off, when they pay them and how much they pay them. I, also, want to know who is missing or presumed dead, or who has been raped by these lowlifes. We need to know every business they operate. The most critical information we need to get is what policemen from the city, county, state or FBI, are on the take. And lastly, we need to find out what judges, city, county, state and federal, are on the take." Doc's voice grew louder as he spoke about the crooked police and judges.

Joe moved in his chair with every sentence Doc spoke, simply amazed at what Doc had to say. The others seemed to react the same way. *"I'm sure glad he knows all this stuff because I didn't even think of half of it. I wonder how he knows so much being a doctor,"* Joe thought, with an inward smile. The thrill flowed through his body.

Jimmy appeared eager to help. "Do you need any of my people? I knows some guys that, flat out, will kick some butt. You want somebody dead? I know them, too."

"I'm not sure, Jimmy, but I'll tell you this, the men we have will be trained to handle these guys. We can't afford to make one mistake. One mistake dealing with these Capuanos is like me making a mistake with a patient during surgery: *YOU'RE DEAD!*" Doc's eyes popped from their sockets, then fell back as he spoke the last two words.

"You're absolutely right there, Doc," Jerry confirmed. His eyes took in his companions sitting in the room. A brotherhood began to take shape amongst the group. Everyone felt it.

Joe cleared his throat. "I don't know too much about these Capuanos, but I believe we should try and work from the outside in. Kinda like herding hogs. You can't scare them or they'll run on you. You have to be smarter than they are or they'll outsmart you. You hit them too hard and they bite your ass. I think we get all this information, herd as many of them to a holding pen as we can, then call the rest of the prime hogs to our turf by feeding them enough corn. If my Grandpa were here, I believe that is the way he would have planned it."

"I like your analogy, Joe," Doc said, with a grin on his face.

"I'll get you the men and all the information I can as quickly as I can," offered Jerry.

"We don't want to rush anything, Jerry," Doc advised.

"I won't be ready to kick any ass until at least June 1st." Joe hated to admit it.

"That's ok, Joe. It'll take that long to gather the information we need," Doc said.

"I'll contact my friend down in St. Louis. His name is Lester Yates," Jerry said.

"When can we eat? I'm hungry as a hog with no corn in the trough," said Joe, looking for the waitress.

The waitress came and they all ordered T-bone steaks. Jimmy and Joe had twenty ouncers, while Doc and Jerry, fifteen. They also had baked potatoes, mixed vegetables and all the sourdough bread they could eat.

The meeting ended with Doc saying, "I'll try and find five good men to start herding these hogs, along with at least two more investigators. We have less than 250 days to get our ducks in a row. June 1st will be our goal." He looked at Joe. "You all stay in touch with me. Here's my card. Call me anytime and leave a message. I'll get back to you as soon as I can."

"Just remember one thing: Those three that killed my Sue are mine and nobody else's," Joe said, with hatred in his eyes.

"We all know how you feel, Joe!" Doc said, looking directly at Joe.

"I want you all to know we have to keep this information just between us and anyone we bring on board. If the mafia gets any inkling of our plan, we are in big trouble. We can't tell anyone, even people we trust," Jerry said, his eyes floating from Doc to Joe to Jimmy and back again.

"Jerry's right," Doc said, looking at the other three as if their lives depended on what he said.

"We'll get these bastards! I feel it in my bones. The only way to capture or kill snakes is by surprising them. The plan must be foolproof. We can't afford any mistakes," Joe said.

"I've lived in the ghetto all my life, except the time I spent at Sheridan and I'm here to tell you, if you make a mistake, you die. There is no second chance. You can't trust anybody," Jimmy said, as he glanced into everyone's eyes with concern.

They left the private room and filed out of Fredrick's. Jimmy and Joe hugged each other and exchanged phone numbers. Jerry and Joe shook hands and looked each other in the eyes, both nodding. Doc shook Jimmy's hand. "I'm glad you're on our side and not theirs."

Jimmy smiled and responded, "me too."

Chapter 52

# ANOTHER DEATH

All the lights were on when Doc and Joe arrived at Joe's house. "Something ain't right, Doc." He flung open the car door and ran to the house. Doc followed right behind him. Joe saw his Mom in the front room crying. Rene sat next to her on the sofa. Joe's heart moved up to his throat instantly, but managed to say, "Hi! Wh-what's going on?" His eyes converged on his Mom's wet, red eyes as she glanced up.

"Your father has passed away, Joseph!"

Joe walked over to his mother, got on his knees and embraced her. "Mom, I think it was for the best; he was never going to get better." Joe could smell the burnt flesh and hair. That awful day seemed like yesterday to Joe. The bile again rose in his throat. Doc stood motionless in the doorway.

"I know, Joseph. I just wish we could have had some time to say good bye," Helen said, as she began to cry again.

Chills ran down Doc's back. Joe couldn't handle much more death. His throat thickened.

"Joe, I'm really sorry about your father," Rene said, as she hugged him and kissed him on the cheek. Brownie stood beside Joe, rubbing his head on his leg.

"Joe, Joe, I don't know what to say. I- I guess all I can say is I'm real sorry." Doctor Knowles' hands gripped Joe's large shoulders. "Mrs. Clark, I'm real sorry." He shook his head, turned and left.

Joe looked at Rene and his mother and wondered if death would ever go away. I don't know how much more I can handle, Joe thought. That damn bean can! He shook his head. His fist tightened.

"You all want something to eat?" Joe asked. He needed to stop the hurt in his stomach. It had been over two years since the lightning had struck down his Pa.

"Maybe, maybe just something to drink, Joe," Rene said, with a small smile.

"What, what would you like, Mrs. Andretti?"

"Soda would be fine."

"How about you, Mom?"

"Nothing, son." She kept her face buried in her hands, a wet handkerchief crumpled in her hand.

Joe grabbed a Coke for Rene and fixed himself a large roast beef sandwich. He grabbed a bag of potato chips from the cupboard. He returned to the front room, sat down in an overstuffed chair and began to devour his food.

The room felt too quiet for Joe. "When are we going to have the funeral, Mom?" Joe's leg ached and his head pounded a beat a second. His stomach still hurt.

"Probably, Monday. I don't know, but the funeral home will probably call in the morning. I called your sister and she said she probably couldn't make it because some sort of schooling she had to take. I don't understand why they couldn't let her come home for a few days."

"She can't make it?" Joe shook his head. He took three more bites on his sandwich before he spoke again: "Probably hold it at the church. All the relatives would more than fill the funeral home."

"Yes, the church would probably be better."

"I think I better go, Helen. I'll call you in the morning. If there is anything I can do, please let me know," Rene said, tears welling up in her eyes as she thought of Sue.

"Ok, thanks for coming over. You've been a dear friend."

Joe rose and hugged Rene. "Thanks for being here." Rene kissed Joe on the cheek, tears running down her aged face.

"Mom, I think we better go to bed. We've got a big day tomorrow."

"You go ahead, Joseph. I want to sit here by myself."

The funeral took place at the Methodist Church. The sanctuary was full. The overflow sat in the Sunday school room behind the sanctuary. Relatives more than filled the church, with the remainder of the people being friends and neighbors of the Clarks. John was laid to rest at the same cemetery where Harry and Sue were buried. Now, Joe had three people to visit. How many more would there be?

Chapter 53

# NEW TRUCK

Joe visited the Ford dealer on Wednesday morning with Brownie, after going to the track and eating breakfast.

"Joe! Joe!" Harry ran out of the showroom toward Joe with his right arm high above his head. Joe never said a word—just looked and gave a partial wave.

"Looks great, right Joe?" Harry said, out of breath as he spoke.

"Yeah!"

"We have some paperwork in my office to sign and you're free to go."

"Whoa! I would like to drive it before I sign any of your darn papers."

Harry swung around, mouth parted. "No problem, son! I'll get you the keys," Harry responded, as he checked his watch for the second time.

Joe took it out on Highway 51 north of town and had her up to 100 miles per hour in less than a mile from the city limits. The truck still had plenty of pedal left. Joe figured he easily could reach 130 mph if he had to. He knew it should be broken in slowly, but he thought it best to run her hard in the beginning. Maybe she would be faster than if he didn't. He had done that to his T-Bird and it ran great.

Joe had had his new truck only three weeks before he and Brownie put on over 2000 miles just riding around. He did drive it to LaSalle to see Doctors Allen and Smithfield about his injuries. Everything appeared to be healing very well and Joe got a clean bill of health from each doctor.

Doc Knowles hired another investigator, Robert Harris, from Chicago. He had spent ten years with the Chicago Police Department before becoming a private investigator in Chicago. He was well-respected and his fees were high.

Harris would handle everything to do with payoffs. He would also be getting information on prostitutes and looking into the pressure being put on businesses. All his energy would be focused on the Capuano organization.

Jerry took a six-month leave of absence from the Tribune and would be handling everything else until another investigator could be hired. The information gathered so far appeared to be far greater than they had ever envisioned.

Lester Yates, the investigator in St. Louis, had gathered information on Tony Torletto, the Italian who had bought Marco's restaurant. He also traveled to other cities; such as, New Orleans, Kansas City, Detroit and Memphis, to line up informants who might have information pertaining to the Capuanos.

All three investigators tried to locate ten good men to herd these hogs when the time came. Background checks and histories of individuals would take some time to decipher.

The Capuanos hadn't paid any income taxes for over ten years. Jerry gathered this information through his brother-in-law, who worked for the Internal Revenue Service. His brother-in-law found the Capuanos' tax forms to be legal. Dirty money generated most of their income, which never got recorded. The Internal Revenue Service had called for an audit several times with the same result: Marco's restaurant and night club and two other retail establishments that sold Italian-imported clothes showed very little income.

# Chapter 54

# THE CEMETERY

Visiting the cemetery, Joe spent most of his time remembering things he had done with his Grandpa. "Grandpa, I'm in kind of a predicament." Joe told his Grandpa about the mafia and Sue. He told him about his Pa dying. "I need your help, Grandpa." A tear ran down his cheek. Joe used the back of his fist to wipe it away. "I wish you were here. I know you could figure out what to do." Joe seemed lost for words. He dug his hands deeper in his jean pockets. "Grandpa, I just need to know if I should go after these Capuanos or leave it alone. I don't think I could live with myself if I do nothing. I know you need to think about it. I'll be waiting for your answer." He got up slowly, stood motionless for a minute, and wiped his eyes. "Goodbye, Grandpa. I'll be back."

Joe left and walked over to his Pa's grave spending a few minutes reminiscing about old times. He managed to forget about the bean can, until the burnt flesh smell returned, making him sick to his stomach. His body froze and his eyelids dropped as the scene took over his imagination. Tears fell to the ground.

With arms stretched out, palms up, and eyes looking toward the heavens, he asked, "Why? Why did you let this happen? He never did anything wrong. You let the Capuanos live. Why?" Whatever beliefs Joe had left had vanished. Rage encompassed his body. He picked up a piece of tree bark and threw it as hard as he could. "It ain't right. I'll kill those bastards." His body shook. He couldn't control it. Drying his eyes for the last time, he walked hurriedly back to his truck with Brownie at his side.

Pausing at his truck, Joe looked toward Sue's grave. He saw her. She was dressed in shorts, driving the tractor with the hay baler behind it. "I'll get them, Sue. I'll get them before next year's end. I'll get them for sure." The door slammed, engine roared, and Joe and Brownie sped away, the sunlight following them.

The next day after working out at the track, Joe got a part-time job, three days per week, at the feed mill. He would work Monday,

Wednesday, and Saturday bagging up hog feed for the hog farmers who lived within ten miles of town. Each heavy cotton bag of hog feed weighed one hundred pounds. Joe would be paid $1.75 per hour, twenty-five hours per week, and he got all the dog food he wanted—free.

# Chapter 55

# HELEN'S DILEMMA

Unsure of herself, Helen decided to seek Rene's advice. "Hi, Helen, come in!" Rene's large smile faded when she saw the concern on Helen's face.

"Hi! Rene, I hate to trouble you, but I am really worried about Joe. I don't know what to do anymore."

"Can I make you some tea or would you like some coffee?" Rene asked, heading toward the kitchen.

"Tea would be fine." Too much coffee upset her stomach. Helen followed Rene and sat down at the kitchen table, looking helpless.

"Ok, Helen, tell me what's on your mind."

Helen fidgeted with her moist hands. She looked at the floor, hoping the words would jump up at her. "Joe scares me, Rene! You know he has such a violent temper. I'm sure as I'm sitting here that he will kill those men, those Capuanos." The grooves on her forehead deepened.

Rene shot back at Helen. "Helen, you have to let Joe do what Joe wants to do. You'll never stop him, even if you gave him all the rhubarb pie he could ever eat." Helen couldn't bring herself to smile at the jest. "He's extremely tough and strong-minded. You'll have to put it in God's hands and whatever happens, will happen." Rene paused. "I hate to say this Helen, but I hope he does kill those Capuanos. The police will never touch them; they have already proven that." The tea kettle whistled loudly. Rene stood and poured the tea. "I know it must be very hard on you, with all the uncertainty. I think, and you may not agree with me, that we both need to support him in whatever avenue he takes. He's standing all by himself out there. I feel sorry for him. He has no support from anyone. I have some homemade cookies. Would you like one?"

Helen shook her head.

"Maybe that Jimmy in Chicago will support him. Joe is only eighteen and, yet, he is man enough to think he can take on the mafia."

Helen stared at her cup of tea.

Rene waited for Helen to speak. "I don't know, Rene. I know I'd like to see those murdering, no-good men punished, but I'm afraid for Joseph. He's never had any experience with these types of people and he knows nothing about Chicago."

"Joe has more savvy than we give him credit for. He'll find a way." Rene's eyelids rose. "You would almost think he had American Indian blood in him. That time spent at Sheridan did him more good than harm. I believe he picked up a lot of cunning skills from his Grandpa. Sue used to tell me what Joe said about Harry. He really worshipped that man. In his eyes, his Grandpa was the smartest man on earth." Rene touched Helen's hand. "He'll be all right, Helen, one way or the other."

"Maybe, maybe you're right Rene. How-how do you think we should handle it?"

"I believe we need to support him right now. Tell him with all the sincerity we can assemble—tell him we want him to do what he thinks is best. I'm sure he'll be shocked to hear either one of us speaking with such assurance."

Helen's eyes shot at Rene. Her heart became heavy. She took a sip of tea. "Ok! Maybe we should do this together." Helen knew she couldn't handle it by herself. "Would you mind if we told him together?" Helen tried to visualize Joe's reaction.

"That would be fine, and the sooner the better. We don't want him standing alone any longer. He used to confide in Sue, but now he goes to her grave to talk to her. A man needs a woman's support. He can't get that from a grave, none of us can. Joe's alone, in the dark, and he needs to know we are here. I don't have to tell you how important that is to a man." Rene wiped a tear that had fallen from her eye.

Helen bowed her head, knowing Rene's thoughts were of her husband.

# Chapter 56

# GOOD NEWS

Joe finished his breakfast and headed upstairs to brush his teeth before leaving for work when the phone rang. "Hello!" He hoped it wasn't Joan.

"Good morning, Joe! I was hoping to catch you before you left. This is Doctor Knowles. I'm sorry I didn't get back to you sooner."

Joe sank back, leaning against the wall. He closed his eyes. The walls had been caving in. Doc's voice forced them back a little. "Oh! Good morning, Doc."

"Joe, I just wanted to give you an update on our progress. Lester Yates, in St. Louis, and Robert Harris, in Chicago, have very strong information that the Chicago FBI has been letting the Capuanos get away with several illegal operations for some time. We have inside information that the FBI put mafia members from St. Louis in prison on the strength of Marco Capuano's testimony. He had gotten ripped off by the mafia in St. Louis when he owned a business down there. When he arrived in Chicago, he gave the information to the FBI. In return for his information, Marco receives protection on his illegal dealings in Chicago. I can't believe the FBI is that stupid."

"Wow! The FBI is on their side."

"Almost certainly. We also dug up information on a Johnny Amato. He's the hit man for Marco and his people. He has murdered over a hundred innocent people in the last several years. This Amato has a brother, Tony, in Peru, Illinois. Tony Amato has two children and he seems to be on the up and up. He owns several laundromats and dry cleaners. He has a daughter, Joan, who works at the County Hospital as a physical therapist." Joe's heart almost stopped. A chill ran through his body.

"You won't believe the next thing. This Tony Amato's son, Vince, or Vinny as they call him, graduated from St. Bede on the Saturday of your accident. The bastards that hit you were drunk from being at that party." Joe's face reddened. The sweat started to run down his back.

*"That bitch! How damn stupid can I get? I'll kill those bastards."* His jaws screwed down.

After a long silence: "Joe, are you still there!"

"Yeah, I-I'm sorry!" Joe said, hating himself for his fling with Joan. Joe thought maybe he should tell Doc about what she wanted for information, but remained quiet.

"Joe, we'll nail these bastards, but we can't expect any support from the law. We'll have to be awfully careful. I'm sure the State police and the Chicago police, at least some of them, are involved with the Capuanos. Robert Harris is working diligently to gather information on who we can trust and who we can't."

"Doc, I need to tell you something." Joe looked at the wall clock. He would be late for work, but he thought this was important. "Doc, that Joan Amato was my physical therapist. She came on to me and was really nice. I had-I had sex with her. I was a complete fool, Doc." Joe's heart raced. "She offered me information on the Capuanos. She said she would tell me everything the Capuanos do, how they do it, when they do it and where they do it. She wanted $250,000 for the information." Joe was out of breath.

"What did you tell her, Joe?" Doc asked quickly.

"I said I didn't need any information and I wasn't interested in killing the Capuanos."

"Great! She probably would have given us false information and then told the Capuanos that you had paid her for it."

"I hate myself for getting involved," Joe mumbled.

"Don't let this get to you, Joe. Men have a tendency to let there ponies get in the way of their heads."

Joe felt relief now that he had told Doc. "Thanks, Doc! It won't happen again."

"I'll stay in touch. You take care of yourself."

"Thanks again, Doc. Call me if you hear anything."

"Bye!"

# Chapter 57

## SUPPORT AT LAST

Helen waited two weeks before she had enough gumption to tell Joe that she and Rene wanted to talk to him. If it weren't for Rene's pushing, she never could have done it.

"Joseph, if you're not busy tonight, Rene has invited us over for dinner."

"Sure! What's she havin'?" Joe asked, as he watched his mother bang her head on the freezer door.

"Ouch! I hate this refrigerator," Helen said, closing the refrigerator door empty-handed.

"Couldn't remember what you wanted out of there, Mom?" Joe said, with a grin on his face.

"What? No, I was just looking to see what we might need from the grocery."

"What time is dinner? What did you say she was having?"

"I don't know what she's having," Helen replied, wringing her hands as she left the kitchen.

"Mom, you alright? You're acting a little strange."

Joe and his Mom left for Rene's house at 6:25 for the 6:30 dinner. Helen nervously stuttered with every word. Joe sensed that something wasn't quite right, but chose not to say anything.

"Hi Joe! How are you? You're looking great! Hi, Helen! Doesn't Joe look like he could just take on the whole world?" Rene, looking at Helen, sensed she would not be much help this evening.

"Hi, Mrs. Andretti. It's good to see you."

They hugged each other and Rene kissed Joe on the cheek. Helen tried to keep her composure, but had a very difficult time, to say the least.

Rene showed Helen and Joe into the dining room while she served dinner. As she sat down, she said, "If everyone will bow their heads, I'd like to say a little prayer. Will everyone hold hands, please?"

Helen and Joe bowed their heads and waited.

164

"Our Heavenly Father, we want to thank you for bringing us together tonight. We ask that you bless this food we are about to eat. We ask, O Lord, that you guide Joe Clark in his future plans, no matter what they may be. Lord, we ask that you protect and watch over him. We ask that no matter what he does, that you look upon it as an elimination of very bad people. Thank you, Lord. We pray in Jesus' name. Amen!"

Joe raised his head and looked at Rene with a wide-opened mouth. She continued to hold his large hand. His Mom sniffled. He finally managed to speak. "Thank you for that prayer, Mrs. Andretti."

Rene smiled at Joe and squeezed his hand tightly. "Joe! I want you to kick those sons-of-bitches from here to the other end of the earth. I don't want you to stop until you do. I know you have what it takes and, with God's help, you will get it done. Your mother and I have discussed this matter at length and have come to the conclusion that we can't stop you, so we need to support you in whatever you decide to do." Tears ran down Rene's face, while Helen's sniffles turned into sobs.

Joe sat there, speechless. Before he could utter a word, his Mom left for the bathroom to finish crying, and Rene retreated to the kitchen.

*"How did they know? Damn! I thought I was keeping this all to myself. I sure feel better that they are behind me. Well, I guess my Mom is behind me."*

Joe thought he had better go ahead and eat before the food got cold. He hated cold food if it was supposed to be hot. Rene had fixed pot roast and mashed potatoes with green beans and homemade bread.

Joe had his plate filled when Rene returned. "Thanks, Mrs. Andretti! I really needed your support. I will get those bastards if it's the last thing I ever do." She gave him a short grin. Joe was about to take a bite of pot roast, as his Mom reentered the room. Joe put down his fork. "Thanks, Mom."

Helen took her son's hand and held it. "Joseph, I have known from the very first night you spent in the hospital that you would probably try and kill those Capuanos. You loved Sue too much to see them walk away. This is very hard for me, but I, too, want to see justice done. I just ask that you please be very careful and watch yourself. I've prayed every night for your safekeeping." Her eyes filled with tears again.

Joe dug into his plateful of food. Helen and Rene managed to get some food on their plates before Joe wanted seconds. When Joe finally finished, he had eaten not only seconds, but thirds of everything. Joe hadn't felt this good since before the accident. Having his Mom and Mrs. Andretti behind him meant even more than having Jimmy beside him.

"Boy, that sure was good!" Joe leaned back in his chair and put his hands behind his head. Joe felt full, but he knew that he still had enough room for some of Rene's dessert, whatever it was.

All three talked for almost an hour before Rene offered dessert.

"I sure am ready!" Joe said, rubbing his rock-hard stomach.

Rene brought out a large piece of homemade chocolate cake with at least three dips of vanilla ice cream. Joe had already filled his mouth with dessert before his Mom and Rene sat down to eat theirs.

On their way home, Joe reached over and took hold of his Mom's hand. Squeezing it, he said, "Thanks again, Mom. I know you'll worry, but let me tell you, I have some people with a whole lot of experience helping me."

"Joe, just remember: If you can't finish the job, for whatever reason, don't push it and get yourself killed. I worry so much about that."

"Don't worry, Mom! We will have it together before we strike. Anyway, Brownie won't let anything happen to me."

"You're probably right about that. That dog is more human, I think, than most people."

Joe slept like a baby, but Helen tossed and turned most of the night, waking several times from dreams of Joe being shot by those awful men. Her bed sheets were tangled and soaked with sweat. A burning pain rode over her chest.

# Chapter 58

# THE MEETING

Christmas came and went and Joe continued to visit the track everyday. He clocked himself at under six minutes now. "And they told me I would never run again," Joe boasted as he ran. His heart climbed out, little by little, of its dark hole. He walked to his truck with Brownie, who jumped up and down. Full of fire these days, Brownie was getting ready to take on the mafia.

The exercises worked miracles for Joe. He weighed 222 pounds and his stomach felt like a steel plate. Joe ran, walked, exercised and ate like a bear everyday, in addition to working at the feed mill. The throbbing had almost stopped, unless he got really mad, or he ran too fast. His right leg got stronger. The pain seemed more tolerable than three months ago.

The Capuanos involved in the accident had returned to their work of killing, raping, bilking, committing fraud, and stealing from anyone they could.

Alex and Eddie hadn't had any more complications from the beating they had received in the hayfield that Saturday night. Jimmy Capuano, on the other hand, was unable to perform in bed. He hadn't been with a woman since the crash.

Jerry Moore, Lester Yates and Robert Harris worked extremely hard and had gathered more information on the Capuanos than Doc could have ever imagined. They knew the hours the Capuanos worked, where they were, what was involved, who ran a particular operation, how it was supplied and how many people worked for them. They knew which police chiefs, officers, judges and politicians were on the Capuano's payroll and created a long list of businesses, which totaled over one thousand in Chicago and its suburbs that paid the organization a percentage of their profits. They knew how many cars were stolen and where they were going. They made a list of hit men, other than Jimmy Amato, along with a list of over two hundred fifty people missing or presumed dead who were linked to the Capuanos. At last count, the list of people who wanted the Capuanos dead exceeded one thousand, not including other organized crime gangs in other cities.

Doc Knowles called for a meeting with Jerry, Lester, Robert, Jimmy Robbins and Joe. They, again, met at Fredrick's in Downers Grove.

Mac Gibson, a former FBI agent who had been injured in a shootout with the St. Louis mafia several years ago, also attended the meeting. Although out on disability, he had a vast knowledge of how the organized crime members operated. Mac was thirty-eight years old and had seven years of experience with the FBI, having served in St. Louis, Kansas City and Miami. Every assignment had involved the mafia. Mac said he had proof that the Chicago mafia donated more money to charity than anyone. Jimmy didn't like what his eyes were telling him, but he kept it to himself, for now. Doc had brought him on board through a contact of Lester's.

The jailed mafia members from St. Louis all had long sentences, except one—Rico DeMarco, the hit man for the St. Louis mob. He served eight years and was scheduled to be released in February, 1961. He had a longstanding vendetta against Marco and wanted him dead.

Lester Yates had spoken to Rico DeMarco several times. Rico had indicated he would destroy the Capuanos before 1961 ended. Rico had several relatives in New Jersey and New York who would help him accomplish his goal.

The meeting at Fredrick's lasted six hours, with the information gathered from the three investigators and the data from Mac being recorded by a stenographer. In fact, they recorded every word spoken. The stenographer would type all the information and have it ready for the next meeting the following month at Fredrick's.

Everyone participated in the six-hour meeting. Jimmy had done some checking on his own. He came up with over six hundred females, mostly under the age of thirty and some as young as thirteen, who had performed sexual acts for customers. These included: Chicago's mayor, several high-ranking government officials, policemen, police chiefs, judges, county and state, and FBI agents, and many other men whose wives wouldn't give them what the Capuanos' girls would.

Jimmy acquired most of his information from his girlfriend, Maggie Newsome. Her sister had been a prostitute for the Capuanos for over ten years. Alex "hired" her when she was fourteen. He had kidnapped her on the north side of Chicago where she had grown up and raped her several times. Alex acquired most of his prostitutes that way. Most of the girls Alex hired were black. The white, affluent males liked young, black girls as their sex toys. Eddie and Jimmy also assisted in "hiring" these young girls. Alex told Maggie's sister she could work for him and he would make her a lot of money. If she didn't cooperate, she would be floating in the Chicago River. She did make good money, but the Capuanos took over fifty percent. She hated them with all her heart and wished them dead. She prayed everyday to get away. She wanted to quit, but the Capuanos wouldn't let her. They would either kill her or beat her so badly she would never be the same again.

Jimmy also had compiled a list of prostitutes that were either killed, had disappeared, or had been beaten beyond recognition. When Jimmy finished sharing his information, everyone in the room, including Mac, were more than stunned to hear about the oldest profession known to man, this time using young teenagers.

The silence lasted more than ten minutes. The stenographer broke down in tears. Doc told her to go to the ladies' room and take her time. The sound of the fast clack of her high heels racing across the hardwood floor toward the ladies' room grabbed everyone's attention. "These Capuanos are worse than we thought," Jerry said. Everyone's eyes agreed.

Jimmy took Joe aside. "I don't like Mac. He is a liar. We need to check him out."

"You sure, Jimmy? He is FBI. Should I tell Doc?"

"Yeah, Doc needs to know."

"Ok"

Jimmy slapped his pal on the shoulder.

Joe shared Jimmy's feelings about Mac with Doc on the way home. Doc said he would look into it.

# Chapter 59

## APRIL 1ST

On April 1, 1961 Joe finished the half-mile run in less than three minutes. "I'll be under two and a half minutes before June 1$^{st}$." Joe had purchased a set of weights and was now bench pressing right at 400 pounds. Working at the feed mill and lifting those 100 pound bags of hog feed made Joe much stronger than before the accident.

While working at the feed mill one afternoon, Joe's sister, Sarah, and her friend, Jim Castillo, came into town unexpectedly. Sarah hadn't said much about her man. Joe had asked his mother several times about the last name. When questioned, Sarah always seemed to change the subject, she told him. Joe had his suspicions, but never said anything.

Joe returned home at 5:10 to find a large, black Lincoln in the driveway. Joe's heart went straight to his throat. He pulled the truck directly behind the Lincoln, pinning the car in. Joe jumped out of his truck and ran to the front porch. He grabbed the front door handle and opened it slowly. He heard his mother talking in the front room. Joe figured it must be Sarah and her friend.

Joe walked in slowly and stood in the opening to the front room, trying to feel the man out. The guy was Italian alright.

"Hi!" Joe peered directly at the large Italian man sitting on the sofa next to Sarah. He wore a light mohair sport coat and dark brown pants. His black hair looked greasy and had waves on the sides.

"Hey! How are you doing?" Sarah said, softly. She looked distraught.

"Hi, Sis, who's the guy sitting next to you?" Joe turned his eyes back to the Italian. Joe's tightened jaw showed he was ready whenever. Brownie growled low and moved within striking distance of the Italian.

"This is Jim!" The Italian never moved or spoke—he just looked at Joe with glassy eyes, like he had had too much to drink.

*"Jim what?"* Joe began to rage inside.

"Jim Castillo," he said, standing up, arms in front of him.

*"I bet he's packin' a gun. Jimmy told me they will stand that way to disguise the gun. He might make six foot and maybe one hundred ninety pounds. He looks like he has more stomach than he's showing. He is probably in his mid thirties."*

Joe would not accept Jim's offered hand. He wanted more answers before shaking any Italian's hand, especially one sitting in his house. Sarah sat, awestruck. "I hear you're in the car business. What kinda cars do you sell?" Joe never blinked nor took his eyes off Jim.

"I don't sell cars! I buy cars for many dealers in Tennessee, Kentucky and Georgia, as far south as Atlanta." Jim's face had that *'don't question me'* look.

"Where do you buy them from?" Joe saw red. He wanted to take this bastard outside and kick him around the backyard.

"Uh-all over." Jim showed a crooked grin and appeared to be lying and Joe knew it. Joe doubled up his fist. *"It wouldn't take but a second to drop this lying lard ass."*

"How about being a little more specific about where you're getting the vehicles." Joe walked closer to Jim, who had begun to fidget.

"Detroit mainly, some from Cleveland. Why do you ask?" Jim rubbed his fingers together in front of him and his left eye twitched.

"How many do you buy from Chicago?" Joe now stood only six feet from Jim. He knew he had him in a corner.

"I never said I bought any from Chicago."

"I asked you how many you bought from **Chicago**," Joe yelled, only one step away.

Jim tried to back away from Joe, but the sofa stood in his way. He couldn't move. His eyes told Joe he was as nervous as a call girl in church. Jim never answered.

"I want to know how many vehicles you buy from **Chicago** and I want to know it now." Joe planted his right fist in Jim's chest as he screamed the words.

Helen and Sarah were in a panic and couldn't speak.

"We buy a few! Why? Why so many questions?"

"How many is a few? Ten cars, a hundred, a thousand, how many?" *"The mafia has my sister involved."*

"I don't have to tell you anything!" Jim shouted back, trying to find somewhere to hide or run.

Joe grabbed Jim with both hands before he could blink an eye. He yanked Jim away from the sofa and slammed him against the wall. Jim's feet dangled five inches off the floor. The whole room shook. Joe slammed him again and two pictures fell from the wall. Joe put his large hand around Jim's neck and squeezed until Jim's eyes were ready to bleed. Joe reached inside Jim's sport coat and found a gun. He ripped it out of its shoulder holster and stuck it in the front of his jeans. "Now, are you going to give me answers, or do I need to take you outside and wipe the street up with your fat ass?"

"I buy, I buy a lot. I buy many cars from Ch-Chicago," Jim said, pissing his pants. Urine ran down his pant leg to the carpet. Brownie caught the scent and backed away, baring his teeth.

"That's better! Now! Who do you buy them from in Chicago?" Joe wasn't even breathing hard. Joe smelled something, but ignored it.

"M-Many, p-people!"

"You son-of-a-bitch, do you want me to bust your skull open?" Joe squeezed harder on Jim's throat until his fat face turned blue. Helen and Sarah ran to the kitchen, embraced each other, and started to weep.

"The Capuanos—they will kill me!" More urine escaped. It began to stink up the front room. Joe wondered whether he had crapped his pants, too.

"*The Capuanos*. Who are the *Capuanos?* Tell me!" Joe slammed him against the wall, sending his greasy black hair flying in all directions. Joe's voice bounced off the walls.

Helen looked at her daughter in disbelief. "Jim-Jim is connected to the Capuanos? Oh, no!" She plopped down in a kitchen chair. Sarah remained silent.

"I tell you! They will kill me. I'm as good as dead. They have me in a vice and I can't get out." He started to cry like a baby.

"You cry baby." Joe released Jim and let him collapse on the floor in his foul-smelling urine. Joe towered over Jim like Hercules over a small dog.

Joe went into the kitchen and asked Sarah, "Did he ever hurt you or lay a hand on you? And don't lie to me!"

She looked at Joe with red eyes and answered, "He had to. I wanted to go to the cops about those men in Chicago that make him buy those stolen cars." Helen gasped and began to pray. Sarah started crying. Joe had already guessed, so he wasn't surprised.

Joe returned to the front room and found Jim still crying, lying in the fetal position with his hands on his groin area. "How many times did you beat up my sister?"

"I never wanted to, but she would have gone to the cops and then we would both be dead. She wanted to tell you, but you would have gotten busted up by the Capuanos." He looked up at Joe. "I'm real sorry. I wish I had never met the Capuanos. They are murderers. They will have you killed for just looking at them cross-eyed."

Joe's heart was in a rush. He wanted those Capuanos. He wanted them now. "I don't want you ever to lay a hand on her again. If you even breathe a word of what happened here today, I will not only castrate you, I will leave you to bleed to death. I will cover you with honey and tie you to an ant hill. You think the Capuanos are mean? You haven't seen mean."

"I want you to continue buying cars from those sons-of-bitches in Chicago until I tell you no more buying. Do you understand me?" Joe visualized dead Capuanos.

"Y-Yes, I understand! Don't let them find out or they'll kill you and me and Sarah."

"I want you to get some cleaning supplies from my mother and get on your hands and knees and clean up this stinking urine. Then, get hold of a carpet cleaner tomorrow and have all the rugs cleaned throughout the house." Joe remembered his Mom had mentioned getting the carpets done the other day.

"Yes, sir!"

Joe headed upstairs for a hot shower. He told Brownie to keep an eye on the fat boy. No matter where Jim moved, Brownie kept within striking distance.

Joe finished showering and came downstairs. "Jim, you need to relax a little. Why don't you go out and get yourself some supper and something to drink." Joe was sure he drank. "Then, I want you to go get a hotel room downtown and get a good night's sleep. Get up in the morning and eat some breakfast. Get back over here by 7:30 a.m. sharp. Any questions?"

"No, sir!"

"Don't try to run away. It will be brutal if you do."

"I won't Joe. I will be here in the morning at 7:30."

Sarah walked over to Jim and laid a hand on his shoulder as he cleaned the carpet. "My brother isn't afraid of anyone or anything. You need to cooperate with him. You want him on your side."

Jim nodded.

Helen never looked at or spoke to Jim. Her heart ached for her daughter.

Jim left after cleaning the carpet. He apologized to Helen several times. Joe felt really good now, but as hungry as all get-out. He said to Sarah and his mother, "Hey, let's go out and eat, my treat."

They went to Josephine's for dinner. They talked through most of the dinner about the old days—the Clark's farm before the bean can incident. They had many laughs. Yet, when John Clark's name came up, it became real quiet. Joe tried to keep the conversation as light as he possibly could; he knew his sister and mother had enough sorrow in their lives. They never mentioned Jim Castillo's name once, nor the Capuanos. Sue's name never arose during the evening, either.

# Chapter 60

# BACK TO THE FARM

Jim Castillo arrived at 7:25 a.m. "Good morning, Joe!" He wore a new pair of slacks. His eyes told Joe that he hadn't slept well.

"Hi!" With his large right hand on top of the door jam, Joe's whole body filled the doorway. Brownie, standing right beside Joe, emitted a low growl. "Let's go for a ride." Joe didn't want to discuss anything within a mile of anyone.

They climbed into the F-100 with Brownie. Joe drove slowly out of town toward the Clark farm. They sat in silence until they reached the outskirts of town.

"I-I'm real sorry about last night. I hate myself for causing you and your family any grief. I know the Capuanos will find out and kill all of us. I just know it." Castillo looked toward the floor of the cab, his voice interrupted by trembling lips.

"What makes you think the Capuanos will kill us or anyone else?" Joe said, very calmly, looking at Jim as he spoke.

"They've killed many people, Joe. I've seen them kill people in cold blood, in broad daylight, for disagreeing with them or lying to them. Or, maybe they just wanted them replaced and out of the way." Jim appeared as nervous as a squirrel being chased by a dog.

"You've witnessed the Capuanos killing people. All of them or just one of them?"

"No, not the Capuanos, themselves. They have hit men to do it."

"What's their *names*?" Joe screamed. The truck's speedometer went from 50 mph to 75 mph.

"The number one man is A-Amato. He's meaner than anything I know."

"Who else?" Joe knew they already had the information on him.

"A guy they call Ziggy. He's from Greece, doesn't speak any English and has a limp. He's almost as big as you."

Joe stopped the truck in the driveway of the old Clark farm and he and Brownie got out. Jim sat in the cab until Joe hollered at him: "*get out*!"

"Describe this, this Greek, Ziggy. I want to know everything you can tell me about him."

"He's a big man, almost as big as you. He's around forty, has very dark hair and a receding hairline. He has a tattoo on his, let's see, yeah, on his right arm. His arms are huge. I think bigger than yours. He wears sport coats with a tee shirt, usually a white tee shirt."

"How do you know he has a tattoo if he wears a sport coat?"

"I played cards with him when I went to Chicago. He only had on a tee shirt."

"His stomach solid, or fat like yours?"

"His stomach, bigger than mine." Jim pointed to his flabby gut. Joe grinned.

"How tall is he?"

"Not as tall as you, but he's a very big man."

"Does he wear jewelry?"

"Oh, yes, they all wear big rings, big diamonds." Jim wore a big ring on his stubby pinkie.

"Any scars?"

"Yeah! He has one on his nose. It looks like it was severed with a knife. His nose is very large."

"Anything else you can tell me about Ziggy?" Joe learned his questioning technique from watching Lee Marvin in *M-Squad* and Jack Webb in *Dragnet* on television.

"I don't know. Yeah, he has one eye that sorta droops. I think-I think it's his left eye."

"Who else does their dirty work?"

"A little guy, his name is Al Falcono. He's probably in his late thirties. His hair is real dark and oily and long in the back. He has a scar on his right cheek and his left ear is funny looking. I think he was born that way. He probably doesn't weigh 160 pounds. He's only, ah, maybe five feet six inches tall."

"Anything else you know about this Al guy?"

"No! I can't think of anything else. Wait! He has a finger missing on his right hand."

"Which finger?"

"His right pinkie. When he smokes it is very noticeable."

"What does he smoke?"

"Lucky Strikes"

"What about the other two?"

"Oh! Yeah! Ziggy smokes a menthol cigarette. I think they're Salems."

"What about the Capuanos? Tell me about them. Let's start with Marco."

"I know nothing. I never met him. I know he's the leader and what he says, you better do, or else. He's very powerful in Chicago."

"You never met him or any of his rotten sons. What about his nephew, Eddie?"

"I met Alex once. I never met Eddie or Jimmy."

"I want to know everything about him."

"I don't know much. I met him once is all, and that was for maybe two minutes. He's very good looking, medium build, probably in his early thirties. No scars. No other marks. He dresses like he owns Hickey-Freeman."

"You never met those other guys? Are you telling me the truth?"

Joe grabbed Jim by his sport coat and pushed him ten feet before Jim replied, "No! I never met them. Alex is the only one. So help me God." Jim managed to cross himself and Joe released his grip.

"Tell me about the stolen cars. I want to know everything." Joe started to get angry. He wanted to get his hands on those Capuanos now.

"I've been buying cars from the Capuanos for eight years. Alex made me do it."

"Why did Alex make you do it?"

"I-I was in Chicago. Please, please don't tell Sarah." Jim's face turned guilty.

"Tell Sarah what?" Joe already knew the answer. "*Bastard.*"

"I met one of their girls."

"You met a prostitute?"

"Yeah!" Jim looked down at his Italian leather shoes.

"Then what?"

"I paid her and all. She asked me what I did and that's when I made the mistake of telling her I bought used cars from the car auction in Chicago. How did I know she was going to tell the Capuanos? She told

177

Alex. They have those girls ask their clients all kinds of questions so they can maybe use them in their operation."

"How did they find you?"

"I was in Chicago for a few days and one night about 11:00 they came to my room."

"Who came to your room?"

"Ziggy and a couple other guys." Jim, not wanting to give out any information, would stall after every question.

"What were the other guy's names?"

"Joe Pictallo and John Brunski. They are the guys I had to deal with."

"So tell me. Tell me what happened in the room."

"Ziggy slammed me against the wall as soon as I opened the door. Then he threw my ass in a chair and the other two guys, Joe and John, told me what they wanted. I was to buy all my cars from them. The prices were 30% better than at the auction. I make good money on these cars, but if the feds ever catch us, I go to jail. They supply me with over two hundred cars a month."

"Where do the Capuanos get these cars?"

"They steal them. They have kids steal them—some boys, some girls. They usually use nigger kids. They are fast and they need the money. They're all late model cars, from Fords to Cadillacs. They change the serial numbers by one number or one letter. You can't tell unless you use a microscope. The papers are changed accordingly and no one ever questions anybody. Once the car is stolen, it's taken to a large garage and sometimes repainted. Then, the car goes to another large warehouse where I look it over before they load it on trucks. They're hauled to Louisville, Atlanta, Memphis, Knoxville, and Nashville. I have buyers in these cities and they pay me."

"How much money are we talking about here?"

"I don't know. Somewhere around $250,000 to $350,000 per month and I make 30 % on almost all the cars. I have to pay the shipping, though. That runs me between $300 and $400 per truck load."

"Where did you get the money to start this operation?"

"They, the Capuanos, helped me out. I started with twenty cars a month and I built it to what it is today. They put the pressure on me. They had Ziggy put the pressure on me."

178

"What about the guys who drive these trucks. Who do they work for?"

"They're just independent drivers. I pay them when the load arrives at its destination. Some of these guys have been with me for eight years now. I pay them good and they also get perks."

"What kind of perks are you talking about?"

"I buy them a lay, or whatever they want, in Chicago every week. The Capuanos give me a discount." Jim smiled.

"So you pocket between, let's say, $7000 and $10,000 per month?"

"No, you have to take the transportation cost out."

"Oh, yes, and the perks."

"Yeah!" Jim grinned stupidly. Joe shook his head in disgust.

"Where else do the Capuanos unload their stolen cars?"

"I get about 40% of the cars. The rest go to a guy in Miami and a guy in Houston."

"What are their names?"

"I know the guy from Houston. It's a funny name, Herby Flusher" Jim chuckled. Even Joe smiled.

"What about the guy in Miami?"

"I never met him, but his last name is Garcia. He's a Mexican, I think."

"Tell me about this Herby guy."

"He's a wheeling, dealing son-of-a-bitch. He talks ninety miles an hour and he smiles while he stabs you in the back."

"How many times have you seen him?"

"Twenty times, maybe."

"What does he look like?"

"He is a slick one and well-dressed. He has a medium build and is about forty. He doesn't smoke and has reddish hair, like yours. He tells me he makes 50 % on his cars. I don't believe him, but that's what he tells me."

"Does Herby buy more or less than the guy in Miami?"

"He buys more, many more. He has an export thing going into South America. He buys almost as many as I do."

"Do all these guys pack a gun?"

"Oh, yes!" Jim looked at Joe. "You still have my piece?" Joe didn't answer.

"Where do these guys who work for the Capuanos live? I'm talking about Pictallo and Brunski."

"Pictallo, I know, lives in the Italian section on the south side. Brunski lives in an apartment downtown off of Dearborn. Pictallo is married and has five kids. Brunski is single, divorced and has a daughter, I believe."

"What about Ziggy?"

"I don't know. He doesn't speak English."

"How do you play cards with him if he doesn't speak any English?"

"He knows the numbers and the faces on the cards. Somebody taught him that. We play mostly poker and gin."

"I want to know where he lives and what kind of car he drives. I want to know the plate number, too."

"I-I don't know, Joe. He would kill me if he ever found out."

"I'll kill you if you don't find out. I want to know the next time you go to Chicago. When are you going to Chicago?"

"Next week!" Sweat oozed from every one of Jim's pores.

"Do you love Sarah or is she just someone to sleep with?"

"Oh, Joe, I love her very much. I never touched anyone since we've been together.

Joe believed most of what Jim had told him this morning. They returned to Mendota.

Sarah, unhappy to hear that Joe insisted Jim leave without her, said "Ok! Where am I staying?"

"I'll tell you later. For right now, you're staying here."

Jim kissed Sarah and hugged her for several minutes. After he left, Joe told Sarah she would be going to Cut Bank, Montana. "Your Uncle Charlie lives up there. He's meaner than any of them mountain lions in the West. I don't want you calling Jim for any reason. The phone lines at his end will probably be tapped. You use a different name. How about Sally Smothers?"

"Sally Smothers! Forget it," Sarah said, with fire in her eyes.

Joe grinned. "Ok, give me a name. I think Sally Smothers is a great name."

"How-How about Virginia Curtis?" Sarah always had the hots for a Jim Curtis in high school.

"Whatever! Just don't change it. It will take a couple of weeks to get your paperwork together."

Her eyes filled with puzzlement. "What do you mean? Will this be my permanent name—forever?"

"Nah, just for awhile! I don't want those SOBs knowing where you're at."

"What do you think you're going to do with those Capuanos?"

"I'm not sure, but I'll handle them, Ok!"

Joe called Doc and told him he needed to get some identity paperwork changed for his sister and mother. Doc let Joe know he would handle it. He would have a guy come and see him. Joe told Doc about Jim Castillo, but made it brief.

# Chapter 61

# THE ATTACK

Three days later, as Joe finished his quarter-mile run in just under one minute and thirty seconds, a man in a blue 1958 Chevy sat waiting for him. Brownie stood right next to the man, teeth ready, as he stepped out of the car. "Wow! That dog bite?"

Joe didn't answer. Brownie wouldn't let the man move.

"You-you must be Joe!"

"Who are you?" Joe wiped the sweat from his forehead.

"My name is Ralph Limpkin. Richard Knowles sent me to see you."

"What about?" Joe trusted no one.

"You need some paperwork done, I believe." Ralph looked puzzled.

Joe became a little sheepish. "Yeah, sorry, I don't trust too many people."

"I guess you're a little skittish, huh?" The man was short, had a small frame, light hair and looked to be in his early forties. He wore a sport coat, an open-collared shirt and light-colored slacks. He didn't look Italian, but Joe knew the Capuanos employed other hit men.

Joe didn't like the remark, but tried to be nice to the man. "I need some paper-How do you know Doc?" Joe thought he felt something strange.

"I went to high school with Rich. We played football together our junior and senior years. Rich was one hell of a receiver. He could catch anything, great hands."

Joe shook his head. "You know, to be working in a bank and all," Joe tested Ralph.

"Yeah, he's been in the banking business since he got out of college."

Joe hit Ralph, or whatever his name was, within a second of his last word, with a wicked right hand that laid him out cold. Joe watched him come around. Brownie sat right next to the half-conscious man. "Wwhat the hell did you do that for?"

"You lied to me, Ralph. I don't like liars."

"What did I lie about?" Ralph held his already swollen chin.

"You know!"

"No! No, I don't. Rich is a banker at some bank in Rockford."

"You're wrong."

"That's what he told me. I haven't seen him since high school."

"Tell me what he told you. Why did he call you?"

"We have mutual friends. Rich and my brother-in-law were, and still are, buddies. I have a printing company in Janesville, Wisconsin. My brother-in-law called me and told me Rich needed a favor. I told my brother-in-law to have him call me. So, he did. I'm telling you the truth."

Joe didn't believe a word he said. "I'll tell you what, you get in that truck and we'll go call Doc. Ralph got in the truck, along with Brownie and Joe. As Joe started up the truck, Ralph pulled out a .38 short nose, two inch barrel and ordered, "Get your hands off that steering wheel." The second the last word came out of Ralph's mouth, Brownie latched onto Ralph's wrist, bit down and twisted. Ralph howled and dropped the .38 to the floor. Joe could hear bones breaking under the pressure of the dog's huge jaws. Brownie let go of the wrist and clamped down on Ralph's throat. Ralph's eyes grew red and his face turned blue. His arms flew every which way. When he finally grabbed at Brownie, Brownie only increased his pressure.

Joe jumped out of the truck and reached the passenger door in a matter of seconds. He instructed Brownie to ease up. Joe dragged Ralph out, smashed his face into the ground and kicked him in the stomach. Ralph laid there like a gunny sack full of oats.

"Good boy, Brownie! I sure owe you one!" Joe hugged his dog while he waited for the man to come to.

Joe reached into the man's coat pocket and pulled out a wallet. He opened it up and found out the guy resided in Cicero, Illinois and his name was George Santos. He grabbed the guy's hair and pulled. His wig came off. "I bet this bastard works for the mafia."

Ralph awakened, tried to reach for his groin with the hand that had the broken wrist and cried out: "Oh, my God! That dog broke my wrist." Joe took his size fourteen shoe and dropped another hard blow to the man's stomach.

"Santos, don't you call my dog anything but 'Brownie, SIR' and the word SIR better be at the end of Brownie. If you want to live for another minute, you tell me who sent you and why." Joe's size fourteen shoes sat just inches away from crushing the rest of this guy's face.

Joe shouted, the revenge escaping from him. "Tell me!"

"The Capuanos have a tap on the doctor's phones."

Joe, shocked to hear they had tapped Doc's telephones, asked "when did they tap them?"

"Yesterday, the first day we heard that Doc called Ralph and wanted identification papers."

"Did you or anyone hurt the doctor?" Joe asked, keeping considerable pressure on George's throat with his foot.

"No! I can hardly breathe. What do you want to know?" Joe dug his foot into George's neck until he turned blue, letting up after several seconds.

"I want everything you can tell me about Alex and I want it now."

"Ok!" George answered with a voice hoarse from a damaged larynx. "Alex is an asshole. He isn't like his father. He has no respect for anyone, except his family. He treats everyone like they're scum from the sewer. He treats me like shit. There are a lot of people who want to see him dead. He rapes all of his prostitutes and beats them regularly. The guy is crazy."

Joe interrupted. "When he's with a prostitute, where is he—in his office, a hotel room, where?"

"He takes them to the Osage Hotel on Randolph. He has a room there on the top floor, room number 1107. I've been there. It's really nice. It's a large suite. It's all done in red and has brass fixtures. He has this huge tub. It holds six people. He sometimes has two or three girls there at the same time. He always has a bodyguard. His name is Rocky. No last name. Rocky is from Sicily and will stick a knife in you before you blink an eye."

"These prostitutes, are they white, Negro or Oriental?"

"They are mostly Negro, has a few white girls and a lot of Orientals. His clientele likes the very young, nigger girls. The very young Oriental girls are becoming very popular. Alex has a connection with some Oriental person by the name of Fu Yen. He's getting the Orientals from over in Thailand. He buys them over there and sells them to Alex."

Joe's face wrenched as he thought about these poor, young girls. "How much does Alex pay for them?"

"He pays a thousand for each girl. They make over three thousand a month each and Alex gets forty percent from each girl. They're a very hot item. He has clients waiting for several weeks to screw one of those slant eyes. Alex said he's going to up the price for an Oriental because of the demand."

"What kind of car does Alex drive?"

"He drives a Cadillac. It's a black, two-door coupe."

"I want the license plate number."

"I don't have it!"

"I want it and you'll get it for me."

"Ok!"

"George, what happened to Ralph?"

"I shot him and threw him in the Rock River. You'll never find his ass. The river moves really fast in the spring. He's probably way south of here already."

Joe's stomach knotted instantly. "I just ought to take you out in the country and string your sorry ass up and let the buzzards peck on you till you die."

"If I didn't kill him and dispose of his body, the Capuanos would have killed me before nightfall."

"What are they going to do to you now?"

"If you let me go, I'll try and gather more information on the Capuanos. I can't stand to work for them, but they have me in a trap. If I do what they want, I stay alive; if I don't, I'm in the river. They have very simple work rules. I can help you! I know I can!" George begged for his life and Joe loved every minute of it.

# Chapter 62

# ROCKFORD

Joe's heart was carrying more weight than he could handle. He had to unload. Jimmy used to tell him to take deep breaths because it releases the blood that clouds the head. His main objective remained to be avenging Sue's death, but now it seemed to be getting all mixed up in his head with his Grandpa's death and his Pa's death. He wanted to get even. He never got the answers he wanted. Somebody had to pay.

"I'm going to Rockford. I need to talk to Doc," Joe said as he stomped down the stairs.

"You be careful. I worry about you," Helen said, gathering up the breakfast dishes.

Joe headed for the door, with Brownie at his heels, and got into his truck. He started the big engine, then remembered. He jumped out of the truck and ran upstairs and got his hickory bat and Bowie knife. He came down the stairs two steps at a time. When his mother saw him, she panicked. "Joseph! What are you going to do with that?" Her hands covered her mouth.

"Don't worry, Mom! Just need a little protection. You never know, somebody might want to try and steal my truck." He grinned; his mother trembled.

Doc would be upset to hear about Ralph being murdered, but Joe knew he had to tell him.

Joe arrived at the city limits of Rockford and pulled into a gas station to look in the yellow pages for Doc's office address. He found it and asked the attendant for directions. He drove for what seemed forever before he found the office. It was a large, three-story building occupied by doctors. Joe went to the receptionist and asked her for Doc Knowles' office. She told him it was on the third floor, room 308.

"Hi! I'm Joe Clark! I need to see Doc Knowles." Her gold name tag read "Bernice."

"Doctor Knowles is still at the hospital in surgery." She looked at her watch. "He should be here in an hour or so. He'll probably have lunch before he comes in."

"Bernice, is there any way you could get hold of Doc? I'm a personal friend and I really need to speak to him."

"Are you a patient?"

"No, I'm just a friend."

"I'll try and call him over at the hospital. Would you like to have a seat?" She smiled.

Joe went over and sat his 235 pounds of solid rock in an arm chair that was just barely big enough to hold him. He picked up an April edition of *Sports Illustrated* and began reading about the upcoming baseball season. He flipped though the pages until he came to the Dodgers and began reading about Sandy Koufax when—

"Mr. Clark!"

"Yeah." Joe got up quickly and approached the counter, still carrying the magazine opened to the section on the Dodgers.

"I reached the doctor and he said to meet him at Marie's Restaurant. Do you know where that is?"

"No, I sure don't." Joe peered at Bernice's open top. Joe could see the tops of her breasts. "*She doesn't seem to mind.*" His head said lay off; his loins spoke differently.

Bernice gave Joe directions to the restaurant and seemed to take her time, maybe giving Joe a longer look. "I think that's right. If you have a problem, please feel free to call me." She gave Joe a big smile and winked at him as she handed the directions to him, with the underlined phone number in larger print than the directions and her name printed at the bottom.

"Thanks very much, Bernice!" Joe winked back and left the office. "*WOW! She was sure nice. I didn't see any rings. I wonder if she's married. She surely has a boyfriend. Maybe I'll ask Doc when I see him.*"

Joe managed to get to the restaurant without calling Bernice. He thought maybe he'd call her anyway just to see if she maybe wanted to go to a movie. He figured he better not.

"Hi, Doctor Knowles."

"Hi, Joe. It's good to see you."

"*I'm sure he won't be saying that when I tell him about Ralph.*"

They sat down in a booth and Joe told Doc about the death of

Ralph. Doc's face turned grey. Silence overrode his emotions as he put his head in his hands.

"I'm sorry, Doc. If I wouldn't have called you, this wouldn't have happened." Joe thought of the bean can and the car wreck and his Pa, Grandpa. And Sue, Sue....it was like a curse on him that anyone near him died. He bent his fork in half.

"Joe, it's not your fault. I believe they have my phones tapped." Doc looked at Joe with glassy eyes.

"Yeah, they do, Doc. The guy that killed Ralph came to see me." Joe told Doc everything he learned. He told Doc what George Santos had said and that he would help them, and why. He tried to straighten the fork back into its original shape.

Doc listened to every word without interrupting Joe. Finally, when Joe took a breath, Doc said, "That's fantastic detective work, Joe! It would be great if we could get a few more from inside the organization to help us." Doc slapped his large hand across Joe's big shoulder. "You're one hell of a man for your age; in fact, you're one hell of a man for any age."

"I still need those papers for my sister and my Mom. Do you think you can get them for me? I have all the information you should need. I got up this morning really early before I went to the track and got into their purses." Joe took the piece of folded-up paper from his wallet and handed it to Doc.

"I'll take care of it."

Joe's eyes burned from fear of another life being taken. "Doc, I think you'd better get your wife out of town. I think if you even fart the wrong way, you're dead."

"I-I know! She doesn't want to leave." Doc bowed his head as if he were praying.

"I'm sending my sister to our Uncle Charlie's in Cut Bank, Montana. My Mom is going to Denver to her Aunt Ethel's. Mom doesn't know it yet. I told my sister. As soon as I get the papers, they'll be on their way."

"I'll take care of this right away. I'll bring them down to you in a couple of days." Joe and Doc ordered. Joe ate his food, while Doc just picked away at his.

Joe's mind wandered when he suddenly remembered Doc's

receptionist. "Say, Doc! I met your receptionist, Bernice. She sure is good-looking!" Joe blushed.

"Yes, she is, Joe, and she just broke up with a guy she'd been dating for some time. She's older than you. I would say, maybe, twenty-six. She lost her parents in a car accident. Maybe you ought to give her a call after this Capuano thing is over."

Joe looked straight at Doc as his expression went from chipper to grief-stricken. "Yeah, I guess I should wait to ask her out, now that you mention it." Joe swallowed hard. "What do you think our chances are with these Capuanos?" No one had asked this question before.

"I-I don't know." Doc's head bowed again. "The Capuanos are murderers. They have an army to protect them. They have burned my home, threatened me, and now they have just flat-out killed an innocent man, who just happened to be doing me a favor. He has three kids still in school." Doc's eyes welled.

"Doc, I don't blame you for being scared. I think about those Capuanos everyday." Joe's hate overrode his fear. "Maybe I'm too damn stubborn or not old enough to be scared. I almost killed that guy this morning. He'll never talk the same again. I won't stop, Doc, until I get these guys. Maybe once we get the plans all set, you and your wife should get out of town, at least until it's over. Jimmy and I have reasons to kill these people. You have a reason, but we have a personal motive against them." Joe stared at Doc as he spoke.

"I have to admit, I am scared. I have never been so afraid, especially now that they have killed Ralph. I might be alright once I get over the shock."

"I'm getting into great shape, Doc. I'm way ahead of schedule. If you want to do this in May instead of June, I'm ready. I think everyone else will be ready."

"No! No! I want it perfect. I don't want anything to go wrong. I want us all to come out of this without a scratch." Doc stared at the ground. "I wish we hadn't been on that road that night."

They said their goodbyes. "I'll tell Bernice." Doc's tiny grin disappeared quickly.

Joe stopped at the cemetery on his way home. He had been stopping at either his Pa's grave or Sue's grave every other week since he started driving again. Since his mother and Rene were supportive of his desire to go after the Capuanos, he had less of a need to spend time at the cemetery. Joe just felt closer to God when he was by the gravesites. The church didn't have the same effect.

Joe had only been inside a church once since the wreck and that was for his father's funeral. He continued to wake up in a cold sweat many nights, smelling burnt flesh and hair.

He still didn't have any recollection of the horrible crash that had taken Sue's life. He remembered only the prom, what Sue wore, her beautiful face and body, and the T-Bird. *"Those bastards will die."*

# Chapter 63

## THE PAPER

Joe's time around the track clocked six seconds slower than yesterday's.

He walked in the door to the sound of the phone ringing. It was the feed mill, wondering if Joe could work today. Joe didn't want to refuse since they had been good to him.

Just as he was about to get into his truck, a black Cadillac pulled in behind him and blocked him in. Joe took a sharp look at the driver and right away spotted Doctor Knowles. "Hi, Doc," he called, walking toward the Cadillac.

"Hi, Joe. I'm sorry I didn't get down here sooner. I've been really busy."

Joe thought Doc looked less upset than he had earlier in the week.

"Hey, before I forget, these are the papers for your sister and mother. I got my wife to go live with her sister in California. After hearing what had happened to Ralph, she got paranoid."

"Thanks, Doctor Knowles! I really appreciate it. I'm sure glad you got your wife to leave, at least until after June first."

"Joe, just call me Doc." Joe nodded and smiled.

They had a short conversation and before Doc left he said, "I almost forgot! Bernice said to say 'hi.' I think you might have something there."

Joe grinned from ear to ear as he put the folded envelope in his jean hip pocket. "I'll call her sometime next week."

"Joe, I've got to go."

"Thanks again, Doc!"

Joe greeted Brownie with a big hug when he got home from the mill. They both headed straight to the kitchen. Joe pulled some juice from the refrigerator and grabbed half a dozen chocolate chip cookies from the cookie jar. Munching on a cookie, he opened up the envelope and, absentmindedly, slipped a cookie to Brownie.

He finished the remaining four cookies and drank another large glass of juice before going upstairs to shower and shave.

Joe thumped his way down the stairs to find his Mom in the kitchen preparing dinner. "Hi, Mom."

"Oh! Joseph, I don't know what I'm going to do with you. You never clean up after you make a mess."

"I know what you are going to do. You're going to Denver to Aunt Ethel's."

"What did you say?"

"I said you're going to Aunt Ethel's."

"And just why am I going to Aunt Ethel's?" Helen placed her hands on her hips.

"I don't want you or Sarah here. Things may get rough and I want you out of here before it does. I got new identifications for both you and Sarah. She's going to Uncle Charlie's in Cut Bank. Her name will be Virginia Curtis. Your new name will be Maria Evergreen."

"What? Where did you get a name like that?"

"Mom, you'll only have it for a few months. You have always liked evergreens.
I have all the paperwork taken care of. I want you out of here this weekend. You can catch the Denver Zephyr on Sunday evening. I already have your ticket."

"What? What if I say I'm not going?"

"You don't have any choice. The Capuanos killed the guy that was supposed to get these identifications for me."

"Oh my, Oh my God! What are we going to do? How are you going to stay alive?" Helen covered her face with both hands; her brow lined with worry.

"I told you—don't worry about me. Where is Sarah?"

"She went to Sylvia's house. She'll be back soon."

"I want you to get packed. Take only what you need for a few days and pack the rest in boxes. I'll mail them to you. You should be home by July fourth."

"I better call Aunt Ethel and tell her I'm coming." Helen reached for her address book.

"I already called her. I told her when you would be arriving."

"When did you do this?"

"The other night while you were at church."

"This is just too fast. I can't even think straight. You have people trying to kill you and your sister going off to Cut Bank. Does she know about this?"

"Yeah. She likes horses and Uncle Charlie has twenty horses for her to ride. She probably will have to clean out some horse stalls while she's there. Just don't tell her she has to get close to any smelly manure." Joe grinned.

"What is today? I can't think straight."

"Today is Friday! Your train leaves at 7:40 Sunday night."

"I need to tell some friends where I'm going."

"I don't want you to tell anyone. The less people know, the better. I'll tell Rene when you get out there."

"I just know I'll worry myself sick while I'm out there. You make sure you call me."

"I don't want you to call me when you're gone. You can call Rene. I'll call you from Rene's house. They may have our lines tapped already."

"Oh, my God, you think they've been in our house already?"

"Mom, you worry too much."

"You have no fear. I just hope you're smart enough to handle these Capuanos."

"I can handle them." Helen retreated upstairs to start thinking about packing.

Sarah came in right after Helen had gone upstairs. "Hey! I got your new identification stuff. You're leaving on the Greyhound tomorrow morning for Rockford. You'll change buses there and go to Minneapolis, then change again for Helena, Montana. At Helena, you'll get another bus to Cut Bank. You got it?" Joe had memorized all the details.

"No, I can't go then. I'm going out with Sylvia and her cousin on Saturday night."

"I'm sorry, but you have to go tomorrow morning, without fail." Sarah gasped as Joe told her about Ralph.

"Ok, maybe, maybe I can go out with them tonight."

"Just don't tell them anything. I don't want anyone to know where you are."

"I understand! I know these Capuanos are the worst of their kind anywhere.

# Chapter 64

# JIM'S CALL

It was early Monday morning. Joe was on his way down the stairs of his now-empty house when the phone rang. "Hello!" "This is Jim! I have some information for you."
"Where you calling from?"
"A pay phone."
"Ok! Shoot." Joe was certain the phone lines in his house hadn't been tapped yet.

"I found out the Capuanos have something really big going down in June. I got this from Al Falcono this past Thursday night when we were playing cards."

"Ok, what is it?" Joe was a little perturbed with Jim's bullshit. *"Just get to the point."*

"Al told me—this is really big! The Capuanos are going to be getting social security checks from the feds after people die. The feds shut your social security off as soon as you die. The Capuanos will receive checks after the first of every month, for up to six months, on deceased people. The Chicago FBI is involved. I should say, a few members of the FBI are involved. The main man of the FBI office in Chicago, a guy named Harold Camel, like the cigarette, has it all set to start up in May. He has two other guys involved with him, Gerald Buckley and Randolph Snodgrass. This scam is worth millions. They figure it will be worth over five million bucks per month once they get started. The money will be sent to a bank in Switzerland."

"Wow! That's a lot of money." Joe leaned against the kitchen wall.

"This guy Al, Capuano's number three hit man, wants out of the organization. He said he'd kill the Capuanos the first chance he got. Alex raped Al's daughter when she was only fourteen. Al had her in the office one day. When Alex saw her, he took her to Osage Hotel's room 1107 and screwed her so many times she almost died. This Alex belongs in an institution."

195

Hearing about Alex and how he raped little girls made Joe livid. "You didn't tell Al about any plans did you?"

"No! No! I sure didn't. I never said nothing. I just wanted to let you know who wants out and who wants in. The Capuanos are tight with their money, except for Johnny Amato and Ziggy. Those guys get paid big bucks."

"How much is the FBI getting out of the social security scam?"

"Al said they'll get half because it was their idea. This Harold Camel has a brother who works for social security, who can change the routings on the checks so they all go to a Swiss bank account. I guess they have several banks over there to send the money to."

"Do you think this Al guy will talk to me?" Joe wanted to get the information from the horse's mouth.

"Sure! In fact, he told me if he could get some guys together, he would fry the Capuanos. He hates them. His wife has been in an institution since the rape of their daughter. The Capuanos haven't paid him anything. Al said he is flat broke. He asked for money from the Capuanos and they told him to go to hell."

"Do you have anything else, Jim?"

"This next thing I'm about to tell you will make you sick."

"Alex has lowered himself even more. He's taking these young nigger and Oriental girls and having them perform sex with each other. He charges admission for the perverts who watch that kind of stuff. He's getting a $100.00 per person, per show. The shows run for two hours."

"You're kidding me!"

"No! I'm not! I've seen it with my own eyes. Those Orientals look to be about ten years old. They have sex sometimes with big buck niggers. They told me that people who pay for this get on the stage and screw these young kids and then they have oral sex with them right in front of everyone."

"Where is this place?"

"On Rush Street, in the basement of one of Marco's businesses. There have been plenty of Marco's political buddies there. Al told me that a couple of priests were on the stage with two of those Oriental girls He said one of them was from his parish."

"I hate these bastards even more. And Jim, they are Negroes. Don't ever use that other word."

"I-I won't Joe."

"Make damn sure you don't."

"How do I get hold of this Al guy?"

"I can set it up. I don't have his number. He will definitely talk to you."

"I want it set up for this Thursday evening. Have him pick the restaurant."

"Okay!"

"Thanks for the info."

"I want out, and I want out so bad I would give everything I have to get out of this hole I'm in. Hey, I almost forgot. Amato killed a guy named Harris, a retired cop. He was snooping around. His ass went in the Chicago River after they castrated him."

Joe froze.

"Hey, Joe, you still there?"

"Yeah." Joe couldn't keep the tremor from his voice. "I got to go." He raced upstairs to the bathroom to throw up.

# Chapter 65

# ANOTHER MEETING

Joe paid a visit to Rene to tell her that his Mom and sister had left for Denver and Cut Bank, respectively. She gave him some homemade bread and offered to fix him some things he could warm up to eat. They talked briefly.

The Dodgers were into their third week of the season. They had all their players back. Koufax and Drysdale were the mainstays. They remained the most feared pitchers in baseball. Joe could hardly wait till he had an opportunity to go to Wrigley Field and see the Chicago Cubs play the Dodgers. Washing his F-100, he hoped that Jimmy, Doc and he could go to a game this summer after they destroyed the Capuanos.

At 10:35 Thursday morning, Doc arrived at the Clark's house. His black Cadillac sparkled, as always.

"Hi, Doc."

"Hi, Joe, are you ready to go?" Doc wore a lightweight blue sport coat, tan slacks and an opened-collared shirt. Joe had on his usual: Lee jeans, long sleeve plaid shirt, tennis shoes and a baseball cap with a picture of a tractor on the front. Joe grinned from ear to ear.

"Yeah, say, I have to meet a guy named Al Falcono at Geronimo's Steak House on Ogden Avenue near Cicero at five o'clock. Maybe we both need to drive. Or, do you want to meet this hit man for the Capuanos?" Joe smiled as he spoke.

"You're meeting a hit man? I can't believe it. How did you arrange that?" Doc looked Joe over. Joe might be a kid in some ways, but he thought Joe was big enough to tackle a rhino if he had to. Doc shook his head. "Who's this hit man? My God, Joe, doesn't that scare you?" Doc shook his head, again, knowing Joe wasn't scared.

"If you can take the time to go to Geronimo's, we can talk on the way to Fredrick's. I have a lot more information that will make the hair stand up on your neck."

"Ok, I'll drive and you can give me the lowdown on everything."

Joe shared with Doc everything he had learned the last few days from Jim Costello. Doc would speed up and slow down, depending on what Joe had to say. He saved the news about Robert Harris until the end. Doc's speed plummeted to 30 MPH.

Doc and Joe arrived seven minutes early for their one o'clock meeting, but Jimmy, Jerry, Lester, and Jolene Groins, the stenographer, were already waiting in the back room of the restaurant. Doc had informed Mac two weeks ago that his services were no longer needed; that the plan had been scrubbed. Everyone waited eagerly for the meeting to start, aching to blurt out the information they had gathered.

# Chapter 66

# AL FALCONO

Jimmy, Doc and Joe headed for Geronimo's in Doc's Cadillac. They talked mostly about baseball on the forty-minute ride. Doc and Jimmy discussed the Chicago Cubs, while Joe got a few words in about his Dodgers.

They pulled into the almost half-full parking lot of Geronimo's Steak House at 4:49. Doc parked under a lamp post so the light shone on his black Cadillac. He didn't want to come out and find it had been stolen.

The restaurant, large and dark, had a stone entrance area and exposed wooden beams. A huge fireplace dominated one wall. The dining tables looked like large, polished picnic tables. The waitresses and the waiters wore black slacks and maroon tops.

The three men were escorted to the rear of the restaurant. Doc noticed that almost everyone was dressed up. He told Jimmy and Joe to remove their hats. People stared at them from all directions. Two guys over six foot five and another man over six foot two made quite a swath. Jimmy seemed to be the only Negro in the restaurant, except for a bus boy. They arrived at their table and, as they sat down, Joe noticed an olive-skinned man sitting at a table to his left. The guy looked to be maybe fifty with dark, greasy hair. He was as ugly as a skunk's butt and looked like he could kill a newborn robin with his teeth. He weighed around 150 pounds.

Joe sat down, keeping his eyes on the man who sipped his drink, while fixing his eyes on Joe. *"I will let him make the first move."*

The olive-skinned man got up slowly and walked toward them, with his drink in hand. He wore a white, silk sport coat and black slacks. His black shirt appeared to be silk, too, and he wore it with an open collar. He had a red silk handkerchief in his front breast pocket. The clothes didn't improve his looks. Joe could swear he saw a gun holstered as the man bent to get up from his chair. It looked to be on his left side. That would make him right handed. Joe's mind was traveling faster than the Denver Zephyr. His pinky finger was missing. "It's Falcono alright," Joe whispered to himself.

"Hi! My name is Al Falcono. I am supposed to meet a Joe Clark. Might that be you?" Al asked, with his right hand lying across his belly button and his left hand on his half-filled glass. He hadn't taken his eyes off Joe since Joe sat down. Joe only saw him blink once.

"Yeah, that might be me." Joe stood up, towering over Al. Al looked to be five-foot seven, maybe.

"You're one big mother ------"

Joe grabbed him quickly by the silk shirt and slammed him against the wall. Al's right arm hung loosely; his glass shattered on the hardwood floor. Al's brown eyes protruded. Joe had raised him two feet from the floor. Joe spoke in a low, menacing voice. "Don't you ever call me that name again! You do and I will attach your head permanently to your ass. Do you understand?"

"Y-yes, I meant nothing! We, Sicilians, just talk that way."

"Not to me you don't."

"Ok, man! Now, put me down." His voice tightened.

Joe slammed him in the open chair. Only a few people, other than Doc, who turned white as a ghost, and Jimmy, who grinned, saw the altercation.

"Al, the first thing I want you to do is to keep your hands on the table until I tell you different. Is that understood?"

"What for?" Al looked at Joe with loathing.

"Because I said so." Joe's teeth clenched.

Al nodded. "I need a drink."

"Al, I want you to look at Jimmy," Joe pointed to Jimmy, "and keep your eyes on him. You got that?"

"Yeah!"

"Ok! You tell us everything you want us to know." Joe leaned on his big arms, taking up an eighth of the table top.

"First of all, I have never been treated like this in my life. You are lucky I didn't eliminate all three of you. Second, who are these other guys? I was supposed to meet a Clark guy only."

"Jimmy, here, is a long-time friend of mine. Doc is also a friend of mine. They rode with me and will watch you to make sure you don't do anything stupid."

"I don't like being set up. Jim told me you were the only one that would be here."

"Keep your eyes on Jimmy."

"Why? I'm talking to you." Al now looked at Jimmy.

"Because I said so, that's why."

"I need a drink!" Al appeared to be much older than late forties. Probably caused by the stress the Capuanos put on him, Joe thought.

Doc asked Al, in a very pleasant tone, what he wanted to drink. "A double shot of vodka on the rocks with a twist and two olives."

"Ok, Al. Jimmy, what do you want?"

"I'll just have a Coke," Jimmy said, keeping his eyes focused on Al.

"I'll have a Coke, too," Joe said.

"I'll get the waitress." Doc appeared glad to have an excuse to leave. The tension at that table felt to be more than that of a leaf spring on a wagon load of corn.

"Talk, Al. We're your friends here. You just have to prove to us you are capable of being our friend."

"I have been with the Capuanos for more than ten years. I kill people. I have killed over seventy-five people since being with Marco. Most of these people were innocent. I hated doing it, but once you get into Marco's ring, you never get out. That Alex raped my little girl and she wasn't even fourteen. She will never have children of her own because he destroyed her plumbin'." Al blinked back the tears. "I would kill him, but then they would have my wife and little girl killed. My wife, she is in a mental institution and probably will never get out."

Doc came back to the table with the waitress and the four drinks. Al grabbed his, took a large swig, and set the glass on the table. He took a deep breath, then picked it up again, gulping the remainder of the vodka. He never even waited for the ice to chill the contents. Al's eyes reddened.

"I want out of this organization so bad that I have thought about even killing my little girl and my wife so they wouldn't be punished by the Capuanos. They will make you die such a horrible death. They are worse than the Indians you had over here. Hitler was bad, but the Capuanos are brutal. I need another drink." Sweat formed on Al's forehead, and it wasn't from the vodka.

Doc offered, "I'll get you two, if you would like."

"Thanks! I could sure use 'em."

Joe glanced at Jimmy. Jimmy's eyes told Joe that this guy was telling the truth. "Al, how would you like to get us as much information as you can without getting yourself or your family killed?"

"I can probably tell you all you need to know. I know everything they do, when they aren't screwing some poor little girls—that damn Alex."

"Tell us everything you know, Al!" Joe urged gently.

Al talked for two hours and consumed four more vodkas on the rocks. He gave Joe, Jimmy and Doc enough information to make their plan much more workable. Doc took notes.

Al told them about the people who needed to be put down. He gave them their names, addresses, what they did for the organization, where they ate, what they drove, married or unmarried, kids or no kids, girlfriends' names, hobbies, what they drank, where they got their shirts laundered, and, of course, their descriptions.

They totaled, including the Capuanos, thirteen. He said they could not leave anyone of the thirteen alive or they would be destroyed. He told them the places where they could find the Capuanos, when they were at the office, when Alex was screwing a young girl at the Osage Hotel, and who ran what operation and how they worked.

Al shared more information about the FBI and the social security scam, along with a change to their stolen car ring. He left nothing out.

The meeting ended with Doc saying, "Al, we really appreciate you coming here tonight. You have given us a tremendous amount of information. We will definitely be in touch with you."

"I think, without a doubt, we can accomplish the destruction of the Capuano organization. Marco messed up by mistreating his own people. Rule number one: Never screw the people who are doing your work for you. Marco's father never learned that and neither has Marco. This could have been bigger than General Motors if Marco had listened to me eight years ago. He just laughed and blew cigar smoke in my face." Al took another drink from his glass, but only swallowed melted ice.

"I have one last question, Al. What about Rico DeMarco?"

"He's getting out of prison in one week and Ziggy will be waiting for him. He is a dead man. Guaranteed! He won't live twenty-four hours after he walks out the gates of that prison."

"What do we need to do to keep Ziggy from getting this guy?" Joe asked.

"A police escort is the only way. You'll have to hide him. If he shows his face, Ziggy will nail him. He is the best there is, other than Amato."

"He is on your list of thirteen. Do we need to take him down before the others?"

"Absolutely not. That's Marco's boy. If he gets taken out, Marco will hire a thousand Sicilians to kill whoever did it. The thirteen have to be taken out together, in a matter of a few hours." Joe and Jimmy looked at Doc and grinned slightly.

They all got up together and walked out of Geronimo's. Al's parting words were, "Who are you guys, anyway? Doc, are you a doctor, or is that just a name?"

"Just a name, Al," Doc answered, with a grin.

"You two guys look like you could kick some ass. Just remember that size don't mean nothin'. A bullet will stop your ass in a second. You better be packin' a rod if you want to stay alive." He patted his left breast.

"Thanks for the advice, Al," Doc said. He was already armed, but had no idea whether he would or could actually use it if and when the time came.

Doc, Jimmy and Joe climbed in Doc's Caddy and headed for Jimmy's house. "The man's tellin' the truth. I sure didn't catch anything he said that was a lie," Jimmy said, sprawled out in the back seat.

"I hope so, Jimmy. I guess we have to trust somebody," Doc said, driving north on Cicero.

"We need to find a way to protect DeMarco when he gets out of prison. We'll need all the hit men we can get. These thirteen may be spread out all over Chicago," Joe said, as he stared out the front window. Joe squeezed his lips together, trying to digest all the pieces of the plan.

"The plan is coming together," Doc said, as they headed north on Michigan Avenue.

# Chapter 67

# DINNER WITH BERNICE

Joe arrived at Doc's office ten minutes before five. He left the flowers he had bought in the truck. He took the stairs up to the second floor two at a time. Joe had called Bernice earlier in the week about coming up.

Bernice was ready to go. Joe felt a little nervous and hoped he was doing the right thing.

Joe followed Bernice to her place, a second-floor apartment about six miles from the office. She drove a 1960, blue, Ford Falcon.

Joe got out of his F-100 with the bouquet of flowers and Bernice said, "You are really sweet. Did you pick these from your garden?" She knew he hadn't.

"Yeah, I hand-picked them." Bernice planted a hot kiss on Joe's parted lips.

Bernice's dog, Blackie, smelled Brownie on Joe and they became friends instantly.

"What would you like to drink?" Bernice headed toward the kitchen to get glasses and open the liquor cabinet.

"Whatever you have is fine with me." Joe had never had a drink, not even a beer.

Bernice filled two cocktail glasses with ice and poured them each shots of Dewar's Scotch, adding a splash of water to each. Joe took a sip, swallowed hard and coughed twice.

"Do you like scotch, Joe?" She wore a warm smile.

"Yeah, I've never had it before, though." Joe tried again—he swallowed a gulp. This one went down easier.

"Joe, do you want to talk about your accident?" She needed to know. Her parents had been killed in an accident.

"You sure you want to hear about it?"

"Yes, if you want to tell me." She reached over with her hand and stroked his arm.

Joe told her the whole story, but left out the part about the

205

revenge against the Capuanos. He told her how he met Doc. "Where did you grow up?" Bernice asked, wiping tears from her eyes, which were more for her parents' accident than Joe's. They hugged each other briefly. Their eyes told that a romantic relationship was in the making.

Joe told her about the Clark farm, the lightning that had struck his Pa, but, mostly, about his Grandpa. "You've had a full life already and you're still a very young man. How old are you, Joe?"

"I'll be nineteen on May 12th."

"That's my birthday, too! I don't believe it!"

"Wow! That's something!"

"Nineteen!" She reared back. "I'm serving booze to a minor! Geez! Why didn't you tell me?" She grinned from ear to ear, but suddenly her smile turned sultry. "I guess you'll have to spend the night. I sure don't want you to drink and drive at your age." Joe got one of those uncontrollable feelings in his groin.

"This is the first drink I've ever had." Joe grinned as if he had just gotten caught with his fingers in the cookie jar. Her eyes went wide and her free hand touched her lips.

"You're big enough to be two men. How big are you?"

"About six foot five and I weigh around two hundred and forty," Joe answered, proudly.

"How did you ever recover from that awful car accident in such a short time?"

"I worked my butt off."

She sized up his broad shoulders, huge arms and massive legs. "I bet you did." *God, what a body.* Bernice felt the heat rise in her body and it wasn't from the scotch. She didn't want to control it; she wanted Joe.

"Let's move to my bedroom." Joe felt her hot breath enter his ear.

A small light filtered from the adjacent bathroom into the dimly lit bedroom. They embraced and she began to undo the buttons on his shirt. The room filled with love as her cries rang against the walls.

Afterwards, Bernice dressed in a short, silk kimono decorated with a print of wild, Oriental flowers and they moved to the kitchen.

She put her hands on her small hips, legs slightly spread and smiled. "Now how am I going to get dinner ready with that hairy chest staring at me? I'll want to make love to you on the kitchen table." They both laughed and embraced each other until the juices started flowing again. Bernice pulled away, "I can't think straight with you half-naked."

They finished dinner and were on their second scotches. They retired to the large sofa in the front room. It was long enough for Joe to lay out straight and wide enough for two people to lay side-by-side without hanging onto one another. The heat of passion rushed in.

They kissed their way back to the bedroom. Her kimono never made it to the doorway. The sheets were still rumpled from the last love session.

With their bodies still embraced, eyes open, thoughts running wild, Joe spoke first. "I haven't—that was—you're terrific."

She kissed him. "I'm sure glad—glad I met—saw you. I'll have to be sure to thank Doctor Knowles." She kissed him several times, slowly, with feeling.

"I'd love for you to stay the night, Joe, but I know about dogs. He'll hold it until you get there. The next time, and I hope it's soon, you'll have to bring Brownie with you." She kissed his ear. Joe's thoughts of Brownie started to fade, but he swung his legs over the bed.

When Joe got home, Brownie headed out the door immediately. He never made it to the tulips across the street. He hit the big oak tree in front of the house, made three circles around the yard and dropped his deposit on the front lawn.

"Maybe next time I'll take you with me to Rockford. Bernice has a large dog like you. I think you'd like him. His name is Blackie." Brownie barked loudly enough to wake up the old and restless in the neighborhood. Joe broke out into a laugh. It felt good to laugh.

# Chapter 68

## SECOND DATE PLANS

Joe returned from the track the next morning around six-thirty. He felt like a young colt that had just gotten out of the barn. Walking through the door, he heard the phone ring as he headed for the kitchen. He answered it on the fourth ring. "Hello!"

"Hi, Sweetie. Did I wake you?"

"Good Morning! No, I've been to the track already."

"You really are disciplined, aren't you? I like that."

"Sometimes, I am. Other times, I need a little nudge."

"I just wanted to tell you, I think you're a real jerk for letting me sleep by myself last night. I woke up at 3:00 this morning and wanted you so bad.

"I slept like a rock. In fact, I slept so well, I thought I died and went to heaven." They both laughed.

"I want to see you soon. When are you coming up?"

"Why don't you come down and bring Blackie?"

"Ok, when?" She had hoped he would say that.

"Anytime, but Thursday. You can spend the night." Already Joe could feel the warmth in his shorts.

"How about Wednesday night? Are you going to cook me something?"

"Wednesday would be great. I can't cook. I can burn things, though." Joe's heart came to life. They both giggled.

"I can bring something and I'll cook."

"I'll take you to the local greasy spoon. It's better than any of the other spoons in town."

"I don't go to just any greasy spoon, now."

"I'll take you to the best one in town. I promise."

"Ok! I can be there by six-thirty."

"I'll see you then." Joe gave Bernice directions to his house.

"Bye!"

"Bye!

He could smell Bernice's body. He knew he needed to get his mind focused. He had to eat and get to work at the feed mill.

He placed the dirty dishes in the sink, knowing his Mom couldn't scold him. The kitchen reeked of burnt bacon grease and hadn't been cleaned since his Mom left. The rest of the house fared a little better.

After a quick hug for the dog, he was out the door and on his way to work. Bernice faded from his mind before the Capuanos filled it. The radio in the truck played, "I'm Gonna Live Till I Die" by Frankie Lane.

# Chapter 69

# BERNICE ARRIVES

Bernice arrived five minutes early, with Blackie by her side. "Hi, Joe." She wore a pair of white shorts and a lilac-colored top.

"Hi, Bernice. You look great. Come on in."

The two dogs looked at each other. Brownie smelled Blackie from one end to the other and vice versa. Once they realized they were both males, the attraction ended and they went in the house and laid down five feet apart.

"Would you like a drink?"

"Sure, do you have scotch here?"

"No, we'll have to go get some. I'll pay; you buy." Bernice laughed.

The trip to Rocky's Liquor Store, the only liquor store in town, was quick, returning to the house in less than half an hour. They had left the two dogs in the house to get acquainted and, upon returning, found them both stretched out on the living room floor.

Joe served the scotch as they sat on the sofa in the front room.

"Did you ever just want to go, to-go, to another country?" Bernice asked. Joe stared at the wall as too many things rolled around in his head. "Like New Zealand?"

Joe turned quickly and released a big old grin. "Oh, yes, I've wanted to go to New Zealand ever since reading about it in geography class in high school. I remember the mountains and the beaches. You could ski in the morning and swim in the afternoon."

"Really, that's when I got the idea that I would like to go there. The coast, the mountains, the lakes, the people speak English."

Joe stared at the ceiling and could see the pictures of New Zealand clearly in his mind, a place without violence or blood. *"A place to raise cattle and a family, yeah."*

"Ok! When do you want to go?" Bernice asked, with her hand on Joe's thigh and happiness in her eyes.

210

"This fall, maybe. No, maybe next spring. Yeah, definitely next year."

"Whenever. I love it that you are willing to explore somewhere other than Illinois. It is so boring here." Bernice could tell things were piled up way too high in Joe's head. He needed a change of mood. She kissed him several times.

They went to a new, locally-owned steak house in town. The name, "KICKAPOO," came from an old Indian tribe that had camped in these parts many years ago. Joe had eaten there before and the food was great. They ordered salads to start. Joe ordered a 16-ounce sirloin and Bernice, a small fillet.

Ten minutes after they had arrived back at the house Joe took a deep breath and turned to Bernice. Joe began to explain why he and Doc became friends. He told her about the Capuanos, the prostitution ring, stolen car operation, social security fraud, cigarettes, illegal gambling, and the murders and rapes—everything. Bernice took in every word he spoke with gasped emotion. Joe mentioned the young girls that had been raped and murdered. Her eyes teared up and her rosy complexion faded as he spoke of Alex and his obsession with young girls.

Joe continued, telling her about the police, the FBI, the judges, political leaders, the mayor, and the priest. "My God, Joe, how have you survived all this? How will you survive from now until they are put away?" She sniffled and Joe wished he hadn't told her.

"Starting with the day the lightning struck my Pa, the death of Sue, my Grandpa's death, to the death of Ralph from Rockford, I have all this hate inside me. I need to destroy these bastards, or explode." He turned his cheek. Did he want forgiveness? He looked back into her wondering eyes. "Does that make sense to you?"

She never spoke, just nodded her head, staring straight ahead. She had hardly touched Joe since he began.

She got up and stood in front of Joe. "I love you, Joe! I don't know how or why, but I do. If anything happened to you, I would just die. Please be careful. I asked Brownie to protect you." She kissed him hard on his lips. Joe's tension faded a little. A sense of peace came over him.

Joe returned Bernice's kiss. "My Grandpa called me the immortal one. I have been through a tornado that carried me and a dog and six pups for more than a mile. I was seven then. I was sent to Sheridan Boys' School for kicking the crap out of a damn minister, who killed my pet pheasant in our garden. I was twelve then. While I was in Sheridan, Jimmy Robbins and I were in a fight in a lunchroom with sixty other boys. Jimmy and I, plus a couple of other guys, were the only ones left standing. Several boys died that day."

"I survived the car accident, survived the lightning storm that killed my father. And I forgot to tell you about being on top of a forty foot windmill when I was five. I would have gotten down without any help, but my pant leg got caught in the gears."

Bernice just shook her head and kissed Joe on his lips, neck, face, and the top of his head. Joe put on a smile, the first one tonight. "Don't worry about me." This was the first time he had shared all of these stories with anyone. Sue had known most of them.

As Joe stood, he placed his large hands on Bernice's shoulders. He looked into Bernice's eyes and saw a future, someone he might be able to love. He needed someone—someone who, hopefully, would outlive him. They embraced for several minutes, their hearts remaining on the same wave.

They awakened by their barking dogs. Joe jumped and glanced at the alarm clock. The time was 2.33 am. Joe flew out of bed and ran over to the window. Before he pulled the curtain back he heard the phone ringing. "The phone is ringing, Joe."

"Yeah, I hear it." You stay here and lock yourself in the bathroom."

Joe slipped on a pair of jeans and ran down the stairs, with Brownie on his heels. Blackie stayed with Bernice.

Joe grabbed the phone, leaving the lights off. "Hello!"

"Joe, this is Al. I just wanted to let you know I took care of Amato. He was coming out to kill you, Joe. I shot him at a stop light after he told me where he was headed. It happened about an hour ago in Yorkville. His foot came off the brake after the bullet entered his fat head. His car went into the intersection and got hit by a semi. The car exploded. I am back in Chicago already."

"Great! Thanks, Al. You probably saved my life. What about Ziggy?"

"Ziggy went to St Louis to kill DeMarco when he walks out of prison."

"Are you going to take out Ziggy when he gets back?"

"Yeah, I'll take care of him. I'll be the only hit man the Capuanos have left. Marco will want me to take you out. He's getting nervous. He'll get some more hit men, but none ever as good as Ziggy and Amato."

"Thanks again, Al, and be careful."

"I'll call you tomorrow, or the next day, after I get Ziggy. Sorry I woke you up."

"No problem, Al. Thanks again."

Joe went back to bed, but sleep didn't come for over an hour.

# Chapter 70

# THE NEXT MORNING

"**D**oc will be here soon! You better get some clothes on." She got up and hugged Joe, as he tried to get a leg into his jeans. He stumbled and fell into a heap on the kitchen floor. The crash shook the floor. A twinge in his right leg shot out. A knock on the door came within seconds. "I'll be there in a minute," Joe hollered. The dogs barked loudly. Joe finally managed to get back up and get his jeans on. He put his shirt on as he headed toward the door.

"Wait! Don't open it yet. I'm not ready for you to open that door," Bernice pleaded as she ran for the stairs with her clothes in her arms, heading to Joe's bedroom. Joe waited with his hands on the knob as Bernice bolted up the stairs naked.

Joe opened the door to see Doc sitting on the porch. "Hi, Doc!" Joe's face was as red as an overripe tomato.

"Hi, Joe, did I catch you at a bad time?" He noticed Joe's shirt tucked in his pants half-assed.

"Nah! Bernice is here and we —

"I didn't expect to find her here. Although, I thought, maybe, I saw her car there in the street." Doc smiled as he stood up.

"Hi, Doctor Knowles." Bernice carried a convincing smile that showed she had fallen in love.

"I guess we better go, Doc. I'll drive today. Wait, I need to go upstairs and get some things." Joe left Doc and Bernice on the porch with the two dogs.

Joe picked up his hickory bat, Bowie knife, the Winchester 12 gauge shot gun and half a box of 00 buckshot. He wrapped it in a blanket so as not to alarm Doc and Bernice.

"Joe, what have you got there?" Bernice stepped in front of Joe and grabbed hold of the blanket. Her face blanched as she felt the gun.

"Bernice, I may need this for protection. I promise I won't use it unless I have to." She ripped at the blanket and the Bowie knife fell to

214

the ground. Her eyes went wild as she looked at the knife.

"Oh, no!" Bernice said, eyes glued to the knife.

Doc walked over to see for himself what Joe had hidden under the blanket. "You, you expecting trouble today, Joe?" Doc's voice quivered and his hands shook.

Bernice headed to her car. Joe could see she had begun to cry. He laid the knife and the shotgun under the driver's seat of the F-100. The hickory bat went behind the seat.

Joe walked over to Bernice. "I'm real sorry about this, Bernice. I wish it was over and you and I could be on our way to New Zealand."

"Oh, Joe, I wish we were in New Zealand now." She wrapped her arms around him. "You be careful."

"We are just having a meeting."

She smiled and kissed him on the lips.

"Please be careful, Joe. I love you."

"I love you too, Bernice. And don't worry, the FBI will more than likely be there today. They won't start anything with them there." He kissed her and returned to his truck, where Doc stood waiting. Joe felt a closeness that he hadn't felt in a long time.

# Chapter 71

# FREDERICK'S

When they arrived at Fredrick's, Joe recognized several Ford cars, some black, some blue. Joe counted them twice—five in all. "Looks like we will have some guests at our meeting today."

"W-who?" Doc looked around, seeing nothing but an almost-full parking lot of cars. A few guys stood around one vehicle. "I-I don't see anyone unusual, Joe." Doc's eyes searched for Capuanos and their body guards. The lines rose on his forehead.

"FBI, they have at least twelve men here, maybe more." Joe calmly got out of his F-100.

"How do you know that, Joe?" Doc asked with a little more pep in his voice now.

"There are five Fords here. They are all the same year and model, three black and two blue. The men are probably inside." There were at least fifty cars in the parking lot. Joe's Grandpa had taught him how to distinguish and count a herd of cattle and to do it quickly.

Doc peered around trying to find even one Ford. "You simply amaze me, Joe."

They met in the same room as the other meetings. The table was set up for eighteen. "There are twelve FBI agents here, Doc."

"I don't see any. Where do you see them?"

"I counted the places at the table. Seventeen places, that means twelve agents, unless the Capuanos were invited." Joe smiled, hoping they would be here.

"Right, I see now. Where are they?"

Lester, Jerry, and Jimmy entered the room and they all greeted each other. The stenographer wasn't there, which told Joe that this meeting wouldn't be recorded by anyone, except the FBI. Joe bet they had sent her home, but had grabbed her notes from the last meeting. They took their seats and waited. Within a couple of minutes, twelve men in dark suits, ties, white shirts, and black shoes walked in. One of the guys had a pad and three pencils. They all looked to be in their thirties or early forties, except one man, who was mostly grey on top and appeared to be in his mid-fifties.

"I have the pleasure to introduce to you the finest law enforcement group in the United States, The FBI!" Agent Freeman said, standing erect, hands at his waist, addressing everyone seated. "On my right is agent Patrick Callahan, the Director of the Midwest Division of the FBI. He has been briefed on the corruption here in Chicago. Patrick is new to this Division. He comes from the Eastern Division. The man he replaced will be terminated. Gentlemen, I am here to tell you that things are going to change in Chicago and Illinois very quickly. I now will turn this meeting over to Patrick. Please hold any questions until he is finished." Agent Freeman sat down before Director Callahan rose.

"Good morning, gentlemen! First of all, Joe Clark, would you please stand up." Joe rose like a lumberjack. "This man is the reason why we are all here today. Joe, I want to say thank you, from all of us in Washington. Robert Kennedy, as you all know, is our new Attorney General. He has been informed about the death, destruction, rape, money laundering, stolen car ring, fraud and, God knows what else, that has been going on here in Chicago. I want to thank everyone else: Jerry Moore, Doctor Knowles, Lester Yates, for your investigation and hard work. A special thanks to Doctor Knowles for his financial support. Joe, you and the rest of your group here, will be honored sometime in the months ahead for the information that you have gathered and for your bravery. Joe, you can have a seat. Thank you."

Still standing, Joe asked, "What about Jimmy Robbins? He has brought more information to our group than anyone."

"I'm sorry, Joe. Who is this Jimmy Robbins?"

"Stand up, Jimmy." Joe grabbed his friend's shirt.

Jimmy stood beside his buddy with a stern look, leaning toward Callahan.

"I'm sorry, Jimmy, I guess your name was omitted from the information I had."

Jimmy and Joe sat down.

Most of the others seemed to be relieved by his opening remarks. Joe showed signs of skepticism. Jimmy caught Joe's eye. Bullshit was in the air.

"We haven't said anything yet to Agents Camel, Snodgrass and Buckley. The three men will be terminated soon. We have a formality that has to be met first."

"We will take these men, the Capuanos, and their people alive, if we can. Only, and I mean only, because they can supply us with information we couldn't gather if they were dead. If they resist, then we are authorized to kill them on the spot. That is from the Attorney General's Office."

"Now, does anyone have any additional information that you think will be helpful to this operation?"

Joe stood up. "What happens to these Capuanos when you don't kill them?" Joe asked with clenched teeth. His eyes waited for the right answer.

"They will go to trial. Believe me, it won't be any local judge on the bench. There will be a federal judge ruling on this case. He will be appointed by the Attorney General. And, again, let me say that this comes from the Attorney General's Office, **THESE MEN WILL ROT IN PRISON."** Doc flinched; he had used the same terminology. "The crimes these men have committed will leave us no other alternative than severe punishment. They will be an example for this country."

Joe sat down. He didn't make any more comments, or give any indication of what he thought about Patrick's proposal. Jimmy slapped him on the back and whispered in his ear. "I'm looking forward to goin' and watchin' the Cubs beat your Dodgers."

Joe smiled at Jimmy, but made no comment.

Doc stood and seemed very much relieved that the FBI was going to handle the Capuanos. "I want to ask a few questions, if I may." He wiped the beads of sweat on his forehead with a handkerchief.

"Of course, Doctor Knowles, you can ask anything you wish."

"What happens to the State police who are on the take, the city police, and the city, county and State judges who are corrupt? And, last but not least, let's not leave out the politicians."

Patrick seemed to be speaking from his heart when he replied, "If we have proof that they were involved in any way, shape or form, then they'll go down with the rest. This also came from Mr. Robert Kennedy. He wants no stone unturned. We are instructed to clean house in this State until it is rid of any corruption."

"When you said 'rot in prison,' did you mean life, without parole?"

A cold smile came over Patrick's face. "Exactly. They are never going to see daylight again, except when they go outside to exercise. They will be sentenced by a Federal judge within days after capture and sent to a Federal prison; no jury in this case. This case will go away very quickly. I pity anybody who wants to start or continue any organized crime in this country, as long as Robert Kennedy is our Attorney General."

"What about Alex Capuano's children? Are they going to be watched closely so they don't get involved in any revenge, or maybe other organized crime?" Doc questioned.

"Absolutely! They, along with anyone the Capuanos were associated with. That is one of the reasons we want these guys alive, so we can interrogate them till the cows come home." Patrick caught Joe's eye and smiled, but Joe didn't return the smile.

"What about the girls who are prostitutes for the Capuanos? Are they going to be helped in some way to find a different line of work? Most of these girls aren't even old enough to work, so what about schooling or education?" Joe asked.

"I wish I had an answer for that, but I'm afraid I don't."

"The amount of money the Capuanos have accumulated over the last thirty years is staggering. Why can't that money be used to help these girls and, also, the young car thieves, who are prisoners in this God-forsaken organization?" Joe suggested.

Patrick's eyes dropped; his hands went palms down. "That-that seems to be a good idea, but, again, I can't answer that question at this time." Joe sensed he was avoiding the question.

The sound coming from Joe's chair as he stood up got everyone's attention. Joe's ears burned and Jimmy knew his buddy would be making a statement. Joe said, without hesitation, right index finger aimed at Callahan, "I tell you what. You go back to Washington and you tell your Mr. Kennedy, or his brother, the President, I don't care. We want the money the Capuanos took illegally from the citizens of this State and other States." Callahan and the other eleven agents' lower lips fell; their twenty-four eyes focused on Joe, their bodies froze. "I want that money given to the young girls for education and to help them get started with a new life. The young girls and boys that were in the stolen car ring, the

219

same thing. We are talking about teenagers here." Joe paused briefly, letting his words soak in. Some of the agents, including Callahan, dropped their heads.

"The remaining money and, believe me, there is a barn full of it, probably several barns full, if you find it all," Joe took a deep breath, "we know for a fact that there are several million dollars involved. I want Jimmy, here, to get a big chunk of it. Jimmy and his sister and four little brothers have lived all their lives in the ghetto in Chicago. Their mother was a whore and got herself killed. Their Daddy is in the State Pen at Joliet. I have been to their Aunt's house. None of us would want to live where this man grew up and still lives."

"You people wouldn't know shit about the prostitution ring or the car ring, if it weren't for Jimmy's sister and Jimmy risking his life. Jimmy's fiancé's sister is a prostitute for the Capuanos. She, too, is risking her neck every single day. Jimmy got a lot of the information you have from her. Jimmy has teeth missing—show them, Jimmy, when he got the crap knocked out of him by Capuano's thugs." Jimmy grinned broadly. Three missing teeth were laying somewhere on a dirty Chicago street.

"My Grandpa was a very smart man and one thing he told me when I was just a little kid was that the government will take your money and the public will never know where, how, or when that money is spent. I don't want you getting in all the barns that are full of money and giving it to the damn government to waste on some stupid-ass thing that doesn't amount to a hill of beans."

"Mr. Patrick Callahan," Joe took another deep breath and blew it out, "I'm giving you until next week at this time, right here at Fredrick's, to tell us what these people are going to receive. We don't want a damn trip to Washington D.C. and a bunch of politicians slapping us on the back, and then taking all the damn money that the Capuanos have." Joe remained standing, waiting for an answer.

Silence and bewilderment choked the room. Everyone looked at Patrick, including the other FBI agents. The ball was in his court and now it was up to him to deliver it to Washington. Patrick's mouth hung open, eyes fixed on the table in front of him. He picked at his fingernail, wrung his hands and wiped the sweat on his forehead with his left hand before answering.

"Joe, that was a great speech." Callahan nodded, flashing a short grin. "I wish I could stand up here and tell you that, yes, the feds will turn over all the money to everyone who was involved, but that is not very realistic in this modern age. The FBI has expenses, too." Joe cut him off again.

"I don't want to hear any damn excuses, Callahan." Rage filtered out of Joe. He spoke from his Grandpa now. "You either deliver or I will tell the papers and the television and radio people everything. Get off the political bullshit and get us that money." Joe pumped his index finger at Callahan.

"You know, Joe, General Patton would have loved you." Callahan smiled, but his eyes didn't.

"You know I would have loved to have served under him. He wasn't a coward and he didn't take any crap. And, I will tell you another thing, this country would be a hell of a lot better off if we had more Pattons in it." That, also, came from Harry Clark. Joe's adrenaline roared throughout his body. He knew he had the feds scared.

Neither Callahan, nor the feds, wanted the media blowing this thing out of proportion. "Joe-Joe, I will take this up with Washington tomorrow morning. I will have an answer for you next week, right here." Patrick knew he had to get answers for these people.

"Thank you, and tell Kennedy that we appreciate him taking the bull by the horns instead of waiting to see if he's stepping on some politician's toes. Time will tell what he's made of. If he hedges, then I don't respect him." Joe made the last statement for Patrick to carry out of the room.

Everyone took a break before lunch, going outside to get some fresh air. Jerry, Lester, Jimmy and Doc talked to Joe and shook his hand. They slapped him on the back and commended him, "You gave Patrick an ultimatum. Way to go!"

Joe remained quiet. He still thought it was too good to be true. He wanted his own revenge. *"Passing it on to the FBI is the best way."* This definitely would make Bernice happy. He walked away from the others, heading toward his F-100, trying to get the cobwebs out of his head. The hate still boiled inside him. He caught a glimpse of his Grandpa smiling.

Joe looked at his truck and everything seemed to be ok. Jimmy walked over to him. "I know what you a-thinkin'. You wants to kill those Capuanos. Me, too, Joe. I think it better we wait till Callahan bring us

Washington's answer." Joe shrugged his shoulders and tilted his head toward his shoes. "That Patrick guy, he scared of you and what you might do. They can't mess with you, man. If they do, they know the papers will tear them up. Hey man, I kinda wanted to go to Washington."

Joe laid a hand on Jimmy's shoulder. "I hope so, Jimmy. They let us down, we will go to Washington. I'm not afraid to tell Kennedy what I think. I just hope he has the guts to put those bastards away." Joe walked away with a lump in his chest.

Patrick approached Jimmy and Joe. "We're going to leave now. I will get on Washington's butt in the morning. You two be careful. We will have this all sewn up by noon on June 4th." They shook hands and said their goodbyes. All five Fords left the parking lot in a single file.

# Chapter 72

## ANOTHER CALL

Joe called Bernice as soon as he got home, but not before he let Brownie out. "Pack your bags. We are going to New Zealand."

"Oh, Joe. You are okay. I was worried sick. Please come and stay with me tonight."

"Ok! I have some things to do here first. I'll be up around 5:00, maybe 5:30."

"Joe, what happened at the meeting?"

"I'll tell you about it when I see you."

"Ok! I love you."

"I love you, too."

Joe took Brownie to the city park. He threw a rubber ball over a hundred times for Brownie to catch on the fly. Joe felt more contented right now than he had been for some time. He was in love again and the Capuanos had only a little more than a month before they would be incarcerated.

Joe thought about Bernice's body—her warmth, tenderness and her touch. His family could come home. Rene would be at peace. Sue could rest at last. Joe hugged his dog. The pounding in his head vanished.

Joe returned home and had just gotten out of the shower when the phone rang. He wrapped the towel around his waist and headed down the stairs to the kitchen. "Hello!"

He could hear heavy breathing on the other end. "Joe, Al Falcono. I just wanted to tell you Ziggy's body is where no one will ever find it."

"Al you are amazing! Thanks again. You be careful. The Capuanos will think you were the one taking out their hit men."

"No way! They think you are the bad ass."

"Thanks again, Al."

"We will have the Capuanos to ourselves."

"Al, you can have them all if you want."

"What's the matter? You runnin scared?"

"Nah! You do such a good job and I'm tired of all the death.

"I understand, Joe. I am, too, but I need to finish them once and for all."

# Chapter 73

# THE CAPUANOS ARE DEAD

J oe arrived at Bernice's at 7:14 p.m. He was ready for a
Dewar's, for sure, and to have her naked body lying on his
hairy chest.

"Hi, Joe, I missed you!" She flung her arms around his neck and pulled
herself up, wrapping her legs around his waist. She planted a kiss on him
that would have made a sailor blush. She wore nothing but a kimono
hitched up above her waist. Her body radiated warmth; a scent and
softness that made Joe's heart throb almost as much as another part of
his body.

The scotch would have to wait. She shed her kimono. They
reached the dimly-lit bedroom. Joe gently laid her down. Her silky, clean
body lay ready. Joe teased her. He did a slow strip. She cried for him. He
made her wait. He slowly entered her. She moaned, then screamed and
Joe's nightmares faded away.

The next evening, after an hour of love making, Bernice and Joe
sat at the kitchen table discussing New Zealand. The time on the clock
read 7:45. The dogs rested on the kitchen floor. Bernice's phone rang. Joe
jumped. Bernice rose slowly, with eyes focused on Joe.

"Hello."

"Bernice, Bernice, is Joe there?"

"Ah, yes, Doctor Knowles." Her eyes widened.

"I need to talk with him, Bernice."

"Okay, just a minute." She put her hand on Joe's arm. "It's
Doctor Knowles."

"Hello, Doc."

"Joe, Joe, somebody took out the Capuanos. They are all dead.
They were in 'Marco's.' Al—Al just called me."

"Are you sure they got them all?"

"Yes, Al tried to call you and when you didn't answer, he called
me." Doc said, out of breath.

"It's all over the news in Chicago."

"Who did it?

"Al wasn't sure. He said it might be people from New Orleans. It will be on the ten o'clock news tonight."

"Why don't you come over to Bernice's before the news and we can watch it together."

"Okay, I'll see you then. God, Joe, I'm so glad it's over."

"Me, too, Doc. We need to celebrate."

"I'll be there before ten."

"See you later."

# THE REVENGE

# Chapter 74

# ALEX

J oe, Doc and Bernice gathered in Bernice's front room at 9:48 for the ten o'clock news. "Today, at approximately 8:28 a.m., it is believed that as many as eight men walked into Marco's Night Club on Rush Street in Chicago and killed nine people. The confirmed dead are Marco Capuano, owner of Marco's Restaurant and Night Club, Eddie Capuano, nephew of Marco, Jimmy Capuano, youngest son of Marco. The other six men have not yet been identified. Three of the unidentified are possible FBI agents. This has not yet been confirmed. Alex Capuano, the lone survivor of the Capuano family, was not at the night club during the massacre. The police originally thought Alex was among the deceased, but later confirmed he was not. Marco Capuano was known for his large donations to charities throughout the Chicago area. Marco was believed to be associated with organized crime in the city, but that was never proven. Alex Capuano was not available for comment." Joe's eyes pierced a hole through the television.

"The police have no suspects at this time. It is, however, thought that another group, possibly a mafia gang, was responsible for the deaths. The police also felt that some of the men responsible for the deaths had been in Capuano's organization. We will have more on this bizarre crime tomorrow at 6:00 a.m."

Joe's face turned grim as he continued to stare at the television. Doc said, "Joe, you were right. This calls for a celebration."

Joe raged—"Bullshit! I'm calling Jimmy. We are going after that scumbag." Again, his head throbbed like a jack hammer. He bolted for the phone.

Bernice looked up at Joe and gave a quick nod. "I'm going too, Joe. You're not doing this with just Jimmy. I'll go change my clothes."

Her demeanor assured Joe she was capable. He nodded with no expression as she headed for the bedroom.

Jimmy answered the phone on the sixth ring, "Hello!"

"Jimmy, did you hear the ten o'clock news?"

"No—ah-no, I was in bed with Maggie. What's—what did the news say?"

"Some guys went into "Marco's" on Rush and killed nine of the people. They didn't get Alex. He was probably raping some young girl at the Osage. I want him, Jimmy, and I want you to help me. I'll be up at your place in two, possibly three, hours."

"I'll be ready. We will get that SOB and make him squeal like a stuck hog. Where do we go first?" Jimmy's voice rose with every word.

"We'll go to Osage first and, if he isn't there, then we'll go to his home and squeeze it out of his wife."

"Ok, Joe! Do you want me to get some help?"

"No, Bernice is coming. She has a black belt."

"Damn! I'll get some sleep for an hour or so. You pound on the door when you get here. I've been up since five this mornin'."

"See you, Jimmy. You have a couple of guns?"

"Oh, yeah, I got guns."

Doc was not nearly as happy as he had been when he had first heard the news about the slaying of the Capuanos. Joe continued his rant. "That filthy, rotten no good son-of-a-bitch will die a slow death. There is no doubt in my mind that he is at the Osage Hotel." His eyes narrowed and his chest swelled on every breath.

"I'll call Al Falcono and see if he can locate Alex." Joe dialed Al's number as Bernice entered the room. She wore tennis shoes, bobby socks, navy pedal pushers and a loose-fitting, white pullover. She showed no fear. "Hello, Al!"

"Yeah, who's this?"

"Who did it?"

"Joe, I'm not sure, but the little rat is still alive."

"Do you know where he is?" Joe wanted an answer now.

"No! I think he might have driven out of Chicago. I didn't check the Osage Hotel, though. I guess I should have, but Alex always goes home on Fridays for the weekend."

"I think he is still there. Did anyone check his home?"

"Yeah, Benedetti checked it out and is still waiting there. No sign of him. I'm staying home, so I can stay in contact with them. My cousin, Vince, will be here shortly. Then, I'm going back out to try and find the rat. I want him worse than you Joe, if it takes me the rest of my life. What about the railroads, airports, bus stations?"

Joe was livid. This guy was now on the run, but where?

"The FBI is supposed to be on top of that," Joe replied. Al laughed. "Hey, does the FBI know who did it?"

"Nah, they think it was some other mafia group."

"I'm goin' to the Osage. Where can I reach you?"

"I'll call the Osage at 2:00 a.m." Joe looked at his watch—it was 10:35 p.m.

"I'll be there."

"If you find the bastard, make sure I get to see him before he dies"

"No problem, the same for me."

"Ok!"

Joe hung up the phone and Bernice hugged him. Doc paced the floor. "We've got to go." Joe stood at the door with Brownie beside him.

"You two be careful. You too, Brownie. I hope you get him before he leaves town," Doc said, as beads of sweat appeared on his forehead.

"Thanks, Doc, we'll call you when we get him."

"Doctor Knowles, will you take care of Blackie?" Bernice asked.

"Sure!"

Chapter 75

# CHICAGO

Joe, Brownie and Bernice left and brought along the hickory bat, the Bowie knife, and the 12-gauge shotgun and a box of 00 buckshot shells.

They took Highway 20 into Chicago from Rockford. Joe drove only five miles over the speed limit. He didn't want to get stopped for speeding.

The F-100 pulled up in front of Jimmy's house at 1:08 a.m. Joe walked up to the porch and pounded on the door. The door rattled. Within a minute, Jimmy appeared at the door with three other Negro guys standing behind him. The other three were damn near as big as Jimmy. "Meet Mo, Lester and Sammy. They want to help. If you don't want 'em, just let me know. This is your show. These guys will kill for starin' at 'em wrong."

"Yeah, we'll take them, but they'll have to ride in the back of the truck."

"They know. They been ridin' in the back since they were born." Joe felt terrible for saying that.

Jimmy and his three buddies got in the back and Joe sped off, hoping he could find the Osage Hotel on Randolph. As Joe drove down Michigan Avenue, a cop pulled out from an alley and followed them for several blocks. Joe racked his brains trying to think of what he would say if they got stopped. They all had weapons on them. Joe's heart beat like a drum.

They turned the corner at Randolph with the cop car right on their bumper. Joe was getting pissed. "These assholes are probably on the take from the Capuanos."

Bernice spun her pretty head toward Joe. "Just keep on going, Joe. You haven't done anything wrong."

Joe drove in silence, his knuckles white from gripping the steering wheel. He kept a steady speed and drove up to the Osage Hotel, stopping in the hotel parking garage. He parked in the first open spot that would accommodate his F-100. The four guys climbed out of the back of the truck. Brownie followed behind Joe. Joe introduced Bernice to Jimmy and his three friends.

"Those cops are still out there. What do we do, Joe?" Jimmy asked.

Joe thought, took a deep breath and blew it out slowly. "I'll go inside with Bernice and Brownie and check things out."

Joe, Bernice and Brownie entered the lobby. No one said anything about Brownie not being on a leash. Joe looked outside as the cops sped away from the curb with their lights flashing. His heart slowed. Joe returned to the F-100, leaving Bernice and Brownie in the lobby.

He retrieved his weapons, placed them in a leather bag and reentered the lobby with Jimmy and his friends. Joe approached the night desk clerk. The clerk looked young, was skinny, and had thin fingers and a sweet smile—too sweet. "You know if Alex Capuano is in room 1107?"

He turned, without saying a word, and answered as he turned back, "Yes, sir! He hasn't notified us that he has left. He has been here a long time, though." Joe felt awkward talking to this guy.

"Is there another exit from his room other than down these stairs or down the elevator?"

"No, sir!"

"What about fire escapes?"

"We have a sprinkler system."

"Do you know if anyone else has inquired about room 1107 other than me?"

"No, sir, at least not since I've been on duty."

"When did you come on duty?"

"Midnight."

"Does he have anyone in his room?"

"I don't show," looking at the register, "that he does."

"Do you know Alex Capuano?" Joe felt like Jack Webb in *Dragnet*.

"Yes, sir, he is here almost every time I work."

"Have you seen him today?"

"No, sir."

"Did you see him yesterday?"

"I didn't work yesterday." The clerk began to fidget, his voice sounding scared. His silky, white hands looked moist.

"If he has a visitor come to see him, does she or he come to the desk first, or just go up to his room?"

"They just go up. He has one or two men outside his door. They won't let anyone in, until Mr. Capuano wants them in."

"What does his room look like inside?"

"It's real nice." His eyes lit up. "It has a very large bathroom, with a big shower and a sunken tub. The bed is so delightful. It is huge. I would just die for a bed like that. It has these silk sheets. Oh! To lay—"

"How many damn rooms?"

"It has a large bedroom and bath and, let me think, yes, it has another room with a, oh yes, a sensual fireplace."

"Are there men outside his door now?"

"I'm not sure."

Joe walked away from the desk clerk and instructed Jimmy and Bernice, "You two keep an eye on that fairy over there. If he picks up the phone, you stop him. I don't want him calling Alex."

"No problem, Joe!"

"Joe, I'm scared!" Bernice said, her hand on his arm.

"Jimmy won't let anyone hurt you."

"I'm scared for you."

"Don't worry about me. Besides, I'm taking these three guys with me and Brownie won't let anyone hurt me." Joe kissed her dry lips and smiled quickly.

Joe, Brownie and the three Negroes started up the stairs. Joe turned and directed Jimmy, "Watch the elevator. Stop anyone getting off or on."

"Got it, Joe," Jimmy responded, with a big grin on his face.

Joe handed the gun case to Bernice. He had the Bowie knife stuck in the front of his jeans and the hickory bat in his left hand. The 12 gauge, loaded with six shells, hung loosely in his right hand.

They continued their journey up the eleven flights of stairs. When they emerged on the eleventh floor, Joe checked the hall to his left. He saw no one standing or sitting outside any door. He looked down the other hallway, and there he spotted two men. They sat about halfway down the hall. They were leaning back, with their heads pressed against the wall. He assumed they were guarding Room 1107.

Joe had to decide how he would handle this. He checked his watch. It was already 1:55 a.m. Al was supposed to call at 2:00. He pondered for a few seconds. "Sammy, you go down and tell Jimmy that I'm expecting a phone call at 2:00 and for him to take the message. You get the message from Jimmy and come back up here. Take the elevator." Sammy nodded.

Sammy left and Joe, Brownie and Lester approached the two men, who appeared to be asleep. Mo stayed behind to keep an eye on the stairs and the elevator.

They were within five feet of the two men, when one of the men sat up. He appeared to be Mexican, wasn't very big, but had the looks of someone who could kill and then laugh about it.

"Good morning!" Joe said, just loud enough for them to hear.

The man reached inside his sport coat, but Brownie grabbed his arm before he even touched his weapon. The bones in the man's arm crunched. Brownie let go and clamped down on the man's privates. Joe used the bat to make sure the noise of the man's cry got snuffed out immediately. The commotion caused the other man to wake up. Lester grabbed him by his shoulders and kneed him in the groin. He began to scream in agony. Joe let the bat drop on his skull with a thud. The man collapsed in a heap on the carpeted floor.

Sammy returned and was on his way down the hall when Joe spotted him. "What's the message?" Joe asked, hoping that Al had figured out Alex Capuano was still here.

"Said he'd be over as soon as he could."

"Thanks, Sammy, you come with me."

234

# Chapter 76

# ALEX IS FOUND

Joe stood back about four feet from the door and whispered, "I'm going to bust this door down. I want you two guys to stand right here and watch. If we are not out in a few minutes, Sammy, you come in. Lester, you stay out here." They both nodded. "If anyone resembling an Italian comes out this door, kill him." They looked at each other with a half-grin.

Joe pumped the 12-gauge to inject a 00 buckshot shell into the chamber. He left the hickory stick with Lester. Joe raised his size fourteen shoe up to a level that would impact the door at mid-way. He slammed his foot against the thick, wooden, oak door. A second later the door sprang open: Two men stood next to one another with machine guns pointed at Joe. They were not more than ten feet from him. Both men were overweight and looked to be in their forties. Joe stared back at them. They looked scared out of their wits. Joe remained as cool as ice. He pulled the trigger and re-pumped the 12 gauge, taking a split second to inject another shell in the chamber. He pulled the trigger again and the two men were riddled into several pieces. Blood splattered everywhere. The noise sounded like a cannon going off in a drum. Brownie crawled all over the bloody, fat men lying on the floor. Joe's heart started to race.

Joe walked into the bedroom. Kneeling on the bed, trying to scream, sat a naked Oriental girl. Her mouth gaped open, but no sound escaped. She looked to be no more than ten, thought Joe. He hoped she was at least sixteen. Her shoulders rose and fell with every breath. Joe approached her and noticed that there was someone else in the room. A man's silk bathrobe rested at the foot of the bed and a pair of slippers sat beside the bed. Joe glanced in every direction, but didn't see or hear anyone or anything. The perfume smell clouded Joe's nostrils. Sammy looked like he had seen a ghost.

Brownie sniffed at the closed door to the large bathroom. He started to paw at it and started barking. Joe knew he had his man in the bathroom. He knew the time had come for him to see the man who had killed Sue. He needed to calm himself. *"Get calm, Joe!"* Heart pounding, he took several deep breaths.

"Open the damn door." Joe's envisioned Sue with her gentle smile.

The silence lasted only seconds. Joe heard the young Oriental girl trying to weep. He raised his large foot and slammed it into the bathroom door. It flew off its hinges.

Joe saw no one, anywhere. He walked closer to the doorway and thought he saw a shadow behind the shower curtain. Sammy followed Joe, when Joe yelled, "You pissing yourself, Alex Capuano?"

No words came from behind the shower curtain. Brownie wanted to get at the man behind the curtain, but stood his ground until Joe ordered him to attack.

"You're goin' to die. You want to die now, or do you want to drag it out?"

Still no movement, then a whisper-like cry could be heard from behind the shower curtain. Joe thought it sounded like a young girl. He took the barrel of the 12-gauge and slid the curtain back, quickly. There stood another young Oriental girl, stark naked and shaking like a leaf, with arms folded across her small breasts. She looked like the other girl. *"Too damn young,"* thought Joe. "You son-of-a-bitch." A flash of Sue came into focus again. Joe screamed, "Where the hell is Alex?" He had the barrel of the 12-gauge pointed towards the Oriental's throat. He wanted Alex now. He'd waited long enough.

She pointed up with her little index finger; her whole hand shook. Not a sound came out of her open mouth. Her lips trembled. There was dry blood on her legs. Joe looked up and saw a trap door in the ceiling. Room 1107 sat on the top floor of the Osage Hotel. He motioned for the girl to get out of the bathroom and for Sammy to stand back by the doorway to the bedroom. Joe took the barrel of the 12-gauge and poked the loose trap door. "Hey, rapist, you coming down or do you want me to shoot your ass out of your hiding place, you bucket of hog slop."

No response. Joe watched as the trap door became discolored. The spot seemed to be growing. "You have three seconds to open that trap door and show your face, or I'll blow your ass out of there with this 12-gauge shotgun." He had two more 00 shells in the shotgun and half a dozen in his coat pocket.

Joe started to count, and by the time he got to two, a voice quivered, "I-I-I-will-pay you a-million dollars to let m-me go."

"No way, Alex."

Seconds later, the door opened and Alex, naked as a skinless rat, shimmied himself through the small opening. Only a weasel like him could squeeze through that hole. Joe's heart skipped a few beats as Alex's feet touched the floor. Oh, how he wanted revenge. He shook his head. *"No! No! Al will kill him."*

"Sammy, you have Mo get Jimmy and Bernice. Have Lester stay by the door. Take these girls out of here. Make sure they get dressed. Have Mo stay downstairs and keep a look out for anyone who moves."

Sammy left. Alex stood on the marble floor of the bathroom in his bare feet. Brownie waited with foam dripping from his mouth. He sat only inches away from Alex's privates. "So, you're Alex Capuano." Joe's body felt numb. He tried to keep from shaking.

"I don't know who you are. I will pay you two million dollars, cash, if you let me go. We have that much money in the safe over at the club." Alex stood around five foot nine and weighed about one hundred sixty pounds. He was a good-looking guy, if you could forget who he was. His eyes darted about as if looking for a way to escape.

"I'm Joe Clark."

Alex's eyes winced. His body slumped.

"You're the country boy. Amato was supposed to have killed you." His brown eyes became wet as he placed his left hand over his privates. "I will get you six million dollars, tonight" Alex said, nervously.

"Gee, Alex, I thought you only had two million. How many safes do you have?"

"We have lots of money. I will pay whatever you want. Please! I have a family."

"You should have thought about that the night you drove your damn car into my car and killed my girlfriend." Joe's voice grew louder with each word. He placed the barrel of the 12-gauge against Alex's hairy chest, punching the barrel several times, knocking Alex backward into the tub. He should just blow his ass away.

"I'm sorry! I was drunk that night. I didn't want to kill anyone."

"Tell HER that, Alex. You tell her that. Get on your knees, bow your head and you tell her you're sorry." Joe's voice grew into a scream.

The air in the room became hard for Joe to inhale. He gasped several times. Tears ran down Joe's cheeks. He quickly wiped them away.

Alex got on his knees, bowed his head and said, "I'm sorry. I'm sorry I killed you. I wish—I wish I could return to that night and not cause your death." Alex bawled as he tried to speak. "Oh, God!"

Bernice and Jimmy appeared at the bathroom door. Jimmy asked, "Is this the SOB who rapes little girls, then kills them if they don't do what he wants?"

Alex looked up at Jimmy. "Who are you?"

"Jimmy Robbins. My fiancée's sister is one of your hookers. You had some of your people kick the shit out of me several months ago. It's goin' to be a real pleasure to watch you die." Alex looked at Jimmy, thinking he could be bought.

"Jimmy, I'll pay you ten thousand dollars if you let me go." Joe busted Alex's skull with the butt of the 12-gauge. Bernice winced. Alex collapsed on the marble floor, blood trickling from the blow. His curled, naked body lay motionless.

"Why did you do that, Joe? I wanted that ten thousand."

"He offered me six million. I didn't think it was quite right, him only giving you ten thousand."

Jimmy kicked him in his privates. "That's payback for my missing teeth, treating my sister like a prisoner and using young girls as prostitutes." Disgust and hatred showed all over Jimmy's face.

"Alex is gonna hurt when he wakes up," Jimmy snarled. Bernice gasped and turned her head. Joe watched Bernice and realized he shouldn't have let her come up. Joe's heart started to calm. The rage in his head began to leave.

"We need to keep this guy alive long enough to go to Marco's club and get some cash. We can help a lot of these girls with six million," Joe said, as his heart rate returned to normal.

"Six million dollars. Wow, that's a lot of dough," Jimmy exclaimed.

"Jimmy, you wait here until Alex wakes up. Have him get dressed and meet us down in the lobby. I'll have Lester stand guard at the door."

Jimmy, hands on his hips, shook his head. Smiling, he asked, "What do you want me to dress him up in?"

"Let him dress in whatever. When we walk out of here, we want it to look like nothing is wrong."

"What do we do with these bodies and all these innards that are splattered around the room?" Jimmy snorted, looking at the gross, bloody bodies of the two men sprawled out all over the floor.

"Al Falcono will get somebody up here to clean this place up. He'll take care of the bodies. They'll have to paint, put new carpet down and get some new furniture."

Joe, Brownie and Bernice left for the lobby. Upon exiting the elevator in the lobby, they spotted Al talking to Mo and Sammy. They had a gun pulled on Al, who didn't look too happy, to say the least. Mo said to Joe, "This here guy says he is a friend of yours."

"Hi, Al. That's Al. He's on our side."

"What! Who are these guys anyway?" Al asked.

"They're friends of mine. We have Alex upstairs. There are two dead and two unconscious. We need to get new carpet, new paint, and some new furniture for room 1107. Can you get someone on it and have it finished by noon? If the FBI comes snooping around here, I don't want them seeing the place all bloody."

"Did you kill the bastard?"

"No, Al! He's unconscious. We are going to take him over to Marco's. He offered us the money they have in their safe."

"Wow! That has to be a big pile of money, probably a couple million." Al's eyes grew bigger.

Joe never responded to Al, but repeated, "We need to get that place cleaned up."

"I'll get right on it. Don't you worry about a thing, Joe. I just want Alex to myself."

"You got it, Al!" Joe had had enough. He got his man; now, let someone else handle him. Joe shrugged, unloading several pounds off his shoulders. His day had come. The Capuanos were finished. Bernice stood next to him, showing no emotion. The desk clerk sat doing paperwork, not paying any attention to anyone.

Joe could hear Al on the pay phone telling someone what needed to be done in room 1107. He used every swear word he could come up with; cigarette smoke exited his nostrils as he talked. Finally, he put the phone down and walked over. "It will be all done by noon, today. The bodies will be disposed of. The FBI won't be able to figure out anything here. Where is this bastard anyway?"

Joe nodded toward the stairs.

Jimmy had Alex's arm in a vise grip as he led him down the stairs; the grimace on Alex's face plainly visible.

Al spotted Alex and pulled his gun out. Joe knocked the gun to the floor. "No, Al, you have to wait," Joe screamed at him. Al glared at Joe as if he wanted to kill him for stopping him, but said nothing. Bernice, the black belt, prepared herself.

Seeing the gun Alex hollered, "Al, shoot the bastards." Jimmy landed his right fist up the side of Alex's head. Alex collapsed. Jimmy dragged his carcass down the remaining stairs.

"Alex! You the one that's goin to get his ass shot," Al said, as Joe picked up Al's gun off the floor.

"Let's get him out of here," Joe said, moving toward the parking garage. "Jimmy, you take Alex in his car. Take Mo and Sammy with you. I'll take Brownie and Bernice. Al, you go up and get Lester and make sure those men upstairs in the hallway are kept quiet. You decide what you want to do with them. Make sure that guy behind the desk over there doesn't remember anything that happened tonight."

Al just smiled. "We'll meet you over at the club. Just don't kill that SOB. I still want him." His tone revealed his anger.

Joe gave a quick grin. "No problem, Al!"

# Chapter 77

# MARCO'S CLUB

Alex was conscious, but a little woozy from the two wallops to his head, when they arrived at Marco's. He unlocked the door to the club and flipped on the lights. They proceeded slowly up a long flight of carpeted steps. The offices for the largest organized crime operation were about to be revealed.

"Sammy, you and Mo stay out here and make sure no one comes in or out, except Lester and Al," Joe instructed.

The offices were huge and had the same cherry wood and plush carpet they saw in the main lobby. Paintings and other art pieces hung on the walls throughout. Marco's office held the wall safe. Alex went directly to the safe, spun the combination lock to the proper positions and opened the safe.

"Okay, step back, Alex," Joe ordered, as he put his hand inside the large wall safe. Joe grabbed bags of cash. He grabbed everything in the safe, handing it back to Jimmy, who placed it on a large table in Marco's office. There were ten bags and two smaller bags of what felt like marbles.

They dumped the money on the table. Joe, Bernice, and Jimmy could hardly believe their eyes. There were thousands of hundred dollar bills. "How much is here, Alex?" Jimmy asked.

"Count it, nigger. I open..."

"I asked you a question." Jimmy clamped his large hand around Alex's neck. No one uttered a sound.

Alex gasped for air. Jimmy let up on the pressure. "Twelve million dollars," Alex managed to mumble.

"Why so much money?" Joe spoke quickly.

"It was supposed to be for the feds that had helped us with a special deal. Marco was to pay them cash. The two bags of diamonds are for them, too. They have a street value of three million." Bernice looked at the diamonds with very nervous eyes.

"Where is the rest of the money the organization has?" Joe asked.

"Fuck you!"

Joe commanded, "Brownie."

Brownie, like lightning, leapt with front feet striking Alex's chest, knocking him to the floor. "Don't let him move, Brownie."

"The money, Alex, or I will give the word to my buddy and your balls will be in his mouth."

Alex stared into Brownie's large mouth. "We have approximately forty-five million in three different banks," Alex replied, as Brownie's saliva painted his face, waiting for Joe's command.

Joe dreamt about it, laid awake many nights thinking about it. The time had come.

"That is some dog you have there," Jimmy remarked.

"Yeah, what banks, Alex?" Joe's heart began picking up speed. Joe wanted to give back to the ones who had suffered from the Capuanos' organization. Alex hesitated. He wiped the saliva off his face. "Now," Joe was raging again.

"The World Bank in Geneva, Switzerland, the Summit Bank in the Cayman Islands, and the Trade Bank in Paris, France, and you can't touch it. The only way to get the money out of those banks is for my Dad, my brother, or me to be there, personally. The fingerprints have to match."

"Great! It looks like we are going to Switzerland, France, and the Cayman's. We want that money," Joe said, thinking of the young prostitutes and car thieves and the ghetto—the ghetto where Jimmy lived.

"Why? Twelve million is not enough?"

"No, it's for the girls that worked for you, Alex. The ones you raped and held prisoner." Joe wanted more, more revenge. He could get it by giving the Capuanos' money to those in need. "The young girls and boys you had stealing cars for your rotten organization. One of them is Jimmy's sister. They deserve it, Alex. I'm goin' to see that they get it all. Every damn nickel of it."

Al came in the room with Lester and spotted the money on the table.

"Holy shit! That's a lot of cash. Why so much cash laying around?" Al looked down at Alex lying on the floor and said in a raised voice, "You didn't kill that SOB did you?" Al lit a cigarette.

"He'll live. There is forty five million in three banks that we want to get before he dies."

"What? I don't give a shit about that. I want this bastard dead. You could never spend that much money, Joe." Al pointed to the table that held the cash and diamonds.

"Yeah, I can. It will go towards the education of the kids in the ghetto." Joe pondered for a few seconds. He looked at Al. "We need Alex to get the money. His fingerprints have to match the prints at the three banks." Jimmy's head spun toward Joe. His heart stood still, then pounded hard. A large grin appeared. "Wow! That would be great, Joe."

Joe put his large hand on Jimmy's shoulder. "They deserve a break, Jimmy." Joe's throat inherited a lump.

Jimmy just nodded.

"Alex, we need a list of all your employees, including the ones that helped you run your corrupt businesses." Joe searched the desk drawers as he spoke.

"They are in that file cabinet over there. Everyone that is associated with the organization is in there," Alex answered. "Please let my wife and children have a million dollars of the money."

Joe stared at Alex before he spoke. He remembered the question that was asked of the FBI at Fredrick's. *"What about Alex's children?"* "We'll set it up for your kids' education; then, we'll see how they behave to determine whether they get anymore."

"What about my wife?" Alex pleaded.

"Should have thought about her years ago, Alex." Alex's eyes closed.

Al's face dropped. The smoke rolled from his nose. "You're something else, Joe. One minute you want to kill people; the next minute you're saving their asses." Joe frowned at Al's comment, but said nothing. He knew what he wanted. Joe was ready to start saving people, instead of letting them die. "I take away. Now, I have to give back."

# Chapter 78

# 3:40 A.M.

E veryone, including Joe, was exhausted. Joe suggested, "Let's all get a hotel room and get some sleep. Al, you go home and get some sleep and pack your bags. When you get up, go to the airport and get us tickets to Paris and Geneva. Who wants to go?" Everyone raised their hands.

"Get ten tickets." Joe handed Al ten thousand dollars. "Bring back the tickets and the left-over cash." Joe figured Doc and Jerry deserved to go. He'd call them later.

"Ok, Joe. Where are you goin' to be staying?"

"We'll get rooms at the Congress Hotel. I saw it on the way over here."

"I'll call you when I get the tickets."

"Great!" Joe felt as hungry as a bear that had just come out of hibernation. "Al, where can we get something to eat?"

"The Congress has an all-night grill."

"Thanks, Al."

Joe spotted three new golf bags sitting in the corner of Marco's office and decided to use the bags for the money. Bernice carried the bags of diamonds clutched to her chest.

"Let's go get some food and some sleep. Jimmy, you take Sammy, Mo, Lester, and Alex to the Congress Hotel. We'll meet you there."

They placed the golf bags in the trunk of Alex's Cadillac. Bernice continued to hold onto the bags of diamonds. Bernice, Brownie and Joe jumped in the F-100 and sped away. The others followed in the Cadillac.

Joe went to the desk clerk on duty and requested three rooms. "We need one for me, Brownie and Bernice, one for Sammy and Lester, and one for Alex, Jimmy and Mo." The clerk seemed a little reluctant to let them have the rooms.

"I'm sorry, sir, but we don't allow dogs."

Joe offered the clerk an extra hundred dollars and he handed Joe the keys.

# Chapter 79

# TICKETS

The phone rang at 9 a.m. as Joe stood watch over Alex. Joe answered it on the second ring. It was Al.

"Good morning! I got ten tickets for Paris. The plane leaves tonight at 7:00 p.m. Brownie has to go into the lower deck. They charged me for him, too."

Joe hoped Brownie liked flying. "Great, Al! We need to put this money in a bank. Are there any banks close-by that we could put this cash in?"

"You need to put the dough into a lockbox at the bank until things cool down. The banks don't care what you put in a lock box. Get a few boxes in a couple of banks. They give you a key and you can get it out at anytime."

"Great, Al! That's what we'll do."

Mo relieved Joe at 9:10 a.m. Joe returned to his room and got Brownie, who needed to be walked.

They got back to the room to find Bernice still asleep. She looked contented, relaxed. Her breathing was soft. Joe wanted to kiss her, but didn't want to disturb her. He new she needed her rest. Joe felt like a zombie, himself. It had been many hours since he'd had any sleep. His eyes felt like sandpaper, but he figured he could sleep on the plane. He left a note for her. Joe called Jimmy's room and told him they needed to get to the bank. Jimmy showed up a few seconds later. The two of them carried the two bags of diamonds and the three golf bags out of the hotel.

They put the money and the diamonds in three banks: The First National Bank, The First State Bank, and The Commerce Bank. Joe and Jimmy each received a key to the lockboxes. Joe retained $10,000 for travel expenses.

Jimmy, Jimmy's fiancée Maggie, Jerry Moore, Lester, Mo, Sammy, Al, Joe, and Bernice received their tickets. Joe kept Alex's ticket.

Joe gave $500.00 to each person to spend on clothes for the trip. They all went shopping at Marshall Fields on State Street.

Joe dismantled his shotgun and put it into his luggage, along with the Bowie knife and hickory bat. He packed the 38 revolver and all the shells in the bag, as well. Joe told everyone else to do the same. He called Doc and informed him of their plans. Doc couldn't go.

# Chapter 80

# PLANE RIDE

Joe hugged his dog and kissed him on the top of his head. Brownie licked Joe's face. They led him away with his new collar and leash that Joe had bought at the pet store a block from Field's.

The airport buzzed with travelers. The ten heading to Paris felt nervous, except Jerry, who had flown many times. Joe's legs felt numb from being so tired.

Jerry laid eyes on Alex for the first time. He never spoke to Alex, just stared at him and wondered how he could rape and kill all those girls. Alex hung his head. They headed to the Pan American Airlines concourse.

The plane taxied down the runway. Everyone's knuckles turned white from gripping their arm rests. Joe whispered in Bernice's ear, "I love you." She kissed him softly on his dry lips.

The plane, a four-engine propeller type, lifted off and they were airborne for Paris. Jimmy managed to blurt out, "I never thought I'd get this high up. No, not ever." The flight would take eight hours and fifteen minutes. Once they reached cruising altitude, the stewardesses started serving the first-class passengers free drinks.

Joe woke up at 4:00 a.m. to a crying baby who needed his diaper changed. He got up from his cramped seat, stretched, and checked on Alex, who was passed out as if he were drugged. Everyone else slept, except Mo, who kept watch on Alex, while reading *The Post* magazine. Joe tapped Mo on the shoulder and asked, "Do you want me to relieve you?"

"Nah, I can't sleep on this plane. Catch you later."

"I'll check on you later."

"Ok!" Mo grinned.

Joe headed to the toilet to get rid of some of the scotch. So far so good, he thought.

Joe returned to his seat and listened to Bernice breathing quietly. He reached for her hand, held it in his, and shut his eyes. *"I wonder if she will snore when she gets older. I hope not. My Mom snores like a cow elk in heat,"* Joe thought to himself. *"I guess I better call Mom. I ought to call her from Paris. She will know the Capuanos are all dead soon. I don't even remember the last time I called her. I'll call when I get back home."* Joe tried to sleep, but thoughts kept bubbling to the surface. Bernice rested her head on his shoulder. He wondered how Brownie was doing.

They were scheduled to arrive in Paris at 9:15 a.m. local time. They would head directly to the Trade Bank of France, which was on the Champs-Elysees near the Louvre. Some kind of museum, he guessed. They should be able to find a hotel near the bank. Hopefully, the French won't give them any trouble.

The plane began its descent. Joe had managed to doze off for a few hours before breakfast. The smell of egg omelets awakened him.

# Chapter 81

# PARIS EXCHANGE

They picked up their luggage and headed for taxis. They occupied three taxis and rode to the Trade Bank of France the same way they had ridden to the airport in Chicago.

Jerry, Jimmy, Alex and Joe entered the bank. Joe was nervous, but no one would have ever known it. Joe instructed Jerry to do the talking. He looked more believable than Joe or Jimmy. "You cooperate, you little weasel, or you will die before you walk out of here," Joe threatened, hating that he and Alex still shared the same air.

Jerry approached a very sensuous, young, French girl, named Monica. She appeared to be in her early twenties and wore a low cut, tight fitting dress that showed almost all of her legs, as well as her breasts. She had a cute smile.

"We need to change ownership on a savings account." Jerry smiled as he spoke.

"We can help you with that. I will get someone who can speak English who will handle that for you." She left with all eyes on her—especially Alex's.

"My name is Claudette. May I help you in changing ownership of your savings account?"

"Yes, if at all possible, we would like to do that this morning," Jerry replied.

They walked over to a room, which housed a long table and several chairs. She instructed them to have a seat and she would get the proper paperwork to complete.

Joe said, "I would like this money transferred to the Jimmy Robbins Fund." He looked at Jimmy. "I want two signatures on this. Jerry, I would like for you and Jimmy to be on it." Joe knew he wouldn't be around since he would be going to New Zealand.

Jerry asked after she had walked away, "What are we going to do with all this money?" Jimmy couldn't believe his name was going to be on such a large sum of money. His eyes filled with tears.

"I'm not sure yet, Jerry, but we'll come up with something. It will be used to help the ones that were held against their will by the Capuanos. Perhaps, the rest can be used to help the people in Jimmy's neighborhood."

Claudette came back and sat down. With a warm smile, she asked "Whose name is the account in now?"

Silence covered the room.

Joe, who sat next to Alex, elbowed him in the ribs. A gasp of air escaped from Alex's mouth.

"I'm Alex Capuano and I would like to transfer the money in our account to the..." "Jimmy Robbins Account," Jerry finished the sentence. He winked at Jimmy.

Alex continued, "Yes, that's it. My family is all deceased and no one is able to sign this, except me."

"Ok, and who will sign the new account?"

"I will and Jimmy Robbins, who is right here," Jerry answered. Jimmy smiled from ear to ear just thinking about being part of this Fund and helping the kids in his neighborhood. They could build ball fields, parks, basketball courts and, oh yeah, a theater. Jimmy hadn't seen a movie since living at Sheridan.

"I will have to pull up the Ca-how do you spell that, please?"

"CAPUANO" Joe had it memorized from the first time he had read the name in the newspaper.

Alex's fingerprints were verified, the paperwork processed and the money transferred to the Jimmy Robbins Fund. The amount totaled $8,269,129.96. Jimmy sat in a fog. His legs wobbled as he stood and his eyes continued to water.

Al purchased the airline tickets for Geneva.

The plane would leave at 8:48 the next morning.

Joe and Bernice stayed with Alex for several hours while the three Chicago studs, Mo, Lester and Sammy, visited some French clubs with the leftover clothing money. They returned to the room, their butts dragging, but with smiles on their faces. Joe asked, grinning, "can one of you stay awake long enough to watch this guy?"

"No problem," Lester responded.

# Chapter 82

# GENEVA EXCHANGE

They landed in Geneva, received their bags and were out the door waiting for three taxis to take them to the World Bank. Brownie wasn't handling the airplane, airports, taxis and all the people very well. They left and had a very pleasant ride to the bank, nothing like the ride in Paris.

Jerry, Jimmy and Joe headed for the bank, while the others waited in a small espresso shop. Dogs were not allowed in the restaurant, so Bernice, Lester and Al took Brownie for a long walk. Sammy and Mo, still recuperating from the night before, stayed in the espresso shop with Maggie.

The females at this bank were not nearly as sexy as they had been in Paris. The three guys just wanted to get this over with.

The paperwork went smoothly. Alex behaved himself. The amount being transferred at this bank totaled $28,457,016.25. Everyone seemed shocked at the huge figure, but didn't let on to the non-cordial man handling the paperwork. No one knew the man's name—he never said and no one asked.

They boarded a TWA plane and headed to New York. Some of them thought they might like to come back someday, especially the girls and Jerry. Joe just wanted to go to New Zealand. Al wanted to get back to his wife and daughter in Chicago. Sammy, Mo and Lester knew, for sure, they would revisit Paris. Jimmy thought about how all this money would help the kids. He remembered having to steal food so his brothers and sister could eat.

They arrived in New York without delay. While on the plane, they voted to return to Chicago for at least a day before they tried to get to the Caymans. Al left to get the tickets for Chicago. It was after 1:00 a.m. and everyone was totally exhausted. The flight was rough; the plane bounced all over the sky. No one had slept a wink. Brownie still was not doing very well at all. Joe figured Brownie had lost ten pounds since leaving Chicago.

"There's nothing tonight, not until 7:00 tomorrow morning. That means we stay in the airport until then, or we get a hotel room," Al reported.

They all agreed to get a hotel room. They grabbed their luggage, got cabs and headed to a Holiday Inn only a few miles away.

Their early TWA flight landed in Chicago twenty minutes late due to bad weather. A series of tornados had been sighted in and around the area. The rain pelted down as they taxied toward their gate.

Everyone retrieved their bags, except Joe. He headed for the animal pickup area. He found Brownie and Joe knew his dog wouldn't want to fly again, unless it was to New Zealand. Brownie appeared to have lost another five pounds.

Joe, while leading Brownie to the baggage area, thought he spotted Mac. *"What the hell is he doing here? And Joan, Joan Amato. I'm sure that was her. The hair, yes the hair. That was her. What the hell?"*

They both disappeared into the crowd. *"Are they together, that bitch? Maybe I'm wrong."* Joe shook his head, bit his lower lip and continued on toward baggage claim.

# Chapter 83

# COMMERCE HOTEL

They arrived at the Commerce Hotel and checked in. Joe had to pay extra again for Brownie. Joe grabbed a paper. The funeral for the Capuanos was to be held that day. Joe read the article, while Bernice headed for the shower. "Alex is dead! Hey, Alex is dead!" Joe went to the bathroom and pulled the shower curtain back and said, "Alex is dead, according to the paper. They are burying his ass today."

Bernice raised her wet brows. "How—who is that man we took to Paris and Geneva?"

"I'm fixin' to find out. It had to be Alex. The fingerprints matched. I'll be back." He raced out the door and headed to Alex's room.

Upon arriving, he called Jimmy immediately. "Jimmy, get your butt down to Alex's room, pronto."

"What's up, Joe?"

"I'll tell you when you get here. Hurry!"

Seconds passed before a loud bang boomed on the door. Sammy flung the door open and, in a flash, Jimmy appeared within three feet of Joe. "Sammy, you and Mo take an hour. Jimmy and I have to talk to Alex."

They left instantly. Alex looked up and shuddered.

"Alex, we want to know where you were the day Marco, Jimmy, and Eddie got iced." Joe stood within inches of Alex's pale face.

Alex sat there and didn't say a word.

"Talk to me you skinny SOB. You have ten seconds, or you're going to hell."

"I-I" Alex tried to catch his breath. "I—was at the—club." Alex gasped.

"Who was the guy that got killed that looked like you?" Joe asked.

"I-I—"

"Spit it out," Jimmy said, placing his large paw around Alex's neck.

"NO!" His expression strained. "He—He was my cousin from Sicily." Tears appeared in his eyes.

"You bastard. You let your cousin take the fall for you?" Joe said.

"No, I went upstairs to my father's office to get the money from the safe. I had just gotten upstairs when the shooting started. My cousin, Anthony Rossini, was just visiting. He was a pianist." Alex wiped the tears from his face. "He played for a big orchestra in Rome."

"So, what did you do then?" Jimmy asked.

"I stayed upstairs for over an hour. I was scared. Nothing like this had ever happened to our family, not in Chicago." Alex took several deep breaths. "Then, I went downstairs and saw that everyone was dead. I called the police and told them there had been a shooting. I changed wallets with Anthony. He was dead and if everyone figured I was dead, then nobody would be looking for me. Shit! I was scared. I figured the mafia from New Orleans was responsible. They hated our organization."

"I'm confused here. How come the ten o'clock news, on the day of the shooting, said that everyone was dead from the Capuano gang, except Alex?" Joe asked.

"The television people had it right that night. The next day the papers had me dead and the television people had me dead. It would've worked, until you saw me at the Osage Hotel."

"So, who told the news people that you were dead?"

"I called a good friend of the family and told him that Alex Capuano had been confirmed dead."

"Who was this guy you told?" Jimmy asked. Alex told the truth, according to Jimmy.

"George Gregory. Please don't get him in trouble." Alex replied, very concerned.

"Why? What's he to you? You're dead," Jimmy said.

"He took a bullet for my father several years ago and my father gave him a lot of money. In return, he was our pigeon. He carried whatever we needed carried. My father never wanted his name disclosed to anyone. That was the arrangement my father and George had."

"So, how did you get over to the Osage Hotel from Marco's?" Joe asked. Joe was getting sick of all these questions, but he needed to know.

"I drove over. When I got to the hotel, Freddy, the desk clerk, must have been in the men's room. I just went upstairs. I have my own key."

"The gay desk clerk that night said you were in your room and had been for a long time," Joe said.

"I was there earlier that day." Alex had a slight grin on his face. "This Oriental babe, Su, was hotter than molten lava rock."

Jimmy and Joe wanted to kill Alex right then. "So, how the hell did you get into the Osage Hotel, get out of the hotel and get back in again without being seen?" Jimmy asked.

"They saw me go in, but no one ever saw me leave or return. I don't think anyone saw us when we left the other night, either."

Jimmy and Joe walked over toward the door and Jimmy confirmed, "The man is telling the truth."

"What about your Cadillac? I don't understand why the cops or the FBI didn't spot your car in the parking garage at the Osage."

"My car was in the shop. I had a loaner car. I was going to call the shop when I got to the hotel, but I was scared shitless."

"Do you think we need to get any more from him now?" Joe asked.

"Nah, it can wait," Jimmy replied. He rubbed his belly. "I'm hungry," Jimmy said. Joe agreed.

Jimmy, Maggie, Bernice, Joe and Jerry left to grab something to eat, while the others remained at the hotel. They discussed the Jimmy Robbins Fund and how the money would be used. "Jerry, are you interested in running the Jimmy Robbins Fund? I believe with your education and background, along with your years with the paper, you should be able to raise even more money to help these kids," Joe suggested. A flash came over Joe—how he had treated Jerry the first time he had met him.

"I would love to. I believe it is a wonderful way to utilize the money." Moisture gathered in Jerry's blue eyes. "What about printing a story about the Jimmy Robbins Fund and how it got started? People are going to wonder how a Negro boy, or man, from the ghetto got all this money." Jerry knew he had to print the story. It would appear in every paper in the country.

Joe's head spun. Bernice reached for his hand and felt his strong pulse. New Zealand was their hope.

Jerry leaned on the table with forearms taking up the place of his plate. "We need to tell the entire story as it happened—from Joe's car accident to the present day. The public will want to be sure that the money is used properly. Television will go crazy on this story. The big three, CBS, NBC and ABC, will have a field day with the whole thing." Jerry smiled.

"I like the idea, Jerry. I just hope it works. My Grandpa told me once or twice that most people are like a bunch of sheep. They will cower when the fire gets too hot. They will be all hot to trot, until someone sticks a gun in their gut. Then they run and hide. If we can get the Feds on our side, then it will work. But, what if the Feds say, 'hey, we want all that money. It's not yours to keep.' Now, you all know what they will do with it. Send it to some third world country and not a damn dime will go towards the kids in Jimmy's neighborhood." Joe started to get angry. He pushed his chair back from the table and leaned back.

"I've been with the paper for twelve years now and I'm here to tell you if you print a story this big, then every paper will print it. If I continue to print something on this story for several weeks, the public will follow it closer than they would follow a war. This story touches people's hearts: from the farms of the Midwest, to the rich and famous movie stars in California, to the stock brokers in New York, to the poor people in the south." Jerry seemed as excited as a boy going to his first little league game.

"You got my vote!" Jimmy said.

"Mine, too," Joe said, with some hesitation. His lips smashed together. Seeing Mac and Joan at the airport entered his head. *"Should I tell the others? Damn it."*

"Should I mention that Alex is alive or should we keep him in the dead stage for a while longer?" Jerry asked.

"Let's keep him dead. I like him dead, anyway!" Joe said, with a smile.

"Yeah, sounds great to me," Jimmy said.

"I think I'll call Doc and give him the good news," Joe said, as he got up from his chair.

# Chapter 84

# CHICAGO

"Hi, Doc."

"Joe, where are you?"

"We're back in Chicago."

"So, how did it go? The paper reported Alex as being killed."

"Great, we got the money transferred. Alex is alive, but barely."

"So, the paper is wrong?"

"Yeah, it was Alex's cousin."

"So, you got the money transferred. That's great, Joe. I'm really happy it's all over."

"We still have the Cayman Islands."

"Oh, I guess—did you tell me about the Caymans?"

"I might have forgotten. We're going down there in a couple of days."

"What are you going to do with Alex?"

"Al will take care of him."

"Joe, I have to run, I need to be in surgery in fifteen minutes."

"I'll call you when we get back from the Caymans."

"Take care of yourself, Joe."

"Bye, Doc."

Joe got ready to take Brownie for a walk. Bernice, not feeling very well, opted to stay in the room. She assumed a combination of all the air travel, European food and stress had taken its toll. Joe kissed her softly on the forehead. "We'll be back in less than an hour."

She reached for his hand and held it. "Joe, I love you so much. I'm going to lie here and dream about New Zealand."

"I love you, too. I'll be glad when this is all over." He smiled at her, knowing he wouldn't be as strong without her. "It won't be long now." He kissed her again. "Let's go, Brownie."

# Chapter 85

## BERNICE MISSING

J oe opened the door to his room and didn't see Bernice. "Bernice, where are you?" He rushed to the bathroom; the door was open. "Oh, shit." He saw a flash of Joan Amato's hair at the airport. Mac, that son-of-a-bitch. He shook his head, trying to get them out of his mind. He went to the window, flung open the drapes, and looked down twelve stories to the street below.

Joe called Jimmy, but no one answered the phone. He called Jerry at his home, no answer. He called Al at his home; again, no answer. Finally, he called Sammy's room, where Alex was supposed be. Sammy answered, "Hello!" At least someone was near their phone.

"Where's Jimmy?"

"I think he and Maggie went out to get some food."

"How long ago?"

"I don't know, man, maybe an hour ago. What's the matter?"

"Nothing, really. Thanks, anyway." How would he find Bernice? Joe paced the room like a caged tiger that had just come out of the jungle. Joe called Jimmy's room every five minutes, still no answer. Twenty minutes went by, still no answer. One hour went by, still no answer. Joe was going crazy. *Where the hell did she go? Did someone kidnap her? She knows karate. She could handle them. She's a black belt.* Brownie could tell something wasn't right.

Joe called Jimmy's room for the fifteenth time. "Hello!"

"Jimmy! Bernice is gone. I-I think somebody kidnapped her."

"I'll be right there, man!" Jimmy hung up and in a matter of seconds, he appeared in Joe's doorway.

"What happened?" Jimmy asked.

"Jimmy, she's gone."

"It must be somebody that knows about the money. They want her for ransom. They want the money. That means they will have to contact us." Jimmy scratched his head.

Joe never did like waiting. Jimmy helped ease the pain. Joe

watched TV to pass the time, but he couldn't think of anyone or anything except Bernice.

Time passed and Joe finally got hold of Al at home. "Al, somebody has kidnapped Bernice."

"Oh, no! The guys are in town."

"Who's in town?"

"DeMarco's men. I told you they have more connections than the FBI."

"So, what the hell do I do? I can't just sit here and do nothing."

"That's all you can do, Joe. They will contact you for ransom money. Probably not till tomorrow or possibly next week." Joe's heart sank clear to his knees. "They want you to suffer so you'll do as they say. DeMarco has been known to do this before. It's usually organized crime people, though."

"What'll I do, Al?"

"Nothing, just wait. Pray, if you're into that sort of thing."

"Thanks, Al." Joe's knees buckled. He plopped down on the bed, hung his head, picked up a pillow and fired it across the room, smashing a lamp.

"Hey! You got to stay calm. Don't get out of control. We will get her back. We just have to wait. Is there anything I can get you?" Jimmy tried to comfort his friend.

"Yeah, I need a drink."

"No booze, my friend. We have to be alert. We may need to be on a plane in one hour. Booze will mess up your head. Need a clear head." Jimmy had his big arm on Joe's shoulder.

"Right, I know!" His head hammered. "I'll kill them, Jimmy." The rage returned, growing stronger by the minute.

Joe waited three days and no phone call. He began having nightmares. He would wake up in the middle of the night in a cold sweat. Still, he stayed put. Joe wouldn't leave his room, even to walk Brownie. Jimmy took Brownie out three times a day and brought Joe his meals. Joe's eyes went wild with every movement, every sound, every time the door opened.

# Chapter 86

# RANSOM CALL

By the fifth day, Joe could do nothing but sit on his bed and stare at the clock. At 2:37 p.m., the phone rang. Joe grabbed the phone in a panic, knocking it to the floor. He picked up the receiver and said hurriedly "Hello!"

"Joe! This is DeMarco. I have your girlfriend."

"Where the hell are you?"

"Easy, my friend. Hey, man, she's a great lay." Joe's face turned grim. DeMarco spoke slowly and softly. Joe found that to be strange. Usually, these guys talked really fast.

"What do you want?" Joe knew he had to stay calm.

"I want you to bring Alex down here. I hear he is alive. Too bad! You bring him down here and I'll give you your girlfriend back. She might be a little worn out. Great body, Joe." Joe thought to himself: "*How did he know Alex was even alive? Mac, Joan, those bastards. They saw Alex at the airport. Those bastards.*" Joe slammed his fist into the mattress.

"I give Bernice back to you and we live happily ever after." His voice grew weaker as he spoke.

"When do you want to meet? Where do you want to meet?"

"We are at the Continental Hotel on the main island, the Caymans. You will love it here. Any taxi driver will know how to get here. The front desk will call me."

"It might be a week before I can get there. Alex is not doing well. He has some sort of infection. Doctor said he couldn't travel until sometime next week." Joe wanted DeMarco to think Bernice wasn't that important to him, which would weaken DeMarco's bargaining position. Would he buy it?

"That's ok, Joe! Take your time. We will be here when you get here." Joe grew furious. So damn slow and soft—like the desk clerk at the Osage Hotel. He also knew that Bernice would die before she would let anyone have sex with her.

"Where can I reach you if things change?"

"I told you where I'm staying, country boy. Call me anytime."

Joe hung up the phone and called Jimmy, muttering to himself as he dialed. *"Country boy, how does he know all this?"*

Jimmy picked up on the first ring.

"Jimmy, come over quick. I've heard from them."

Joe's legs felt like they were encased in cement. He tried to get to the door when Jimmy knocked, but could hardly move. "What did they do with her?" Jimmy asked, as he walked into the room.

"They're in the Caymans, Jimmy." Joe relayed the whole conversation to Jimmy.

"We'll get them, but we'll need another twenty guys at least, Joe. We want to be prepared. This will be a war." Jimmy's voice grew stronger with each word. "I can get twenty guys faster than Jackie Robinson can steal second," he said without hesitation.

"I told him that Alex was too sick to travel so we could have some time to plan this."

"Great! All I need is twenty-four hours. When are we leaving?"

The knot in Joe's stomach loosened somewhat, but the rest of his body remained rigid. Joe walked over to the window. He thought about Bernice possibly being mistreated, raped—"No! No! Why did this have to happen?" He punched the air with his fist and picked up a lamp, smashing it on the floor. Joe stared for a minute at the mess on the floor before falling on the bed and burying his head in the pillow.

Jimmy sat on the edge of the bed and put his large hand on Joe's back. "Joe, Joe, she will be ok. We'll get those bastards."

Joe turned over and stared at his friend for several seconds. Finally, he reached a decision inside. He nodded. "Thanks, Jimmy, you're a great pal."

# Chapter 87

# CAYMAN ISLANDS

It took thirty-six hours to get everyone ready to go. Jimmy assembled a crew of twenty-one Negroes, gang members that lived in his neighborhood. Some had spent time in prison. Joe told everyone going on the mission they would be paid $10,000 each. If they were killed, their money would go to whomever they chose. Joe had put it all in writing. Jerry Moore kept the list and stayed back with Brownie. Joe didn't want Brownie to have to endure flying again, unless it was to New Zealand. He hated leaving Brownie behind and hoped it wouldn't be a mistake.

Jerry agreed to carry on the Jimmy Robbins' Fund, in case Jimmy didn't make it back. Al was eager to go along. He picked up Benedetti and one other guy they both knew.

The plane, a four engine Pan American, left O'Hare airport for Miami at 10:37 a.m. on May 11th, the day before Joe's twentieth birthday and Bernice's twenty-fifth. They would change planes in Miami for a direct fight to Owen Roberts Airport on the large island.

The final head count of Joe and Jimmy's marauders totaled thirty, including Jimmy and Joe. All came armed and ready to fight, till death if need be. No matter what happened, the Jimmy Robbins Fund would continue.

Joe figured they would scope the place out before they tried to overtake the DeMarco gang. Joe had no idea how many men he had. Al figured he would have at least twenty or thirty, possibly more. "I think we need to get them on our turf down there.

The plane landed at Miami on schedule. They had a two-hour layover. They would arrive on the island at 4:46 p.m., local time.

Joe attempted to sleep. He'd doze for a few minutes, but then his head would fill with thoughts, bad thoughts, too many 'what ifs.'

# Chapter 88

# DeMARCO SPEAKS

Upon arriving, they retrieved their bags and headed for the taxis. It took six taxis to get them all transported to The Ambassador. Joe had instructed everyone before they left Chicago to stagger the time they departed the Cayman Airport for the hotel. They didn't want to look suspicious.

They checked into fifteen rooms. Two guys stayed with Alex, who slept on the floor. Al wanted a private room. Jimmy and Joe shared a room. They hadn't slept in the same room since being at Sheridan.

Jimmy and Joe grabbed their revolvers, checked to see if they were loaded and headed down the street, on foot, toward the Continental Hotel.

"Joe, if anything happens to one of us—oh shit, forget it. Nothin's goin' to happen. We be ok." Jimmy's voice sounded scratchy.

Joe heard the fear in his friend's voice. "You ok, Jimmy?"

"Yeah, I'm ok. You been a great friend." Jimmy put his arm around Joe's shoulders.

"You, too, Jimmy." Joe's body turned cold. "Bernice will be alright. Won't she?" His body felt numb.

"She be ok, Joe." He patted Joe on the shoulder.

Joe and Jimmy strode right in the front door. The desk clerk smiled and greeted them: "Welcome to the Continental Hotel."

Joe wished he had brought Brownie. "I almost feel naked without my dog, Jimmy." Joe's thoughts of Brownie faded before he reached the desk. Joe took a deep breath, exhaled slowly and asked the desk clerk for DeMarco.

"I will ring him," the lady said in perfect English. "Whom shall I say is calling?"

"Joe Clark and Jimmy Robbins"

She handed the phone to Joe. "We're here."

"Great! How was your trip?"

"Where is Bernice?"

"Oh, I think she is in the crib with one of my men. Such a wild one, she is."

"Cut the bullshit, DeMarco. Let's get this over with."

"You're a tough guy! I didn't know they made country boys that tough."

Joe tightened his grip on the phone. He took another deep breath and blew it out away from the mouthpiece. "If Bernice is harmed in any way, you're dead meat."

No response. "You got Alex, the pretty boy, with you?"

"Yeah, we got him."

"How many men did you bring with you, country boy?"

"Just me and Jimmy. I want to speak to Bernice."

"You're lying, country boy. I say you bring maybe thirty." He gave a short laugh.

*"How did he know that?"*

"I will meet you at the north end of the island. It's called Paradise Trail. You can't miss it. Let's make it tomorrow, noon, just you and Alex and your friend. Who'd you say?"

"Jimmy! We'll be there. Now, let me talk to Bernice."

"Is Alex feeling ok?"

The rage inside Joe continued.

"Yeah, he's better. I want…"

DeMarco hung up. Joe and Jimmy left for The Ambassador.

Back at the hotel, they consulted with Al. "I think it might go down easier than we may have guessed. DeMarco has to be greedy for money. When he was in prison, his girlfriend took off with all his money and headed for some place in South America with some Latino." Al puffed on a cigarette as he spoke.

"Well, let's hope so," Joe said, with a lot of concern on his mind. Getting Bernice back remained his primary purpose. The money in the Cayman bank became less important.

# Chapter 89

## MEETING SET

The next morning Jimmy and Joe arose at 5:00. Neither one had slept well. They each took a shower and shaved and went down and got some breakfast. They ate slowly, with hardly any conversation.

Al joined them in the dining room. "I just got a call from a friend of mine. He said DeMarco was shot up real bad when they hit the Capuanos. He's crippled, won't ever walk again. The bullet hit him in the spine. They say he probably won't live long, either. It tore the hell out of his kidneys."

"That's probably why he talked so slowly and softly. He sounded like a girl," Joe said, somewhat relieved to hear about DeMarco's incapacitated condition.

"What are you goin to do with DeMarco?"

"If Bernice is ok, I'll let him have Alex and go home."

"Let's hope so!" Al exclaimed, as he did his Hail Mary. "I wanted Alex dead. I wanted to kill him. I guess, now, I just want to get back to my family." The smoke sprinted from his nostrils. "DeMarco will kill him for sure."

Joe and Jimmy returned to their room. Jimmy slouched in the chair, while Joe lay on the bed, head propped up with his right hand. He hated waiting.

"Most of the time in the streets, the action is upon you before there's time to think." Jimmy licked his dry lips, then swallowed, trying to relieve the dryness in his parched mouth. "You scared, Joe?" Jimmy's voice sounded like sandpaper.

Joe's eyes snapped toward Jimmy. Joe had never admitted being scared to anyone. "Maybe a little." Joe's eyes switched to the floor. "I'm more frightened for Bernice than myself," Joe responded, trying to wave off any fear he held inside. Joe jumped up from the bed, walked toward the window, and flung open the drapes. He said a quick prayer. And then, "Grandpa, I need your guidance today." He turned toward Jimmy a few

265

minutes later. "We'll get through this."

"I scared Joe. I got this gnawing in my belly. I didn't have time to be scared at Sheridan. The street fights I've been in were quick, no time to think. It was over before I got scared. This time, I have too much time to think." Jimmy's eyes dropped.

Joe looked at his best friend. "Jimmy, let's try and think of something else." Joe laid his right arm around Jimmy's shoulder.

Jimmy looked at Joe, gave a short smile and a quick nod.

They started to talk about baseball, trying to ease the worry.

Joe still hadn't mentioned to anyone that he had seen Mac and Joan at the airport in Chicago. That was strange, very strange. He'd leave it be.

# Chapter 90

## NOON MASSACRE

At 11:00 a.m., Jimmy, Joe, and Alex left the hotel in a taxi for Paradise Trail. They wanted to get there early so they could check things out, just in case things went south. When they arrived, they instructed the taxi driver, Ramon, to park behind the bushes over to their right. "You wait for us. Stay in your taxi until we need you." Joe wanted control of the situation. Joe's heart pounded faster than he wanted it to. "Damn, I wish Brownie were here."

Jimmy nodded, but made no comment.

Ramon left them standing in the middle of the road. Joe had his Bowie knife and the 38 revolver stuck in his pants. He hoped he wouldn't have to use them.

Jimmy had two hand guns stuck in his jeans. He also carried a six-inch switchblade that he could throw twenty feet with accuracy.

Joe checked his watch. They still had ten minutes before DeMarco would get there. Al promised to have ten men in the bushes within shooting distance of the meeting point. They walked in pairs to avoid attention.

Al kept ten more at The Ambassador for backup. He placed five guys inside the Continental Hotel just to ensure DeMarco would be killed if things didn't go their way. One guy remained outside the Continental Hotel to observe. Al would follow DeMarco from the Continental to the meeting place. Al would be riding down Paradise Trail as Joe and Jimmy were making their deal with DeMarco.

Twelve o'clock came. Joe and Jimmy felt ready. Alex turned white. DeMarco's car, a large black Cadillac limousine, pulled up about thirty feet from where Joe, Alex and Jimmy stood. Joe and Jimmy had their hands positioned to grab their guns in case DeMarco didn't cooperate.

Joe's heart rose up to his throat, but he remained calm. At least, he thought he was calm. Jimmy put a false grin on his face. Their eyes squinted in the sun.

The front passenger door opened revealing a thin, Italian man, who exited the limousine and opened the rear door. DeMarco sat in a wheel chair facing the front of the car. He looked sick, very sick. Joe couldn't see Bernice.

"Hi, Joe, this must be your friend, Jimmy. I didn't know you had a nigger friend, Joe. They have them kind out in the country where you are from?" His voice quivered.

Joe's tongue froze; Jimmy's false grin disappeared. Jimmy took two quick steps toward DeMarco. Joe stopped Jimmy's forward motion. Jimmy's body stiffened. "Where's Bernice?" Joe asked, with clenched teeth.

DeMarco lost his phony smile. His eyes flicked past Joe and rested on the last Capuano. "That must be Alex. Hi, you SOB. I missed you the other day we iced your father, that asshole. I spent a lot of years rotting in prison because of him. That piece of shit little brother of yours, that guy Eddie, had some balls, but one of my guys blew his head off. The guy who looked like you wasn't supposed to be there. I'm real sorry about him. They blew his brains out, too." DeMarco spoke, but couldn't hide the pain he felt.

**"What about Bernice?"** Joe's fist doubled.

"Oh, yes, the redhead. She sure is a feisty one. Joe, she loves the hell out of you. Promise me one thing: Take good care of her." He managed a quick smile.

Four rapid shots came from behind Joe, Jimmy and Alex. Joe and Jimmy hit the sand after the third shot.

The second shot hit Alex in the back of the head. Blood blossomed all over the limo's bullet-proof side windows. Three shots struck the limo. Joe and Jimmy weren't sure where the shots had come from. They scrambled to the other side of the limousine. "Who fired those shots?" Jimmy asked.

Car doors slammed. Joe never did get a glimpse of Bernice, still in the back seat with DeMarco. The unseen gunmen continued to fire at the limousine, blowing out all the tires. The limousine sat paralyzed in the sandy road.

"Come out with your hands up." A man's voice echoed through a bull horn.

No one came out of the stranded limousine. "You have ten

seconds to come out with your hands up."

Joe asked Jimmy, "What do we do here? I don't want them killing Bernice." His heart pounded, mouth covered with sand. They both had scrambled for cover in some bushes after the limo had sped away.

"You have three seconds."

From the bushes and palm trees, more than two dozen men with guns appeared. They walked toward the limousine, circling as they got closer. They were no more than eight feet apart from one another. Joe and Jimmy heard nothing but their breaths, and the sliding of sand beneath their feet. They got within three feet of the limousine, surrounding it from all sides.

Joe and Jimmy managed to stay hidden in the brush about twenty feet from the limousine. They were being sliced up by the one-inch, razor sharp thorns on the bushes. Joe managed to press his mouth close to Jimmy's ear and whispered, "I think they want DeMarco. They don't care about anyone else."

"Who are they? I don't recognize anyone," Jimmy said. "They aren't FBI." His voice trembled.

Joe knew that the two of them didn't stand a chance against twenty-four armed men. "Where the hell is Al, and where are the guys he was supposed to have here?" Joe said, starting to panic.

The men had the limousine surrounded. One of the men demanded, "You come out with your hands up or we'll blow the limo up with you in it." Three of the men began pouring—"*God, is that gasoline?*"—around the outside of the limo. "We've got to move fast!" Joe said. The smell of burnt flesh and hair from that awful day on the back forty entered his nostrils.

"DeMarco, open up or the limo goes up in smoke."

"Bernice!"

Gunfire erupted. The men surrounding the limo fired frantically at whoever fired at them. Dead bodies began falling. The gun fire continued. Joe's heart pounded like a base drum. Jimmy finally managed to say, "I can't move, Joe. I—I never been so scared."

"I have to get to that limo," Joe said. He pulled himself through the thorny bushes, ignoring the rips in his clothes and skin, and headed for the car. Jimmy swore, then began following him, staying about five feet behind. The men closest to the ditch had their backs to Joe. Before

Joe could reach the men, he spotted a light. Within a second, a deafening explosion erupted and the black limo was engulfed in flames. The whole back end of the limo disappeared. Black smoke filled the air. The flames made it impossible to get to the limo. The men on the ground screamed, rolling in the sand trying to stop the fire that burned their bodies.

"Bernice! Bernice! Bernice!" Joe screamed. Joe couldn't do anything, but watch. "Bernice, oh my God." The limo's paint disappeared, melting like butter. Joe froze in horror. He never even heard a scream from inside the flaming limo, not a scream. The nightmare returned. The bean can. Too late. Joe turned and shouted. "Stop! Stop! Damn you!" His eyes overflowed with tears.

Jimmy grabbed Joe, pulling him away from the fray. Jimmy tried to comfort his buddy. "Joe, she wasn't in there. She wasn't in there." He shook Joe's arm vigorously. "She would have tried to get out if she'd been in there." But, Joe did not respond. He merely stared at the spot where the limo stood and sobbed, silently.

"Get your hands up!" The voice came from somewhere behind Jimmy and Joe.

"That sounded like Al!" Jimmy said to Joe, still insensible. Of the twenty-four, there were only three men left standing, the rest lay on the ground, their clothes still smoldering from the fire. "The rest of them must be dead," Jimmy said.

"Jimmy! Get their guns," Al yelled, as he walked toward the three men. Six of Jimmy's friends accompanied Al.

Jimmy grabbed the guns from the three men and threw them in the bushes, where he and Joe had hidden. "Al, do you know where Bernice is?" Jimmy asked, hoping he knew.

"Yeah, she's in our hotel. I have Mo and Sammy guarding her. What's with Joe? He looks like he's seen a ghost," Al said, lighting a cigarette.

"Joe, Joe!" Jimmy slapped Joe across the face three times before he blinked his eyes. "Joe! Bernice is ok! Bernice is ok!" Jimmy grinned.

Al came over and told Joe, "Hey, man, get hold of yourself. The war is over." He blew smoke into the hot air. Joe stared at him, blankly. A second later, Al was dead.

# Chapter 91

# JOAN RETURNS

Abullet had struck Al Falcono in the back of the head. He collapsed immediately. Jimmy and the others grabbed their guns and looked around, wondering where that single bullet had come from.

Without hesitation, Jimmy turned and shot the remaining three men. Al was his friend and he wanted revenge. "Let's get that SOB! Spread out and head toward those bushes and trees over there." Joe stood silent as if he had been drugged.

The seven, including Jimmy, searched the area where they thought the bullet had come from. Jimmy caught a small movement out of the corner of his eye and swung around. "Get up!" Jimmy yelled, holding his revolver not more than three feet from the back of the man's head. He could see the man's body wasn't very big, and that he had dropped his rifle in the sand beside him.

The trembling man turned his face slowly toward Jimmy. He was a SHE. "Who are you?" Jimmy was shocked to see this pretty face out here in the sand.

She lay there, directing her defiant gaze at Jimmy. "Did I kill the bastard? Did I get the SOB? That country boy wouldn't listen to me," the voice said.

"Who you talking about?" Jimmy asked, still shocked.

"Joe! Joe Clark!" the female voice replied, her face coated with the white sand she laid in.

"You missed, bitch! You got Al!"

"*A'mbola!*"

"What did you say? You tried to kill my best friend? Damn you!" He wanted to kill her now.

"What's your name?" Jimmy asked menacingly. His finger rested on the trigger of the 38; his hand shook.

"Where is he?" Her chest heaved. "*Voi beledo! Voi merdu! Voi burati!*" She tried to get up, but Jimmy placed his size fifteen shoe on her chest. She had used a Winchester 30-30 semi-automatic. One, hollow point bullet was all that was fired from the 30-30. It had exploded on the way out of its target.

Jimmy grabbed her right arm and lifted her straight up like a rag doll.

"How did Joe get hooked up with you anyways? Jimmy dragged the woman behind him as he talked.

Jimmy found Joe in the same place he had left him. "Who the hell is this? She's the one who shot Al. It was meant for you, Joe." No response from Joe. "Somebody tell me what's goin' on."

Joe turned his head to look at Jimmy, but never said a word. He seemed to have heard, but couldn't respond. "Come on, Joe, get hold of yourself. We're safe and Bernice is safe."

"What's your name? You have ten seconds or you're shark bait." Jimmy had his 38 revolver against the lady's temple.

She looked at Jimmy, tears ran down her sand-covered cheeks. "Joan Amato."

"Who is Joan Amato? Joe, Joe, come on. Al is dead! What do I do with this woman?" Jimmy turned his head and signaled to Albert, one of his friends who stood nearby. "Go get that taxi from the bushes so we can get the hell out of here."

Jimmy managed to get Joe in the back seat of the taxi.

Jimmy turned to shove Joan into the back seat of the taxi when an array of gunfire sprayed the area. Joan took a hit behind her left ear. She slid softly to the ground. Her eyes stared, suddenly empty of hate and life. Jimmy gasped as he let go of her soft arm. A chill ran down his spine. "Go! Get the hell out of here," Jimmy screamed, jumping into the car. Jimmy instructed the others to get their butts back to the hotel.

The taxi roared off as Jimmy pulled the door shut behind him. Joe, still in shock, slumped in the back seat of the speeding taxi.

As they sped away, Jimmy saw the other guys from his neighborhood breaking for the car that Al had driven there. Jimmy slapped Joe's face, trying to get him to come out of his trance. Albert had the accelerator pushed to the floor, leaving Joan in the sand behind them.

# Chapter 92

# THEY SURVIVE

The sound of the car's engine roaring accompanied the rush of palm trees by the windows. They were about a mile from the horrific gun battle. Jimmy continued to try to bring Joe to his senses. "Wait! What is that sound? Stop, Stop the car!" Jimmy screamed. He broke out into a cold sweat. "Get out, Albert! Run!" Albert slammed on the brakes and dove out of the car. Jimmy pushed the back door open, dragging Joe from the back seat. He managed to make it several feet before the taxi exploded into thousands of pieces. Jimmy slammed Joe down on the ground, covering him with his large body. Pieces of metal dropped around them. Several jagged, sharp pieces hit Jimmy, piercing his legs, back and the back of his head.

It lasted only seconds. Jimmy pulled himself to his knees to look at what remained of the taxi. He saw four rims, two axles, a transmission, the engine, one rear end and a pile of scrap metal. "I don't believe it." Jimmy scanned the area, expecting more gun fire. "Albert, Albert, where are you?"

"I over here," Albert answered. "You ok, man?"

"Yeah, I'm ok. You ok?" He stood up and pulled Joe to his feet. "We need to get out of here."

Jimmy rose to his feet and, once again, heard gun fire. Before he realized where it was coming from, a bullet had struck his head above his right ear. Jimmy went down in a large heap, bringing Joe with him.

The gunman ran toward the two ex-cellmates. He stood within forty feet of them as a taxi carrying Sammy, Mo, Lester and Bernice, turned onto the sandy road and barreled toward them. Sammy, Mo, Lester and Bernice were in the taxi. The taxi driver was in the trunk, tied up and a lemon stuffed in his mouth.

Four more men came running from the same direction as the first gunman. Lester continued to speed until spotting Jimmy lying face up. "That's Jimmy!" He slammed on the brakes and turned the steering wheel to the right to avoid running over his friend. The taxi slid to a stop between the five men and Jimmy and Joe. Lester bailed out of the car and headed over to his friend. He knelt down and upon seeing the blood from Jimmy's head screamed, "They killed Jimmy. You bastards will die." He charged toward the oncoming men.

"What—where's Joe?" Bernice screamed.

Lester began firing at the five men, who now stood only twenty feet from the taxi. Mo and Sammy jumped out of the taxi and joined Lester in the fray. Bernice ducked to the floor of the taxi. The gun battle lasted no more than a minute. Lester took a bullet to his chest. Mo and Sammy looked at the three men they had just killed. Lester had gotten the other two.

Bernice crawled out of the car seconds after the last bullet was fired, heading over to Jimmy and Joe. She assumed Joe must have been killed to be lying so still. "Joe! Joe! No! Please! Oh, God, no! Joe!" She tried to shake Joe first and then Jimmy, lying lifeless on top of him. Her heart pounded. Tears welled up in her eyes. Her throat swelled with fear. She couldn't speak.

Mo and Sammy approached Bernice, who sobbed uncontrollably. Mo felt for a pulse on Jimmy's neck. "He's still alive." He reached over to Joe's large neck. "He's alive, too."

"What! My God! He's alive?" She wanted to kiss him but couldn't get to him with Jimmy perched on top of him.

"Help me! Help me get Jimmy off him."

Mo rushed over to Lester and felt for a pulse. After a few seconds of silence, he stood. "He was a good man. He always tried to help those in need." Mo's eyes began to water. After Sammy rolled Jimmy off Joe, he came over and placed his arm around Mo's shoulder.

They picked Jimmy up and laid him on the taxi's back seat. Bernice tried to turn Joe over, afraid of what she might find. Mo and Sammy managed to roll him over. Joe's eyes were open and glassy, but he wasn't focused. Bernice kissed him several times and said, with tears running down her cheeks, "We need to get him to a hospital. What's wrong with him? He isn't shot. Hurry, oh, my God!"

Lester removed the taxi driver from the trunk, leaving him lying on the sandy road, tied and gagged, with the lemon still in his mouth. Mo sat in the back seat, holding his friend's upper body in his lap. Bernice sat on Joe's lap, wrapping her arms around him, kissing him, and talking to him, trying to bring him back to life. Sammy drove.

Jimmy regained consciousness before they reached the hospital. "Where's Joe? Joe! The bomb! Where's Joe?" He tried to sit up but the flesh wound on his right side prompted him to lie back in Mo's lap.

"Joe is ok! He's up front with Bernice," Mo answered, in his deep voice.

"Should we take Jimmy to the hospital? Is he still bleeding?" Sammy asked as he drove through the city.

"Nah, he has a hard head! Let's go to the hotel," Mo said, looking down at his buddy.

"Yeah, the hotel will be better. I believe Joe is just in a state of shock. We'll just take him to his room," Bernice agreed, still trying to revive him.

They got Jimmy and Joe up to their rooms without making too much of a scene. "I want to go back to Chicago. The ghetto is nothing compared to this. I never want to see another mafia guy as long as I live," Jimmy remarked to anyone who would listen.

"Is it all over, Jimmy? There won't be any more killing, will there?" Bernice asked, eyes pleading for the right answer.

"No more killing, Bernice! I think it's all over." Jimmy wasn't sure, but it felt better saying "no more".

Joe came around three hours later, with Bernice lying beside him on the bed. "Bernice! The limo! What happened?" Joe asked, looking up at Bernice. "You ok?"

"Yes, I'm ok, Joe." She kissed him hard on the lips, but received no reaction.

"What the hell happened to Al?" Joe demanded.

"He was shot in the back of the head while you and me stood right beside him," Jimmy said. Joe's eyes swung around towards where Jimmy sat.

"Who shot him?" Joe said, trying to get off the bed. "Who shot Al?"

"I—I don't know, Joe." He didn't want to mention Joan's name in front of Bernice.

The three of them left for the hotel restaurant to get something to eat, leaving their guns behind. Joe thought he was hungry, but wasn't sure. Bernice had taken care of Jimmy's head wound where the bullet had grazed his scalp. She also tended to the scratches they had received from the thorny bushes.

# Chapter 93

## SHARK BAIT

Jimmy, Joe, and Bernice returned to Joe and Jimmy's room. Jimmy opened the door and froze. Sitting in the overstuffed chair was Mac Gibson. Joe's lungs wouldn't let any air in. Bernice remained calm. She didn't know Mac.

"Come on in, boys. You too, young lady." Joe didn't like the smell of the room. As Joe turned to look, he spotted two more men. They stood inside to Joe's left.

"So, how did it go? It looks like you got a little scratch there, Jimmy." Mac had a big grin on his face. "Joe, you look like you had a fight with a mountain lion."

Joe and Jimmy both searched to see where they had left their weapons. Mac must have picked them up, Joe thought. He remembered seeing them on the dresser in front of the beds.

"What are you doing here?" Joe asked, walking straight toward Mac.

"Not so fast there, country boy. The FBI wants your ass for murdering these men. They told you not to take the law into your own hands."

"You're a lying piece of shit, Mac," Jimmy said, as he scanned the room again, looking for the weapons they had left.

"Those are pretty strong words coming from someone who will probably rot in prison."

Bernice prepared herself mentally for what appeared to be a fight in the making. The hours of karate instruction drilled into her to remain calm. She took deep breaths to relax. Her head took control of her body. The adrenaline flowed. She scoped the room. The two guys now stood beside her. She knew for sure that she could take out one of them, but two would be very difficult. No weapons had been drawn yet. Joe looked sharply at her and sensed that Bernice was about to give a lesson in karate to everyone. Her pedal pushers sat just below her knees. Her top fit loosely; that would give her enough flexibility to kick. She wore slip-on shoes. Maybe she would do it barefooted. Joe's thoughts turned to Brownie, wishing he were with them.

Mac remained in his chair, grinning. Joe moved to his left to get a better view of the two guys behind him. Jimmy could easily reach Mac's head with his foot from where he stood. Joe figured he would bull-dog the man farthest to his left and to Bernice's left. The two men stood about four feet apart. Still, no one had shown a weapon. They surely were armed. Joe glanced, again, at Bernice. He shot her a half grin. Her eyes told Joe she was ready. Jimmy stared at Mac.

"Kick ass!" Joe screamed. Jimmy smashed his size fifteen shoe alongside Mac's head. He slumped in the chair like a rag doll.

Bernice kicked the man closest to her with her bare, left foot, slamming him unconscious against the wall. Joe dove for the third man, barreling his head into the man's privates. The man gasped as he went down flat on his back. Joe punched him as hard as he could on the side of the head. The guy was out cold.

"Now, what do we do with these morons?" Jimmy asked.

"Let them come to. We'll question them," Joe said, as he held Bernice, thanking her for breaking the man's jaw. Bernice responded with a kiss.

Jimmy tore a sheet up, tied their arms behind their backs and tied their feet. Jimmy searched them, taking their weapons. "Where are our guns, Joe?"

"I don't know! They have to be here some place."

"Here, they're in the tub," Bernice said.

"I'm getting real tired of this whole thing. I sure wish we were back in Chicago, so I could hug Brownie, and then get out of the country," Joe said, gazing out the window as if he could see New Zealand in the distance. The last few years zoomed through his head. His Grandpa lying on his death bed brought an ache to his heart. When he remembered his father climbing the windmill to rescue him, Joe's eyes blinked back the tears. Sue flashed before him—in his arms on the dance floor at the prom. His throat became thick; his lungs lacked air. *"I must leave it all behind me."* He turned toward Bernice and smiled, glad to have her in his life. The bean can sank to the bottom of the sea.

"It won't be long, Joe!" Bernice said, as she hugged him.

Joe's body shook as she touched him.

Mac woke up first and looked around the room. Jimmy stood over him looking into his eyes. "What happened, Mac?"

"You guys will answer for this. I'll make sure of it," Mac said, with a tightened voice. He twisted and turned, trying to relieve the pain caused by the bed sheets holding his wrists.

"We'll see how you talk when your butt is down at the bottom of the ocean," Jimmy said, with a grin.

"Why, Mac?" Joe now knew that he had seen Mac in Chicago. "We thought you were on our side. What made you change?" Joe asked, expecting an answer that wasn't a lie.

"I wanted the money in the Caymans."

"Sorry, somebody took out Alex. Without him and his fingerprints, you can't get the money out of the bank," Joe said.

"You're wrong! The bank down here doesn't require fingerprints. I checked," Mac replied. "The Capuanos are the ones requiring the fingerprints, not the bank."

Joe and Jimmy shook their heads.

"Alex told you that to buy some time. He wanted to live a little longer," Mac said, with a grin.

"You lie," said Jimmy.

"I'm not going to argue with you, Mac. You're going to hell shortly," Joe said.

"Let's split the money, Joe! I—I will never tell what happened here." Mac pleaded for his life.

"Jimmy, call Sammy and Mo and have them get rid of these three. They are really making me sick."

Sammy and Mo appeared at the door within minutes of the phone call. "Where do you want us to take them?" Sammy asked as he entered.

"Take them for a boat ride," Jimmy answered, grinning.

"Mac, I have two more questions. Did you tell the Capuanos that we were trying to end their organization?" Joe asked, with his face only inches from Mac's.

"You have three seconds to live. I want an answer." Joe deliberately stuck the Bowie knife an eighth of an inch into Mac's neck.

Mac finally answered, "Yes! I—I worked for the Capuanos. They knew everything. I was a double agent. They paid me well for the information." Joe pulled the Bowie knife out of Mac's neck.

"Second question: Who were the men that blew up the car?"

"They were from New Orleans. I was working for them, also. They all paid really well." Blood dribbled down to his chest.

"That money won't be doing you much good where you're going," Joe said.

"Mac, was you and Joan Amato in on this together?" Jimmy asked. Joe's head spun quickly. Bernice waited for an answer.

Joan Amato and Mac. *The airport, yes, the airport.* Joe asked before Mac had a chance to open his mouth, "Mac, were you and Joan at the airport when we got back from Geneva?" Bernice wondered who Joan was.

Mac grinned and then laughed. "You're right, country boy. She said you were stupid. She and I were going to stay here on the island, with Capuano's money." He laughed, again, until Jimmy grabbed him by his shirt, pulling him out of the chair. "The bitch is dead. She took a bullet from your New Orleans' friends. Her ass will be shark bait, just like yours, Mac."

Mac's face sank. Jimmy slammed him back into the chair. He said nothing.

"Sammy, Mo, feed the sharks," Joe said, looking out the window. Everyone in the room gasped for air.

"Will do, Joe," Sammy said with a broad smile on his lips.

Bernice paced the floor, breathing hard and making quick glances at Joe. "Who's Joan Amato?" Jimmy was all ears. His eyes switched to Joe.

"She was my physical therapist." He walked toward the window. "Her uncle was a hit man for the Capuanos." He hung his head in shame for having gotten involved with her. Bernice could tell Joe regretted whatever had taken place. Joe walked back toward the bed. "I saw her and Mac at the airport." He looked at Bernice and shook his head. "I should have known better." Joe slumped into the overstuffed chair.

Jimmy grinned at his friend and looked at Bernice with the same grin, before turning discreetly toward the door.

Bernice waited, then gave a small smile. "Happy Birthday, Joe." She bent over Joe's slumped form and kissed him gently. Pulling back, she looked into his face.

Joe looked into Bernice's eyes and returned the kiss. "Happy Birthday to you, too!"

"God, I miss my dog! Let's get out of here." He put his arm around Bernice and followed Jimmy out of the room.

# Epilogue

The year after the Capuanos had been laid to rest, Joe and Bernice married in Mendota and honeymooned in New Zealand. They found a farm for sale and put a down payment on it, using some of the mafia's money Joe had taken out of the Capuano safe. They moved to New Zealand a month later with Brownie and Bernice's dog, Blackie. They raised two boys and a girl.

Jimmy and Jerry started the Jimmy Robbins Fund. With Jerry's news reporting, the whole country became aware of their work and money poured in from all over, including the Capuano money from the three foreign banks. The Feds felt they had to turn it over to the Jimmy Robbins Fund or be ridiculed by the public. The crime rate in Chicago's ghetto dropped considerably the first year and was virtually nil after five years. Other major cities in the US wanted to follow Jerry and Jimmy's pattern after seeing what they had accomplished. Jimmy, along with his wife, Maggie, and their three boys have visited Joe numerous times.

Helen Clark never remarried and stayed in Mendota, but did visit her son and his family in New Zealand many times. She remained very good friends with Rene, who remained happily married.

Joe's sister, Sarah, moved to Texas and married a cattle rancher, but never had any children.

Doctor Knowles continued to practice in Rockford and worked diligently for drunk driver reform.

# About The Author

Upon graduating from high school, I spent three years in Germany with the United States Air Force. After college, I spent my entire career selling and managing salespeople.

I spent a year, part time, under the direction of a Doctor of English learning the skills of writing. I attended a six month working seminar in Boulder, Colorado headed up by an experienced author and teacher.

I have traveled to five continents covering over forty countries and have spent time exploring all 50 states. Articles on my travels have been published in a US newspaper and a European paper, as well. I currently reside in Florida.

# Acknowledgement

I would like to thank everyone who inspired me to write this novel and also express my appreciation to the people who have helped me along the way.

Made in the USA
Middletown, DE
19 July 2015